I0583850

THE FIRST CORONATION

CARLTON JAMES

Black Rose Writing | Texas

©2020 by Carlton James
All rights reserved. No part of this book may be reproduced, stored in a retrieval system or transmitted in any form or by any means without the prior written permission of the publishers, except by a reviewer who may quote brief passages in a review to be printed in a newspaper, magazine or journal.

The author grants the final approval for this literary material.

First printing

This is a work of fiction. Names, characters, businesses, places, events, and incidents are either the products of the author's imagination or used in a fictitious manner. Any resemblance to actual persons, living or dead, or actual events is purely coincidental.

ISBN: 978-1-68433-577-0
PUBLISHED BY BLACK ROSE WRITING
www.blackrosewriting.com

Printed in the United States of America
Suggested Retail Price (SRP) $18.95

The First Coronation is printed in Garamond

*As a planet-friendly publisher, Black Rose Writing does its best to eliminate unnecessary waste to reduce paper usage and energy costs, while never compromising the reading experience. As a result, the final word count vs. page count may not meet common expectations.

ACKNOWLEDGEMENTS

The United States of America was founded upon a document created by brave and brilliant men. For 31 years I served to protect every American's rights in upholding the principles of the U.S. Constitution. Seeing the flag waving in the breeze in front of my home still brings a warm glow for what it represents. I give thanks to God for having been born in this free country. That American spirit of freedom makes it possible to write a novel on any desired subject, including this one. I pray that we nurture these freedoms or they will be lost.

THE F*I*RST
CORONATI**O**N

CHAPTER 1
PRESIDENTIAL ELECTION - MINUS THREE MONTHS

Beijing, People's Republic of China
1430 Hours Local Time

The most powerful man in the People's Republic of China looked cautiously at the figure bowing deeply before him. He knew this man was his most valuable servant and, conversely, his most dangerous threat. He contemplated the man for several more seconds before speaking.

"Lao, when will our renegade province be returned to the China?"

"General Secretary," Lao said respectfully and quietly, "there has been no change since our last meeting, however, our special source has revealed a strong likelihood of a Fontaine Presidency. When she is elected, it will expand our options."

Nodding his head, the General Secretary used a similar quiet voice to say, "And the probability of this dangerous operation becoming known by the Americans? Will this penetration lead directly to war?"

The tension in the air was palpable. With both men knowing the stakes involved, however, it had long ago been determined the rewards were worthwhile.

"The assessment from our handler in Washington and by my small hand-picked staff overseeing this operation shows confidence that if she wins the Presidency, which seems likely the threat will be surprisingly low. I chose the Charm School girl myself and she has proven to be superbly effective." In hushed tones Lao continued to provide details, which brought a very rare smile to the lips of the General Secretary.

"Keep me informed, Lao." With that, the General Secretary turned and walked away.

Washington, D.C.
2300 Hours EDT

He couldn't take his eyes off of her silky, black hair moving over his chest and lap. His excitement had been growing since he had arrived at the hotel room. In that time she brought him three fresh drinks while she delighted in hearing silly stories from the campaign. With each drink, her robe slid open a little more. Her beautiful China-doll skin and imprints of her nipples in the silk made it difficult to focus on what he was saying. Pouring out his frustrations from the campaign over the first fifteen minutes, resulted in her cradling his head between her magnificent breasts in one of the many special ways she used to make his troubles go away.

She listened eagerly to his forty-five minutes of rambling, and he had to admit to himself, he liked to talk, before she plopped herself down in his lap, quickly and skillfully opening his pants. In his mind, all he could think about was how he would best use her outstanding talents tonight, or maybe he would just let her take those matters in hand without his guidance.

The Mountains of Eastern Afghanistan
1930 Hours Local time the next day

"Great Leader," Hadi said with sorrow and a hint of fear in his voice, "the men you sent to attack and gather weapons from the Afghan Army patrol failed and paid with their lives. I found their bodies and one badly wounded survivor four hours walk to the West. The survivor claimed they had killed at least two of the soldiers before a drone spotted their positions, quickly followed by death raining down on them from above. He believed there must have been a Godless American with the patrol that brought about their deaths."

Hadi bowed his head and looked at the ground, feeling the penetrating gaze of the Great Leader bore into his head. Expecting to feel a bullet plow through his brain, it surprised him to hear only a resigned sigh.

"Hadi," the Great Leader sighed, "we have not been kept alive by Allah, his most merciful, for this many years only to be killed, a few men at a time, until we are all blood soaking into the desert sands. I will pray, and opportunity will come to us. We *will* bring great glory to Allah and kill many infidels. Allah Akbar!"

CHAPTER 2
PRESIDENTIAL ELECTION - MINUS TWO MONTHS

Fontaine Campaign Headquarters
Washington, DC
1330 Hours EDT

"You fucking son of a whore," shouted the enraged, high-pitched voice of the first female presidential candidate to be leading in the polls in U.S. history. "How in the hell could you not get those numbers? Can't you *see* how important they are before this next *speech*?" Showering spit had escaped her mouth as she shouted into the face of her campaign manager. Almost two years on the campaign trail had hardened him to these tirades, including her propensity to use profanity.

"Katherine, please keep your voice down," Stetson responded quietly. "There are press people right outside the door who would just love to smear your image."

Silently to himself, Stetson said, "Either the conservative news channel or on talk radio." It had been a very close call a few years earlier when the attempt was made by the newly elected Democratic Congress to impose the "Fairness Doctrine" on the radio waves. After all, it hadn't been liberal commentators' fault that no liberal talk radio show had successfully competed for audience share. Several had tried and failed miserably to attract either a steady audience or adequate investment in the form of advertising.

"*Damn* those bastards in the media, demanding a profit be made when our message is so critical." Stetson thought bitterly. It was only right and proper that Congress muzzle those conservatives by directing the Federal Communications Commission to *make* radio stations give equal time to the right-minded, more intelligent people.

"Katherine, your numbers are up, and the plan to highlight Donnelson's massacre in Afghanistan has, like, totally given you the lead." Don Stetson spoke in a hushed voice in the vain hope that by his use of a quiet tone, it would persuade Katherine to follow his cue. Stetson was referring to the brilliant, of course it was brilliant, since he had been the one to make it happen, the media campaign highlighting the interviews of Taliban widows. The series of interviews described how a special operations unit, led by Republican Presidential nominee James Donnelson, had "massacred seventeen unarmed and innocent men" from an Afghan village during an insurgent clearing mission.

At the relatively young age of forty-nine, Stetson was well versed in handling of prima donna candidates. "You *know* how effective those Taliban widows were in front of the camera. Not to mention how it was the European media that has been pushing this narrative. Now please, let us do our jobs," Stetson hissed. The point about what had caused the spike in Katherine's popularity was calculated to soothe her out of her tirade.

"Don't you hush ME, you fucking little weasel," she hissed back. "I *still* can't believe Donnelson's people haven't been able to expose what I presume was al Jazeera's doctoring of the videos."

Grudgingly giving credit, Katherine said, "My God, it was impressive to come up with the footage… then to get the Euro-media to sweep away the objections… the way they could completely ignore the obvious… masterful! Add playing up the sympathy from Walter's stroke…" Katherine's husband, Walter Fontaine, had been Vice President when he had suffered a stroke two weeks before leaving office.

Pausing, Katherine seemed to come to another decision, turning to Stetson with her most penetrating gaze, "And tell me again exactly *who* it was that planned this whole operation?" Stetson seemed to pale, just a little. He could feel in his gut that Katherine was intent on drilling until she exposed his earlier embellishment about his own part in the "truth dissemination" campaign.

"Well, Katherine, um," and he sucked upon his teeth, just like he always did when caught in a subtle lie. "You know that my whole staff works as a team. We all contribute. We brainstorm," he said in his most weasely voice. Stetson had long ago concluded that at his relatively young age, this tone of voice sometimes took the worst of the sliminess out of his words.

"Cut the shit, you miserable worm," she stormed back at his meager attempt to explain. "Goddammit, I told you to tell me *who originally* came up with the plan!"

Katherine spouted the last phrase with the characteristic mist of spittle, for which she was privately dubbed, 'Katherine the Great... Spitter.' The original designation Katherine the Great was a throw-back to the Russian Tsarina of a similar name, mostly because of the Tsarina's reputation for utter ruthlessness. Since it became popular within her staff to use the moniker, shortened to TG, for "The Great," (at least in her own mind), the different bastardizations of the phrase quickly followed. One of the brighter staffers was secretly recording each of the new nicknames in chronological order–probably as juicy tidbits for a future book.

"Katherine," Stetson said with a little less of the sickening whine than he had just used, "I told you the new kid, Marc Baxter[1], came up with the idea. But I'm the one, well, maybe with a little help from Towanda in our media section, to take the idea and make it truly effective. Baxter never would have taken the idea to the point of using footage from al Jazeera, or sending out a carefully picked film crew to get the additional interviews and footage."

Almost under his breath, Stetson continued, "He's so young he's still wrapped up in all of those damned journalism ethics courses." Then in a more confident and less conspiratorial voice, "He just doesn't understand that we must do certain things to insure a win before the very best candidate for President can do any good!"

Stetson had changed to his soft, forced, and almost hoarse voice he used to most adamantly drive home his point.

"Oh, please," Katherine uttered in disgust, although she felt more than a bit of appreciation for Stetson's stroking. "You know I get annoyed when you do that." Stetson bowed his head in what he hoped looked like a genuine sign of contrition while astutely observing that "she who protesteth too much" had dropped her voice and had visibly calmed.

"But, whatever, I think you should plan to put the boy, Baxter, on the staff. Fresh young minds are just what we need in the White House," pausing briefly to look at the ceiling. "Now,..." giving Stetson an appropriate pause for effect, "this boy has shown no propensities, for, you know, letting those ethics get in the way of getting things done..." Katherine let the phrase drop off. She was a master of saying things without saying them, which gave her plausible deniability.

"Of course not," Stetson hissed under his breath. He thought at the same time this was another of the thousands of details he should have followed through to resolution, but he couldn't tell Katherine. Instead, like most of his assurances to

---

[1] See Appendix A for character description.

Katherine, he tried to be just like the doctors that had assured his father his mother would quickly recover from the infection she received during minor elective surgery. They had been *so sure,* and his father believed them, until twenty-four hours later when her fever spiked to 104 degrees. She died on the way to the hospital. At least, he thought, those bastards had also paid dearly for their incompetence. It may have killed his father with grief, but his mother's death had allowed Stetson to collect enough money to assure his place in politics with the settlement from those arrogant assholes. Like the doctors, however, Stetson had learned most people—sometimes even Katherine—would appreciate a calm, assured voice in response to their fears. He just had to be careful not to use the coveted voice-of-assurance too often.

Stetson continued, "Katherine, I have already spoken with the boy, and he understands how nothing matters more than getting the right person elected. He'll play ball, all right. But yeah, sure, it's a great idea to keep him available and primed for a place in the Press Secretary's office."

"Of course he does have a nice, tight little ass," Katherine mused before plunging into other details, such as putting on her public smile and checking her underarms for sweat stains. "Everything must be just right before going out to greet my adoring fans, I mean my voters."

CHAPTER 3
PRESIDENTIAL ELECTION - MINUS TWO MONTHS

The Mountains of Southeast Afghanistan
1830 Hours Local Time

A light wind blew cold across the rocks and scrub that made up the hillside in Eastern Afghanistan. The few birds were quiet as darkness descended upon the gray, rugged canyons. Stars were gleaming through the cold, clear air. The sun position was just right for the phrase "Allah be praised" to be intoned, as it sank below the farthest mountain peak.

Ahmed loved and hated this time of night, sitting upon his prayer rug kneeling to Allah and Mecca. At the same time he kept a wary eye on the sky, watching for any potential plane or the American CIA's Predator drones. The drones were known to bite as hard, or harder, than the planes with human pilots. It seemed even more evil to have a fighter killed by a machine rather than by a man pulling the trigger. Although it was also somewhat fitting. How better to guarantee that Allah will be merciful and provide the virgins in heaven than to die in glory at the hands of the great Satan, by way of accursed cannon fire from a machine?

The two shivering figures were surrounded by Ahmed's "revolutionary guards," who were so named to reflect their status as similar to Iraq's former dictator Saddam Hussein's elite troops. They had waited over an hour for Ahmed to finish his last meeting and then his required worship of Allah. This wait was fitting for unbelievers. It was especially appropriate for those that were not just unbelievers, but not even considered "people of the book" - Christians and Jews - who were present on the earth before Mohammed. Godless scum, and worse than camel vermin these infidels might be, but they may yet be useful. The Jihadists of the Prophet, or JOTP, continued to have many needs. The taller one had the black eyes of the devil, but those, too, could be used, if properly guided, to do the work of Allah.

Like most evenings in Afghanistan, the wind not only continued to blow but seemed to pick up strength. This must be yet another test from Allah to insure the faithfulness of true believers, Ahmed thought. It was necessary to suffer in this life, to earn the glories of the next one. Fine grains of sand flew through the air, eating away at the smooth skins of these infidels' slant eyed faces. It caused them to look away from him and his oneness with Allah the Merciful. Either these infidels could not grow the required beard of a true man or chose to keep their child-like faces. Just one more example of why they should be scorned and ignored, possibly even killed to incite the infidel masses.

But no, thought Ahmed. Allah the Most Powerful had brought the two men here for a purpose, and it was necessary to tolerate their ungodly presence. These men had suffered nearly enough in the cold to earn a small cup of boiling tea, strong and bitter, before he heard what they came to say. Ahmed's chief lieutenant, Hadi, had told him the two infidels had come with important news and useful materials in the fight against the great Satan—America and its surrogates, the Zionist pigs in Israel.

Ahmed wrapped his face against the wind and blowing sand. He could not but think of the hard thirty-one years that had passed since his mother had born him in a refugee's tent. Maybe Allah was bringing better opportunities to kill in His glory.

Ahmed faced the two men, sitting cross-legged by the fire near the main entrance to one of their less frequently used caves. Hadi had just served tea to the infidels, which was cradled in their hands for warmth, but had not been tasted. Good. They were cautious. After a full fifteen minutes of looking each in the eyes, Ahmed felt the taller one, who was obviously the leader, would not break his gaze after two weeks of such treatment. Ahmed slowly turned to Hadi, and said, in his best, somewhat unschooled Arabic, "Have them tell me what they offer us in our fight to bring Sharia-law to the world. And be quick, so we do not have to suffer their unclean presence any longer than necessary!"

Hadi turned to translate what Ahmed had said, and was interrupted by the larger of the two Chinese men, who spoke directly to Ahmed in flawless Arabic, "I am happy to meet someone that so clearly understands Mohammed's directions as to the treatment of strangers, even if they are, in fact, unbelievers." The momentary expression of horror that spread over Hadi's face was quickly masked in response to Ahmed's intense scowl.

"So you lied to Hadi about your ability to speak the true tongue? What other lies have you told, and what lies do you intend to tell, to the desecration of Allah? Allah Akbar!" Ahmed boomed across the fire.

Both he and Hadi rose, and they could hear the guards bringing their AK-47's to their shoulders, some toward the infidels and some toward the outer perimeter.

The tall one remained both seated and calm, despite the tiny beads of sweat appearing on the face of his companion. He then bowed his head toward Ahmed while maintaining a faint smile. "I did not intend to offend, mighty warrior," the tall one continued in his cultured Arabic. "To the contrary, I have great respect for both you personally and your men, who have showed their cunning and abilities to kill and survive in their fight against the Americans."

The tall one paused, letting the meaning and courtesy of his words sink into Ahmed and those around him. The words, the calm presence, and the subtle, personal air of command had the desired effect. At a motion from Ahmed, safety levers were returned to the safe position on the AK's, and even Hadi uttered an audible sigh of relief.

The tall one continued, "As Allah is merciful, he is also wise in allowing us this opportunity to discuss the future of the world." Pausing again, the tall man politely asked, "Did you find the AK-47's, ammunition, and four trucks to be useful?"

Ahmed sat quietly, battling within himself to summon the fire and hatred he was certain should be present when dealing with this man. All he could think about was the incredible courage and air of command on display. The man neither bowed down in fear nor displayed any show of concern. Such arrogance should have brought Ahmed to a killing frenzy, and yet, it didn't. The sheer force of the man's personality, even with his slanted eyes, made everyone at the mouth of the cave want to believe this man was the benevolent leader in charge. Him!

A few more moments passed before Ahmed could summon a slightly gruff voice to say, "They should be useful and are what has, so far, allowed you to live."

Over the past five years, Ahmed's word, which was the practical application of Imam Abdullah Muhammad's scriptural interpretations, had the effect and power of Allah's law. A simple word had resulted in the death or torture of countless pawns of the Americans. Yet before this tall man, his words sounded hollow and tentative. This very fact should have driven him into a rage only sated by the beheading of both these infidels! Yet, his only thoughts were how reasonable and beneficial this man was. While these thoughts whirled around his head, the man spoke again.

"I, too, believe Allah works in mysterious ways. Allah truly wants not only the American infidels to suffer for their crimes against His will, but also those decadent and undisciplined Europeans. These weapons I bring for your fight against the American infidels are a small token of what I can do for you." The man's voice rose. "Only by crushing the American infidels will you cleanse the Earth of their arrogant taint!"

The tall man's words echoed against the hillside. All who were present could not help but be swayed and driven by them. He continued in a calm, almost soft, but powerful voice. "In order for this cleansing to happen, we knew we must find not only true believers in this cause, but those that could also achieve great things."

The man's spell drove all present to feelings of glory not felt since the successful massacre of the American-led patrol ten months earlier. He then lowered his tone until it was barely audible. Only to Ahmed he said, "But exactly how this great action will occur will require private discussions between only the two of us, and will require the patience I know only you and your followers have in abundance."

Again, Ahmed was swept along with the man's conspiratorial tone. He dismissed all except for Hadi away from earshot. The three men moved closer to the small fire.

Sitting quietly by the fire, Ahmed studied the tall man again with new respect. Infidel, yes, this man was. He stared at Ahmed with his slanted, black eyes, eyes that were both foreign and exotic. This was a man whose presence spoke of confidence and automatically drove one to believe, or want to believe, that great things could be accomplished if one would only follow his vision. The high cheekbones showed some aristocratic background, but his face also showed some Chinese peasant blood. It was the eyes, however, and the voice that commanded respect. His eyes saw right into a man's soul, shining a brilliant light on one's core beliefs. They left the recipient of his penetrating gaze with the feeling of having been measured, and in this case, of having passed the test.

The tall man spoke again, smoothly in the true tongue for a moment, before Ahmed's somewhat dazed mind deciphered the words, "... and the blow you need to strike against not just the Americans, but all who would exploit your people should be swift and devastating on a scale not seen since the time of Mohammed.

This blow should come with the severity of retribution for all the killing of believers, worldwide! Do you know how Allah has designed this blow to fall? This plan must not," he emphasized, "be discussed openly, even among the most trusted true believers. The blow will come in the form of one of the greatest plagues of all time. It is fitting that the smallest cell, a simple virus, will bring down the mightiest evil empire of this time."

Once again, the tall man paused for effect. "But like all great events, great leaders and great patience will be required. Realize that it will take up to a year, or possibly two years, before preparations can be made, but there is much to do in the time you have."

The tall man stopped to look up into the sky, appearing to appeal to Allah himself for inspiration. "In this war against the infidels," (overlooking temporarily that both he and his subordinate were also infidels), "just how many of them do you believe Allah would have you kill?"

Ahmed's eyes shone with the beginnings of fervor for which he was well known and responded, "All of them!"

The tall man paused for several seconds, seeming to contemplate the enormity of what Ahmed had just said. He then asked, "Do you have twelve men, of the strongest faith, who are both dedicated and capable of learning to move about in the decadent West?"

He then continued with the broad outlines of the plan. It would require patience and strict secrecy for there to be any chance of success. Ahmed again found the true strength of his convictions running through his veins. While the plan was being described, he thought about just the right man to help make it even better—all without the knowledge of the tall man before him.

Ahmed had only three wives, even though custom allowed up to four. His first wife was old, in her mid-40s. She was uncertain how old she really was. He had been prevailed upon to take her as a wife by his Imam many years earlier. She had needed a husband to take care of her. His third wife was only twelve. They had been married for three years. Again, the Imam had strongly suggested he take her, supposedly to care for him when he became old and frail. She had proven to be not too ugly and was learning to be a proper, subservient wife.

Ahmed's second wife had attracted him with her flashing, challenging eyes. Jasmine had to be periodically beaten when she spoke out of turn. She had eventually learned to save her sharp tongue until times when he had her exclusive company for the evening, and no one else was listening. It had taken two beatings before she learned not to speak out, even before his other two wives. She had learned these bad habits from having attended school. He tried to forget she had nearly graduated from college in Baghdad. Jasmine's brother was finishing his studies in the United States, and with the right incentive, just might have the ability and knowledge to make the changes that were necessary.

The tall man finished his business with a promise to supply two additional trucks of untraceable plastic explosives requested by Hadi to make roadside bombs. To go with the plastic explosives, he also promised 1,000 untraceable cordless telephones for use as triggering devices.

Back on the road toward Kabul in the noisy truck, the tall man, Chinese Major Cho Chong, looked at his assistant and commented in a Cantonese dialect, "I think the lizard dung sitting next to you will likely become very uncomfortable upon his return to his superior." This statement was made with a smile and nod, before informing Hadi, in Arabic, that he had hoped no offense was taken concerning his ability to speak Arabic. Since his assistant did not speak Arabic, it was only polite to request Hadi translate into Chinese Mandarin.

Hadi returned the man's smile, commenting in Arabic, "It was a surprise, but anyone who speaks the true tongue, by implication understands the true people much better." Hadi maintained his smile, despite thinking how much better this arrogant piece of camel's dung would look with his head on a pike, while his entrails seeped into the desert sands.

The truck drove away back toward the mountains after dropping off Cho and his assistant. Cho walked a circuitous route toward their hotel, allowing them a few minutes of uninterrupted conversation in Cantonese. "Cho you were masterful, as expected," gushed the assistant as they moved down the muddy street. "They were as pliable as your informant had said they would be,"

Cho responded, with a rare tone of approval seeping into his voice. "General Lao and even General Hu will be quite pleased with the outcome."

Cho's assistant couldn't help himself once again overly complimenting his superior. Many in the People's Republic of China's Ministry of State Security[2] considered Cho to be the most brilliant talent to appear in many generations. Both knew this was the double-edged sword upon which Cho teetered. Because of his

---

[2] The MSS is the intelligence and security agency of the People's Republic of China. It was modeled after the old Soviet KGB and performs similar functions to a combination of the CIA and FBI.

abilities and sheer brilliance, they assigned him only the most difficult tasks. Conversely, such tasks reminded him he was both expendable and susceptible to termination should his ambitions not remain firmly in check.

Cho wondered if the difficult work was done in this case. Now it would be up to the scientists, Lao, and his ability to keep the General Secretary on track. It would also require the strictest secrecy seen in the People's Republic of China since Chairman Mao had closed the doors to the West.

CHAPTER 4
PRESIDENTIAL ELECTION - MINUS TWO MONTHS

The Fontaine Estate
Outside of San Francisco, CA
1700 Hours PDT

In the Fontaine estate, former Vice President Walter Fontaine felt the familiar thrill after replacing the telephone on its cradle. He prided himself with refusing to submit to the popular craze of technology that seemed to sweep the country and insisted the household telephones be no more cutting edge than mere cordless. The Secret Service seemed to hate his cordless telephone. Something about security, he thought absently. They were always griping about something involving security. He had just been informed by his Chinese business contact that a certain lovely lady had been asking about his health and whether she might have the honor of polite conversation with him. Looks like his trip back to Washington would indeed have a happy ending.

"Damn," he thought, remembering how wonderful the lovely lady had been during the last year of his Vice Presidency. She had replaced the previous girl with even more beauty and delicious expertise. In the beginning, it had been so easy to arrange for meetings. While serving as junior Senator in California there were no Secret Service, or "knuckle draggers," and Katherine had always been out-of-town working on some legal deal or other. The first girl had been young and supple, and she was almost like an innocent little girl, which were the very traits that appealed to him. Most importantly, she did whatever he wanted her to do, including the rough stuff. They had assured him nothing was off limits and there was no chance of any media blow-up. It wasn't until the last year of his Vice Presidency that the girl returned home to China. For three torturous months, there had been no one to rub his neck and listen to his problems in the dark of night. Then he was introduced to his current lovely little China doll.

It had been a major operation, using the talents of a trusted aid and quite a bit of ingenuity, for him to meet his new China doll the first time. She was older than the first girl had been and was a Master's Candidate at American University in Biochemistry. She was also somewhat taller than the first girl, with a rounded figure and elf-like features. Her lips were full and could do the most exquisite things.

Sam, the head of his Secret Service protection detail, had never forgiven him for ditching the four-man team that evening. It had been reported to the President who briefly mentioned it in passing. It had been unfortunate he had to remove Sam and make it clear to his replacement that bad things happened to those who messed with the Vice President's privacy.

But my God, Walter thought with distinct pleasure, it had been worth it! She was exquisite in every detail. From her perfectly formed breasts to her supple, slim but rounded hips, she could practically make him come simply by stretching and gracing him with her delightful little giggle. He found that he enjoyed receiving some pain-pleasure treatments she devised. She could even hold an intelligent conversation. The woman knew biochemistry, but she was also interested in politics. He was careful, however, to never talk about things that were too sensitive.

The Mike Broehm Residence
Outside of Cronin, Kentucky
2110 Hours EDT

Mike Broehm could only sit and listen patiently as his wife Lauren vented her frustrations from the homeowners' association meeting. Long ago, Mike realized a husband's primary duty was to listen whenever Lauren needed to vent about the trials and tribulations of her various projects. She had left her job to become a dedicated housewife after the doctor's report on the probable cause for her severe abdominal pains. The doctor had been almost sheepish when he spoke to Mike in the waiting room following Lauren's laparoscopy. He asked whether she was under a lot of stress. The doctor had evidently forgotten Mike was a research biochemist with enough education to be aware of the horrendous toll stress can take on a person's health. The doctor explained his little camera, wandering through Lauren's belly button into her abdomen, had found nothing that could have caused her pain. All of her organs were healthy, even the neatly tied fallopian tubes. At least they were certain she wasn't suffering from any of the dozens of female-related problems that could prove fatal. Instead, the doctor seemed to believe stress, probably due to work, had been the main culprit in her discomfort. For Mike, that was simple enough. He walked into the recovery room, and after finding a blanket for his shivering wife, he announced to her he thought it was time for her to retire.

Obviously, Lauren's retirement had not resulted in her slowing down, nor had she suddenly spent more time doting on him. Of course not, he mentally sighed. Instead, she had jumped into one project or charitable group after another, leaving even less time for maintaining the house and taking care of him than before she "retired." Listening, he reflected on how the homeowners' association was just another example of her quest to feel needed. "Just like all of us," he mused to himself.

"I just couldn't believe Kerry DuBois," she said again for the third or fourth time.

"He keeps hammering on the idea the neighborhood should contribute to the Howards and Perrys, just because Alan and Jerry have lost their jobs. As if that is what the association and what little money we have is for. And that isn't the only thing he keeps pushing. He's so damned liberal, he's just hell bent on finding someone else to pay for helping out people he thinks are in need." Lauren continued to fume.

"And then," Lauren continued, having just caught her breath, "he tries to tell everyone he couldn't possibly contribute fifty or a hundred dollars to the families personally, because his job is looking shaky, too, and he doesn't have any savings, and…" Lauren paused again and seemed to see her husband for the first time since he arrived home.

The torrent suddenly stopped, and she took in a deep breath, then sighed. "I'm sorry, Mike. I know you weren't there and really don't think Kerry should be able to upset me like this. But, damn it, he just does! He's so sanctimonious! He tries to paint everyone but himself as a heartless person, while he's some voice of reason for the poor or something."

This last phrase was uttered with a resigned, but frustrated string of words. "Over and over," Lauren continued, "he keeps trying to paint anyone that doesn't support his personal crusade to help anybody and everybody as someone that doesn't care about anyone but themselves. If he keeps this nonsense up, he'll be having us all fighting each other while he comes out looking like the good guy instead of the one causing trouble."

Years earlier, Lauren had taken a college course on Marxist theory. For a short time, she had been willing to believe the utopia painted by Marx and his dialectic theory and *Proletariat Revolution*. She had even attended two American Communist Party meetings. Fortunately, she was awakened by her military theory instructor the next semester. With a military intelligence background and a Ph.D. in Soviet Studies, Dr. Bishop had the right credentials to go with a brilliant mind. He could interpret exactly what the Soviets, later to become the Russians, were doing and why. Mike was sure Lauren was bright enough to have seen through the rhetoric over time, but Dr. Bishop made it crystal clear. On the first day of his class, he explained there was a logical reason virtually no one wanted to get into the Soviet Union and most wanted to get out. This thought was followed by a well-articulated description of what total control over the press could do in the hands of a cold, motivated group of tyrants. Total media control was even more effective when you added a professional *active measures*, or focused propaganda campaign. Insert nearly unlimited funding for control of the masses, at the detriment of all but the most basic necessities, and you got the Soviet Union.

Dr. Bishop then described a particular Soviet active measures campaign designed to implement the theory of death by a thousand tiny cuts. This description, and a class exercise crushed any further possibility Lauren would be fooled. The Soviet spy network was scattered all over the world. It was tasked with spotting and identifying the young idealists in the journalism schools. First, an "Uncle Ivan" would help a little with a struggling student's tuition. Then he would pay for a few drinks here and there. All the while, he would feed the ego of his target by saying how powerful the press was. There was a duty to prevent the big money grubbers from having all that power, planes, and the ability to purchase the pretty bubble-headed girls to stroke them whenever they wanted. It was so easy to fan the fires of envy. This message was repeated thousands of times, causing the targets to buy into the Communist Party line to the point they would accept simple instructions. These instructions came from Moscow, but they didn't need to know that. They just needed to move in the direction where they had been subtly manipulated. They would question or cast doubt on everything from the mental capacity of the current American administration to blurring the line on exactly who really was the bad guy. After all, weren't the American industrialists the virtual slavers who forced people to work for substandard wages while they lived it up?

Dr. Bishop pointed out that if only one or two people were spreading this propaganda, it would have been ineffective. But with first a whisper, then so called open debate shouted from thirty different publications with subtle perseverance, even the normally conservative American people could change their minds. It worked during the war in Vietnam.

Mike also thought it was probably the simple idea that truth didn't matter to the communists quickly doomed Lauren's brief swing to the left. Dr. Bishop ran a class project to prove just how effective their methods could be. First, he identified and asked one of his best students to write and present the logical theme that his or her qualifications and productivity should determine a person's pay. Randy, one of the best students in class, willingly took on the task. Then he clandestinely asked four students to tell veiled lies about Randy's nefarious past and his greedy motivation for giving the presentation. These four moles then suggested the whole reason Randy believed this proposition was he wanted to make only a few people rich to the detriment of everyone else. For three weeks, they worked continuously to defame Randy. When the class was polled regarding their opinions concerning the presentation, they overwhelmingly voted against the proposed system, quickly followed by ridicule targeting Randy. The way Dr. Bishop ended class was Lauren's awakening and one of the most powerful turning points in her life.

Directly following the theory presentation and polling, Dr. Bishop waited patiently at the podium for the class to quiet. He had to wait for the raucous humor and pens and erasers to stop flying in the general direction of poor Randy. One particularly loud woman had even shouted to Dr. Bishop that Randy should be expelled.

The crowd quieted, faced with Dr. Bishop's quiet, friendly eyes. He then posed the first of several astounding questions. "Are you all enjoying your current display of mob mentality?"

After a ten second pause, during which complete silence ruled, he asked, "Are most of you now ready to begin using your mind?" Confusion was obvious on the faces of virtually everyone, waiting for what wisdom, or perplexing question, Dr. Bishop would present next.

"Tell me, please. Did any of you really feel young Randy here should be expelled for merely presenting a theory?" Again, Dr. Bishop was met with a stunned, confused silence.

"Am I correct you feel strongly that what Randy said was both wrong and potentially evil?" Again silence, while the ventilation fans blowing air into the classroom suddenly became very loud. Only a few heads nodded this time.

"Now, let's look at this issue using simple logic. First, let me hear specific, articulate reasons pay should not be based on capability and performance." Five raised their hands with varying degrees of confidence. Unlike most college courses, Dr. Bishop's class had always enjoyed widespread participation by the students during class. Two of the reasons suggested were judged potentially valid by class consensus and placed on the white board next to the podium.

Dr. Bishop continued, "Can anyone give me a specific, articulate reason pay *should be* based upon capability and performance?" A dozen hands went up, with additional hands going up to add to the list over the next several minutes. Dr. Bishop dutifully noted over a dozen reasons supporting the theory on the white board next to the two written earlier.

"Does anyone still believe the original proposition is wrong or evil?" No one raised their hand or nodded their head. "Does everyone now believe the theory is, in fact, valid?" Almost everyone raised their hands, although there were two or three that sat quietly with confused looks on their faces.

"It would appear under the light of reason and logic," Dr. Bishop continued while pointing at the lopsided whiteboard, "it becomes easy to make an informed decision. But, the more important point here is exactly how Soviet style active measures were used to influence even a bright, well-educated group like we have here. At my request a few of your peers were recruited by me to use crowd control and manipulation techniques to overcome logic and reason by turning the issue into something motivated by emotion and class envy."

Throughout the entire class, the four students tasked by Dr. Bishop to influence their classmates had quietly sat in their seats. At first they were curious and excited to see the results of their roles in this experiment. Over time, they began to pale and eventually all looked either in their laps or at their hands on their tables.

To further clarify the point, Dr. Bishop had used the additional example of an advertising campaign, then popular on television. He suggested advertisers were constantly searching for just the right hooks to sink into the public to sell their product. The best ones worked but were always tempered by a free press, which had the ability and responsibility to expose the untruths. What happens when the free press does not do its job?

Lauren, along with most of her fellow students, was only partially listening, their minds racing through the different ramifications of how they had been so thoroughly duped. No one wanted to be a member of a mindless herd. Lauren now understood they had all been part of the herd going over a cliff.

It was a very sober class that filed out of the classroom. Both Mike and Lauren were among them. Lauren neither forgot, nor forgave herself for having been the one who shouted out for Randy's expulsion. Mike felt similar guilt for having been one of the four "Commies" used by Dr. Bishop to dupe his classmates. The lesson was a life-altering moment which changed them both forever. It also drew them together over hot coffee and twenty minutes of quiet time they shared after the class. Thinking back, now Mike could really understand Lauren's tremendous frustration. He was building a quiet anger toward not just Kerry, but all the Kerrys in the world.

CHAPTER 5
PRESIDENTIAL ELECTION - MINUS ONE MONTH

A Major Kentucky University
0730 Hours EDT

Ali al-Hadiz was both flattered and perplexed at the most recent letter received from his sister, Jasmine. He had reasonable respect for his sister, who had almost finished college in Iraq before the American invasion. But then she had become the second wife of a man he believed was either a brilliant leader of men or a crazed maniac. Ali could never be sure which was the case, or if both were true.

Ali knew his brother-in-law, Ahmed, was somehow involved with Jihad and taking the fight to the Americans in Afghanistan, but he knew little else about him. Ali had no contact with Jasmine for over two years when he suddenly received her letter. It included a cashier's check for travel expenses back to Kabul. From there he was told he would meet a man sent by his sister at a particular hotel. The man would provide transportation to their location. Jasmine claimed she strongly missed her brother, and Ahmed had agreed to finance the visit to allow him to see their little girl. The invitation was for the following summer, which Mohamad thought was a long time in advance for such an invitation, but he saw no reason to refuse.

After further thought, Ali believed his sister was considerate in making the invitation far enough in advance to allow for him to finish his Ph.D. and hopefully find a job with an American firm willing to sponsor his quest for a green card. His sister must have spoken with their mother and knew he would finish his Ph.D. in Pharmacy the following May. His thesis involved Nano-technological research to alter genes in particularly nasty viruses to make them attack only abnormal cancer cells.

Ali wasn't interested in finding a job working for an American firm for twelve or fourteen hours per day, but he realized such a job was the second easiest way to U.S. citizenship and the ability to stay in the U.S. The easiest way to citizenship was to find an American wife. Ali was intelligent enough to realize his complete lack of social skills prevented his ability to find a satisfactory American wife on his own, and he didn't have the money to purchase one–if only for the two years required to get his citizenship. That left a future with a low-paying job, even though it would pay much better than he could make back in Iraq, while avoiding suicide bombs. The job would have to come with an H-1B, or specialized work visa, which would allow for his eventual green card and pathway to citizenship.

Having given the matter the requisite amount of thought, Ali quickly wrote a note back to his sister showing his intention to come to Kabul the following summer.

Washington, D.C.
0925 Hours EDT

Su Ling sat in the coffee shop feeling for the thousandth time like a trapped rabbit waiting for the fox. Uncle Sung had just left after having informed her that her services were required once again. The evil man, "likely the reincarnated spawn of a cockroach," she thought bitterly, had been the third MSS Officer to demand she once again become a whore.

Thinking back, it had all seemed like life would proceed according to *her* plan. Success in school, both academically and in athletics, had helped her to think she was making her parents forget their longing for a son. Competing against the better students in Shanghai had given her confidence she was more than a pretty face.

It had all come crashing down that day when, at 17, she was called in to receive her college entrance test scores. Such a summons was usually reserved for only the very best students or sometimes, the worst. With cold precision they had told her she had failed, yes, failed almost all of her tests. In an instant, her world had come crashing down upon her. Failed! She was told her best hope was to find a semi-important official to marry once she was assigned to a collective farm. It wasn't until later; it occurred to her, someone in the Party had the power to change test scores.

Su cried softly until her school guidance counselor had come into the room. He sternly told her someone from the government had come to see her. Confused, she looked up through her tears while the counselor barked an order for her to straighten herself up and make a good impression with this man. He could be, she was told, someone who could find a way for her to overcome her "shame."

The man sat behind the table in the small room reading something in a notebook. No chairs were visible, so she approached his table and bowed her head, looking at her shoes.

"So you have shamed yourself and your family by your poor test performances last week," he began without preamble. Su felt like she had just been punched in the stomach. Her knees shook and a lone tear escaped from her left eye.

"Do you know the shame your mother and father will bear when they hear of these failures? Their daughter, a candidate to become a peasant farmer… Do you?"

He shouted at her while glaring up into her face. He fired the last two words at her like a pistol, making her shoulders jerk while she tried unsuccessfully to suppress her tears.

Su glanced up only once in the next several seconds to find the man glaring at her from behind his black-framed glasses, his round, pig-like eyes boring a hole into the top of her head. After what seemed like hours, he said under his breath, "Although…, there might be some hope…"

Su's reaction to this whispered phrase was strong and immediate. She felt like a drowning monkey grasping at reeds of grass. She was too intelligent to look directly at the man or voice her willingness to do anything to mitigate her shame. Looking back, she realized weakness and shock were natural reactions for a naïve village girl.

Again, the man spoke softly, thinking out loud, "She is not an unattractive girl… and there *may* be some ability to learn simple things…" he trailed off again.

Finally, after an interminable wait, the man said, "Should I save you from the collective farm, girl?" He paused again before grunting in disgust. "Should I even try to save you? Look at me, girl!" he shouted into her face.

Her body shook with her head bowed. She looked into pig-like eyes and did not like what she saw. No pity or any spark of positive human feeling was visible, only the look of disgust that made her heart sink once again. She could even see the depths of cruelty dwelling ever so close to the surface in this man, a man who would pluck one wing from a butterfly and enjoy watching it flutter in agony, too cruel to even kill the poor thing to relieve its misery. In fact, he would enjoy prolonging it. Even under these traumatic conditions, her innate ability to read people allowed her to see into the man's character.

After another long wait, the man began again. "There is a way you might, just might, be able to serve China other than by slopping pigs." She missed the irony of someone like him referencing pigs, considering his strong similarity.

Pausing purely for effect, he continued, "There is a school that might take a girl like you. Hmmm. Could you, no would you, do what it takes to succeed? All for the greater good of your family and China?"

Mr. Wong had looked again off into space, almost ignoring her. It was then his turn to give a minor start, recognizing the bug was still on the laboratory table. "Well, girl, will you do what it takes to overcome your shame? Answer me, girl!"

Su recalled the flood of hope welling up within her at this chance offered by the man. Neither knowing nor caring what would be required of her, her response could only be utter compliance.

Su sat by herself in the Washington, D.C. coffee shop. A chill ran through her body considering what had next happened in her life.

"Excuse me, are you all right?" asked a pretty, strawberry blonde girl in a plain white blouse and jeans. Su brought herself back into the present once again with a faint pang of fear. She realized she had lost the iron control necessary to keep her life intact.

"I'm sorry. I didn't mean to disturb you, only, well, you seemed to be upset after the man left your table," the blonde girl said with a friendly but concerned smile.

After a pause she said, "I'm Lisa, Lisa McIntyre," while holding out her hand with a friendly gesture.

Su had been constantly reminded throughout her several years of training she must *never* make friends with any American. Contact with anyone was to be avoided. Despite that mandate, Su couldn't help but instantly like this friendly girl. Su's instructors had repeatedly told her if anyone approached her, she was to say in slightly broken English, "I OK," and then walk away. But after over two years of contact with only "Uncle Sung," and Walter, the man to whom she was a whore, her emotional walls seemed to recognize a good heart and friendly smile for what it was. Here was a genuinely good person who wanted to be a friend to someone in need of one.

After a quick look around the coffee shop to be sure no one else was watching, Su said, "No, but thank you for asking." After another pause she continued, "That was my uncle... Uncle Sung. He's my only family here and sometimes he upsets me." Whether or not it was conscious, Su could never say. For reasons she didn't fathom, she had dropped her usual thick Chinese accent while talking to Lisa.

"Tell me about it," Lisa said with a roll of her eyes. "My dad can drive me completely *crazy* sometimes, especially when the topic is a guy!" This mental image brought both a smile and a small giggle to Lisa, which almost instantly became contagious.

It was like two kindred spirits suddenly met for the first time. The conversation skipped the usual questions about hometowns and majors. Instead, they jumped right into what their professors were like and what desserts they had to guard against most in the constant battle to eat healthy and stay trim. Five minutes turned into forty-five minutes, while the two girls bonded in ways transcending words and cultures. Both discovered they had a love of 60s rock music, surviving another bout of giggles when they relived the gyrations of Elvis and Mick Jagger on stage. Both loved their parents deeply, but knew instantly they lived in a different world which their parents would never understand. Both were in graduate school studying subjects that mostly attracted college boys, who were far too nerdy to be considered men. They commiserated over their complete lack of interest in any of these boys, nor did they want to waste time on any of the dozens who awkwardly kept attempting to attract their attention. They shared the need to dress down, avoiding make-up and not styling their hair. Otherwise, the boys' attentions would become even more bothersome. It was at this point Su again became distracted as she considered the ways she used her training to insure she did not attract any of the American, or even any of the Chinese, Indian or Middle Eastern boys at their school. She thought it was interesting Lisa seemed to decide on personal actions to avoid undue attention. Su could tell Lisa was really a beautiful girl, with a rounded figure that could attract a great deal of attention from the boys if she wanted to. Instead, Lisa dressed down and almost looked plain in an elegant way.

A quick look at the time left the two girls with only a minute to exchange telephone numbers before each had to hurry off to class. Su thought about her new friend, while hurrying all the way across campus for her next class. For the first time since she was seventeen, she felt her heart lift and believed, if only in a fantasy-like dream, there may be some rays of light in her life. If only she could convince herself, she could allow an American friend into her life. Then maybe she could find some small amount of happiness in what, so far, had proven to be a frightening and miserable life.

CHAPTER 6
PRESIDENTIAL ELECTION - MINUS ONE MONTH

Outside of Cronin, Kentucky
1000 Hours EDT

For Mike, the world was a fairly simple place, especially when it came to the preparations for deer season. All the mess of politics going on in the country just then, Lauren's frustrations with that dimwit Kerry DuBois, even the hassles at the university, were all put on hold as he gathered his equipment together to head up to the farm. Even though it was still over a month away, just thinking about it seemed to help his mood. He packed the warm weather gear in case Mother Nature dumped on his parade and sent balmy temperatures and cold weather gear for potential ten-degree mornings.

The other thing Mike couldn't help thinking about was the conversation with two of his hunting and drinking buddies. Jim Carson and Rollie McDermott were the guys everyone wanted for a friend. Mike had known both men for over ten years and would not only trust them with his daughter, but even with his wife. For the past several years they had all observed many things going on in the world that made them very nervous, especially in the aftermath of 9/11/2001.

Right after 9/11, Rollie had posed the questions of whether his friends were prepared for a more widespread attack than had happened in New York City. "What do you mean?" Jim asked.

"Well," Rollie explained, "I don't rightly know. But one thing's for sure. If I was to lose electric and maybe running water for any amount of time, me and my family would be royally screwed!"

This statement lead to what became a running discussion of both what might happen and what they might do about it. It evolved over the next few years to preparations to meet potential threats, including everything from an earthquake on the New Madrid fault to financial collapse and the anarchy that might follow. Even though each of them refused to consider themselves "preppers," all three men began making preparations for emergencies each viewed like "insurance." Just like life insurance or car insurance, no one expected to either die early or total their car, but everyone wanted to be covered if such a thing would happen.

Mike's first move was to go to Sam's Club to stock up on canned goods. He was proud of himself for the first year until it occurred to him many of the cans would expire and possibly spoil before they were needed. Neither he nor Lauren could stand wasting good food, so his strategy had changed to purchasing freeze dried food in cans. Freeze-dried food vendors hawked their products' 25-year shelf life.

Over the next couple of years, deer camp prep conversations also included the possibility they may need to "bug out" or abandon their homes for an alternate, safer location. The challenge would be on both traveling and having a destination that was safer than their homes. Rollie and Jim would be in trouble if they sheltered in their homes in town and law and order broke down, not to mention if electric power shut down. Too many people in towns and cities were not prepared for anything, much less a major catastrophe. High population areas would suffer food riots and general anarchy.

"Hell," said Rollie, "I may have a gun or three..." The comment brought chuckles from the group, "but if there was more than one bandit, or even a few hungry neighbors, my house isn't defendable. Folks get hungry, or have kids to feed, we'll have desperate people willin' to do desperate things." Jim and Mike both nodded in agreement.

Mike, "If Lauren and the kids were hungry, I think I'd do almost anything to get food for them." Mike silently made a mental note he could not allow such a thing to happen. He had the time to take care of that contingency right now.

"Say, Mike," said Rollie, "do you think maybe we should expand deer camp?" Mike had initially been thinking much along the same line.

"No, I don't think so," said Mike. "Looking around here, there just isn't enough room or secure storage for us and our families. Look, guys. As much as I love this place, the square footage alone would have my wife shooting one or more of us within two weeks, not to mention what it would be like to live here without power or running water. And it's a long walk up the hill to the cabin to lug water five gallons at a time. But I've been thinking..."

"Whoa, there boy!" said Jim with hands up and a grin on his face. "Every time you get to thinking, it either gets expensive or involves a lot of hard work, or both!" He and Rollie were used to Mike's various schemes, almost all of which involved serious financial investment. What made them even more annoying was they were almost always good ideas, and worth the investment in money, time and effort, which usually meant he and Rollie bought into the plan, hook, line and sinker.

"Yeah, yeah. I hear you," said Mike. "But anyway, what would you guys think about maybe looking at my place in the neighborhood as our retreat?"

Both Jim and Rollie knew Mike lived in a big, all-brick house located in a neighborhood in the country that was ten miles outside the nearest town. It even sported a steel roof. The homes in Mike's neighborhood were on acre-plus lots. "If you guys want to invest in some long-term storage food and help me build an insulated storage shed or pole barn to store some clothes and such, you could come out and live with me. It would be a little tight, but there would be room for you and your immediate families. And at least there would be someone living on the premises to protect the place." He let that concept sink in for a good thirty seconds.

"What do you say?"

It only took a quick glance between Jim and Rollie to seal the deal. "Sure works for us!"

Bringing himself back to the moment, Mike thought about what was going on in the world. With the election about to happen and that crazy bitch looking like she might even win the Presidency, maybe he should start spending more time on the group "insurance" policy. He had been thinking about starting to include some neighbors in his planning. The first man to come to mind was Fred Callahan, Chief of Police in the nearby town of Cronin. Fred, age 52, was married to Penny, who loved dogs and had doted on her two Labrador retrievers since her son had grown and gone off to the military. Typically, when inspiration struck Mike, he acted quickly. He picked up the phone to invite Fred and Penny over for drinks.

Washington, D.C.
1100 Hours EDT

Katherine had looked smug while out on the campaign trail for the past week. At least she did when she was away from the press and was not terrorizing her staff. Stetson balanced whether it was time to, once again, insist Katherine listen to the latest version of how important her so called "caring image" was to the "gold ring." She was becoming more and more flighty in her focus. Earlier in the campaign, Stetson merely needed to mention the "gold ring," referring to the Presidency. This reminder would bring her back to focus and reign in her natural inclination to look down her condescending nose at everyone around her. Graduating from an Ivy League university, coupled with power brokers constantly stroking her ego, gave her the attitude of entitlement.

Katherine's poll numbers continued to drift slowly but steadily in the right direction. From a position of trailing by three percentage points six months ago, she had steadily climbed to a position of an eight-point lead. Stetson had to admit Marc Baxter's campaign using the Afghan widows had reversed falling poll numbers. However, Stetson was also convinced the huge state-by-state turnout of social media committees was just as likely to have positively moved the numbers.

Stetson also recognized, but didn't want to give too much conscious thought to the more clandestine work done by local party bosses, particularly in swing states like Florida. In previous elections, the mainstream media ignored subtle little facts like when individual precincts had more votes cast than registered voters. They had also avoided noticing almost all absentee votes having been cast for only one party, despite the precinct voter registrations listing an even split between the two parties.

Wondrously, Stetson thought, those precincts always seemed to lean heavily toward his party. It was even more astounding the way right-wing shouts of complaint were buried or outright ignored.

The potential illegal alien voting numbers were not discussed either openly or even privately, unless it was a very secure environment between trusted political operatives. Stetson knew there had been a significant number of voters assisted to the polls by party bosses in the past. Hell, sometimes they even voted in more than one precinct! He had also been told by one such operative about the hundreds of dead people who voted in the last election.

Fortunately for Katherine's campaign, the vast majority of Americans failed to understand election laws in most states specifically prevented organizations like the FBI and even Attorney General's offices from posting impartial observers at polling stations. Even the most blatant election fraud could only be observed by designated members appointed by each party, when they were not restricted from observing the polls by an apparently well-meaning Sheriff or deputy. By the time complaints of irregularities were reported to the Secretary of State's Office in each state, witnesses forget details or couldn't be found and, if luck held for those committing these bad acts, the complainants would have given up on the notion of anything being done about the misconduct. Stetson took pride in knowing these types of shadow votes accounted for over ten percent of the votes in some precincts and almost always favored Katherine's party.

Stetson had meticulously followed Katherine's demand to include Marc Baxter in the planning sessions and all phases of the campaign, at least so far as Katherine and Marc were concerned. He knew that with Katherine the Great as a candidate, a straight up election was not winnable. Therefore, he had to ensure Marc saw what he should see and didn't get involved in areas where his naïve principles would be offended.

Stetson had brought in Marc to discuss Katherine's mandate a month earlier. He had begun by trying to outline for Marc some of what campaign operatives did with state and local campaign offices that might be considered on the line. Marc had reacted with surprise, followed by a deep frown at hearing what he considered potential fraud. Stetson quickly explained such activities were carefully held to fall short of the legal line. His justification was that sometimes doing good things for the little guy took getting your hands dirty. Marc had been adamant he would not take part in anything illegal. Stetson, in his most fatherly way, had instantly agreed if Marc observed anything of that nature, he should report his observations immediately. They would both address the issue before it got out of hand.

Two weeks earlier Marc had come to Stetson when he learned from a stupid loudmouth in a South Florida precinct some early military absentee ballots had been "accidentally lost." Both men knew the military voted overwhelmingly for Donnelson. Stetson was able to stage a faux firing of that precinct captain by using a private conversation with the idiot during one of Katherine's campaign swings through the area. The fool had seen the error of his ways and removed his name from the party list, just in case Marc checked. Otherwise, Stetson kept Marc appropriately insulated.

Marc listened intently to Stetson's explanations, just like a young martial arts student would listen to his master. Stetson's reputation for getting people elected was legendary. Thinking to himself, Marc could see the importance of bending a few rules to get the right person elected. Hell, you can't make an omelet without breaking a few eggs. Lurking in the back of his mind was the feeling the whole campaign flew in the face of doing what was right. It was more like the ends justified the means. Wow, he hadn't thought about the morals he learned as a child since he went away to Columbia University. Now everyone around him seemed to be swept up with changing the world and damn the people who were trampled.

CHAPTER 7
PRESIDENTIAL ELECTION - MINUS ONE MONTH

New York, New York
1845 EDT

Walter Fontaine was almost cheerful, sitting beside Katherine during the private donor campaign dinner at the Waldorf Astoria. At $50,000 per plate, this dinner intentionally targeted wealthy donors to solicit more money for Katherine's campaign and to offer them one last opportunity to plant a seed in Katherine's (and several of her potential staff's) ear about specific policies they believed were important. Walter had hated these things when he campaigned himself and still hated them on general principles. It seemed the candidate was nothing more than a prize mare to be examined for either running or breeding potential. Stetson had even tried to subtly remind him how much he owed Katherine for his own political success. He also mentioned a few of the benefits of living in the White House and having a taxpayer vacation budget.

Such reminders, which ordinarily would have driven Walter into an absolute rage, were met with a simple cold stare. Stetson had finally relented, apparently feeling he had made his point. Not even this indignity had made Walter lose his cool. Tonight, he would see his beautiful little China doll again. Mr. Sung had arranged it, with a strong word from Walter to his Secret Service detail that when he retired to his room, he did not want to be disturbed.

The evening had finally ended at the Waldorf. The wing of the hotel he affectionately thought of as the Presidential Wing was used by several Presidents in the past, and the Secret Service had dutifully revised the security plan for the building several times. By unwritten understanding, more than one President had arranged to escape from this wing, at least for an evening or night, to get away from the strangling feeling of the constant tight security. Forays out into the public without heavy security protection was a risk, but it was one that was occasionally taken. So long as no one knew about it and steps were taken to insure the President was not recognized while outside the hotel, the security threat to the most powerful man (or woman) in the world was minimized. Walter was well aware of these procedures and found that since he was merely the prospective First Man, it was even easier than it had been when he was Vice President.

When Mr. Sung brought him up to the small suite on the seventeenth floor of the nearby Grand Hyatt hotel above Grand Central Station, Walter was already breathing hard in anticipation. Entering the room, Mr. Sung closed the door behind him. The room was bright, with at least four lamps by the leather couch and chairs and overhead lighting in the bar area. Su Ling had heard his muffled steps on the carpet. She was already at the bar fixing him his Glenfiddich 21 single malt scotch on the rocks. While she stood at the bar, ice cubes gently tinkling into the highball glass, he had to consciously draw a breath. His chest was tightening, and he knew if he didn't take deep breaths, a heart attack could be the result.

Admiring Su's trim shape in the beautifully form-fitting white silk robe brought back all of his adolescent fantasies and multiplied them by 100. "My God, she's beautiful," he thought, admiring her petite 5'4" figure. Her dark hair was long, just like he liked it, and as silky as her robe. He didn't know Mr. Sung had threatened her when she had wanted to cut off some of her hair. The bruise on her wrist had taken two weeks to heal. The thin robe, with gold dragons beautifully displayed all over it, clung to her body, emphasizing her medium-sized breasts, while Walter observed her from across the room. From experience, he then imagined her firm and supple flesh just under the silk, with no underwear to mar the perfection of either her skin or her other succulent attributes. Walter had once commented on the lines left on her flesh from her underwear. Miraculously, every time after that the lines had been missing. Momentarily, Walter had a feeling she might even abstain from wearing underwear all together, even when she was not here with him. That thought quickly morphed into the sensual thought of her walking toward him on the street without underwear.

Su turned toward Walter and carried the drink over to place it in his hand. She held a glass of wine which she had previously refilled twice before he arrived. Mr.

Sung insisted she be ready for Walter at least two hours before his scheduled appointment.

Mr. Sung's microphones had picked up on Walter's comment concerning the underwear lines, and he had instructed her to ensure they were never present again. He then insisted she appear well before the appointed time to be physically inspected. His only softening of the rules was allowing her up to two glasses of wine before Walter arrived. He had apparently decided she would be more affectionate if he allowed this minor alteration from the rules. It also helped her keep what small amount of food she had eaten in her stomach.

"Walter," Su said in her well trained, China doll voice. Using the accent in keeping with her character, she continued, "It has been too long since I see you. But I see you no eat properly," she said with what sounded like true concern in her voice.

"You lost at least two or three kilos."

Walter took both of their drinks and placed them on the coffee table. Then, without fanfare, he gathered her up in his arms and kissed her deeply while his hands moved over her body. Today, he didn't seem to be able to decide where to fondle. After what seemed like hours to Su but was actually less than a minute, she broke away from him followed by a deep sigh as if she too was succumbing to the throes of passion. "No, no Walter," she said in her most subservient voice. "You know how much I like for you to climb the mountain slowly so when the volcano explodes, even dragons cover ears." Her delivery was so sincere and her promise so explicit, Walter almost forgot how much he wanted her right that moment.

"First, I must hear of everything you do since you held me last. Please, leave nothing out." Su settled herself down onto the couch. Walter naturally laid himself across the couch with his head in her lap. He was reveling in what he could feel beneath her silk robe before her skillful questions moved his mind to the annoyingly hectic campaign trail.

It wasn't long before, in response to her innocent questions, he poured out his complaints of the stupid things happening in his life and stupid strategies in use by Katherine's campaign. There was something about Su. Maybe it was that she was from a different culture, and maybe it was because he knew what was soon to come. He just found it easy to tell her everything happening in the campaign. It never occurred to him how skillfully she was questioning him. He described the embarrassing moments when Katherine had made the politically incorrect comment to a donor in front of a microphone. These stories were but the teasers before he got into the campaign strategies, which seemed to get Su the hottest.

The Mountains of Southeast Afghanistan
0745 Local Time the next day

Ahmed had just begun creeping out of his cave as the sun peeked over the mountain. His hatred for the great Satan, the Americans, had been affirmed once again. Following his usual routine, he had been awake before dawn and was making his absolutions to Mecca when his sensitive ears had heard the distant sound of either a drone or a not-so-high-flying aircraft. Ahmed's reaction to the potential threat was immediate and incredibly quick. He literally dove into the cave and rolled another ten meters to come to rest behind a large rock. The sound he had heard was probably just a jet traveling somewhere within earshot, but he was secretly proud of his quick response to the potential threat.

The previous year, he had seen his close friend, Muhammad, nearly vaporized by an American missile. Muhammad had been sitting outside of a cave, using dawn's light to fix the firing mechanism on his Russian made RPG or rocket-propelled grenade. Ahmed was just about to return from answering the call of nature when he first heard the distant aircraft. Almost immediately, he saw the blur followed by Muhammad virtually disappearing in a ball of fire. He wasn't able to hear well for several days. Over the past several years, he had scraped the remains of too many of his fellow jihadists off the desert rocks to have less than a very healthy respect and hate for the Western infidels' air power.

His second wife, Jasmine, had listened to his earlier description of the two Chinese infidels with rapt attention. Over the past month, she had displayed cunning that made Ahmed proud but left him with the deep-rooted fear he might have to have her stoned to death for her knowledge of the ways of the infidel. At least she had learned to save her ideas until they were alone in their bed. She was the one who had suggested a true believer who had lived in America be found to teach twenty-four of the most fervent believers to speak the English language and learn skills necessary to move about in America.

"You stupid girl," Ahmed had told her. "It is far easier to send my twenty-four believers to a Pakistani school for a year than to find a teacher to come here."

Months ago Jasmine would have immediately lashed out with why this plan was wrong, resulting in yet another beating.

"Oh, yes, my husband," she responded instead. "You see so much more clearly than I. It had not occurred to me how difficult it would be to find a teacher with the skills needed. There are many schools who teach the great Satan's language. I am confident you will be able to stop each of your martyrs from sipping too much from the cup of lies they will also teach in these schools. It will be just like you have taught me to follow the true will of Allah." This statement was made with her eyes properly looking at the floor and with the greatest of humility.

Having planted the seeds of doubt in her husband's plan two days earlier, when he came to her again, she chose the time when he was completely spent to ask, "My husband, could not an international aid worker be taken who could teach only the language and skills needed to your twenty-four believers?" She patted her slowly growing belly containing her second child. She said with a loving grin, "You can be *very* persuasive."

After a pause, Ahmed's mind caught up with her point that a kidnapped aid worker could be persuaded to teach his believers only what they would need for the great mission. This time, he would slap her behind only twice, followed by favoring her with his seed a second time for her having appreciated his good idea. Even the Prophet had recognized discipline of a wife must be lessened when she is with child.

CHAPTER 8
PRESIDENTIAL ELECTION - MINUS TWO WEEKS

Outside of Cronin, Kentucky
0700 Hours EDT

Mike Broehm always found the neighborhood association board meetings to be tedious and annoying. These feelings meant he avoided them whenever possible. This evening was one he had promised Lauren he would attend. Also, there were a few things he wanted to bring up himself. It wasn't just Kerry DuBois and his crazy ideas that bothered him about most meetings. It was all the unimportant, nit-picky ideas people brought up to the board that really didn't matter. The Presidential election was coming up in two weeks, and the country had a U.S. Congress incapable of getting anything done. It seemed to him the country was going to hell in a handbasket before everyone's eyes. Worse, no one seemed to want to change it.

With the beginning of the meeting, Mike's mind wandered. Mike was a student of history. He remembered stories of the economic and political situation in the years leading up to and just after World War II. The country went from the Great Depression to fighting a World War on two separate fronts. Through it all, the United States was nearly bankrupt. Maybe it was the dire circumstances of the time, but the government operated differently then. President Roosevelt could schmooze what he called the loyal opposition into working with his Democrat Party to promote the purchase of war bonds. For the first time, the American people financed a major war themselves. It was all done in a spirit of helping our boys over there.

The minutes of the last board meeting were read, and the Board President droned on. Mike continued to consider how the United States leadership had failed in its ability to bring the factions together. During the years following World War II, the United States rebuilt Europe, including Germany that was totally destroyed by the war. In addition, the country also rebuilt Japan and enabled President Eisenhower to build the American infrastructure. He always considered creation of the Interstate Highway System to be what allowed the country to become the greatest nation on the planet. These amazing projects were done at the same time the Cold War began and the Korean peninsula erupted into war. During these times, politicians came together for the sake of the country.

Listening to the Board President going over old business, Mike thought the threat of Communism and the Soviet Union played a key role in squashing socialist ideals during the 1950s. Ultimately, it drove the American Communist Party and sympathetic socialists underground, crushing the Soviet Union's goal of starting a version of the Soviet revolution they called the American Proletariat Revolution.

The Soviets failed to convince the American people of the oppression brought onto them by the upper classes, so they backed off and instead set out a 45 step plan to achieve Communist domination worldwide.[3] Number 15 involved the capture of one or both of the political parties in the United States. These changes even spilled over into the new Fontaine administration. It scared Mike to realize how many of the 45 steps to Communist world domination had already been accomplished.

Mike considered how much the Communist thinking had infiltrated the United States and even the US Congress in today's politically correct society. A complete lack of unity was blatantly apparent. Many portrayed the capitalistic ideals that had built the strongest, most technologically advanced country in the world as unfair. Congress was split between two general factions. One faction felt government was the answer to the country's woes, and big business should pay more of their fair share. The other faction saw nearly half of the population of the country receiving some government benefit. This second faction had an overwhelming mandate from conservative voters to halt what they felt was the headlong plunge toward full socialism. Further complicating the mix was a small, but radical group of anarchists who were always lurking in the background. They were waiting for an excuse to take to the streets and commit wanton destruction for their own entertainment.

---

[3] See Congressional Record, Appendix B.

It seemed to Mike he spent most of his time lately watching the national leadership fail in their efforts to get anything meaningfully accomplished. He just couldn't decide what he should do about it. Through discussions with his close friends, there did not appear to be anything they could do to change the current political climate. It was time for everyone to begin preparations for whatever disaster or major challenge was coming next. The starting point would be here in this neighborhood.

Somewhere during this line of thinking, Kerry DuBois had gotten up to espouse another plan for the association. Today, he wanted the neighborhood association to pay for upgrades in the neighborhood common areas. He then wanted the association to pay to bring out inner-city kids to enjoy the new facilities.

The President of the Board seemed to be intimidated by Kerry, which resulted in Kerry dominating many of the board meetings. Most of the prior competent board members had stepped away because of him. Kerry continued to wax poetic on how wonderful it would feel to see these disadvantaged children enjoying the new playground equipment until Mike couldn't stand it anymore.

Mike interrupted Kerry by saying, "Well, that's very interesting, Kerry. Do you mean you will pay the cost of shipping these kids out here to enjoy what our neighborhood dues have built?"

"Wh, what, Mike?"

Mike repeated, "Are you going to finance the transportation and supervision of these kids you want to bring out here?"

"Why, Mike, you know I don't have that kind of extra money," Kerry back-pedaled.

"So this feel good project is another plan for you to spend all of our money, but you won't be contributing," Mike said, letting the words sink in slowly.

"Well, if you have no compassion, Mike."

Again Mike cut him off, "What I have is compassion with my money, Kerry. I don't take other people's money so I can feel good about myself." After a moment, Mike continued, "Kerry, how much money of your own did you contribute to charity last year? You know, don't you? Didn't you deduct it from your taxes?"

Mike had seen Kerry use the compassion line before. Mike's simple question, asked in a soft reasonable voice, left Kerry glaring at him. Mike looked at Kerry and waited. If there was one thing Kerry could not stand, it was silence.

Suddenly looking around at the others present for the board meeting, Kerry could tell they were waiting for him to say he had given thousands of dollars to charitable causes the last year. In the heat of the moment, it didn't occur to him to lie. In a huff, he got up and stomped off toward his house mumbling, "You people just don't care…"

"I'm sorry, Earl." Mike said to the board President after Kerry had left. "Just couldn't handle any more of that stuff."

Earl was feeling somewhat embarrassed he hadn't had the guts to cut off Kerry himself. He said, "Thanks, Mike. Now, on to new business. Anyone have anything for the board?"

Only the board members, Mike, and one other neighbor were present at the meeting. "Yes, Earl," said Mike softly. "If you don't mind, I do have something I think might be important to all of us."

With a genuine smile, Earl said, "Well go ahead, Mike!"

"You all know me and Lauren and know I don't make suggestions much. When I do, I'm willing to put my own sweat and money into it." The six other people present all nodded their heads.

"I've been talking to some friends and most recently to my financial advisor. Frankly, I'm more than a little troubled. I think some kind of emergency or disaster is likely to come our way. It's not if, but when. And I don't think most people would handle it very well. If it were really bad, most folks would suffer horribly or even die." Everyone was now giving him their full attention.

Mike continued, "Now I'm not expecting the end of the world or anything." He smiled reassuringly. "Maybe something on the scale of hurricane Katrina or if a bad earthquake hit our area. Well, if that happens, damned few folks, even in this neighborhood, are prepared. One of my buddies in state government even told me about a federally funded program called CERT or Community Emergency Response Team. Natural disasters aside, the news is full of stories about several groups of terrorists that are out to get us. Heck, what would happen if we were to lose power for two months? Like most houses in this neighborhood, mine is all electric."

Suddenly, Joe Ryan, a neighbor who almost never talked during board meetings, spoke up and said, "Mike, don't the power people and the Governor have, you know, like contingency plans?"

Mike said, "Well, there have been commercials on TV and the radio lately telling people to be prepared for emergencies. You know, like at least three days' food and water for everyone in your household. I just kind of figure three days isn't enough. If the whole area lost power for four weeks, there's no gas pumped, no groceries delivered, and depending on the time of year, it'll get awfully hot or cold. When folks get cold and hungry, especially if it affects their kids, they can get pretty ornery. I know I would!"

Everyone seemed to think about Mike's words. Mike let it all sink in. "I'm not saying there's going to be Armageddon or anything. I'm just saying we should get prepared." The next half hour was taken up with discussions of what direction their preparations should take. Mike's respect within the neighborhood and his quiet leadership qualities ensured it wasn't a question of whether they would go along, but what needed to be done and how each could do their part.

CHAPTER 9
PRESIDENTIAL ELECTION - MINUS NINE DAYS

Washington, D.C.
Fontaine Campaign Headquarters
0945 Hours EDT

Katherine woke with a start. She had briefly dozed off at her Arlington Virginia campaign headquarters desk. Prior to her impromptu nap, she had been thinking how gridlock in the dysfunctional U.S. Congress could easily derail her plans for the country. In the current political climate, driving the short-sighted legislators to move the country in the right direction seemed like an impossible task. In her dream state, she was not just elected, but crowned by her adoring subjects. They all cried out for her to seize control from the money grubbing industrialists and bankers and give their ill-gotten gains to those in need. She awoke from her vision with the euphoria replaced by panic at the thought of losing the election and any chance of imposing her will on the country.

"Stetson! My office. Right now!" Katherine screeched.

At least her political radar was functioning better than usual, Stetson thought ruefully. The group of reporters had just left after getting the days comments on the campaign. Two weeks ago, she had not timed it so well, which resulted in Stetson calling in favors with three reporters who had stayed behind after the early afternoon meeting. All three were of the opinion the exclusives he had given them over the years did not nearly cover their refraining from publishing anything about Katherine's outburst. He had agreed he owed them one, and each made a short note on their iPads. The bastards even turned their notebooks around for him to see the words, "Stetson owes me," "Stetson favor," and "DS owes me a big one." When the first two saw the third note, they changed theirs to read the same.

Bastards! It wasn't until ten minutes later he realized there was nothing on their pads about Katherine's outburst.

Stetson walked into Katherine's office and couldn't help but wonder how she could keep things so neat and organized. Then he saw Susan Cassel, her lawyer and personal assistant, diligently counseling a young intern in the office's corner. He caught only two phrases about keeping up a professional workplace image and how we have to find things. Stetson was impressed with Susan, who seemed to be organized and could keep Katherine focused.

Occasionally, Stetson had thought Susan was like Dwight D. Eisenhower's wartime secretary, Kay Summersby. Even though Eisenhower's biographers and close friends denied there had been anything sexual between them, Stetson had his doubts. The doubts included both Eisenhower and Katherine. He didn't even want to think about what went on between Katherine and Susan behind closed doors. He trusted Susan would look after Katherine's reputation, even if Katherine didn't.

Directing his attention to Katherine, he found her standing by her desk in a muted yellow Brooks Brothers pant suit. She wasn't a tall woman, so the extra twenty pounds she had gained over the past year was even more noticeable. Her blonde, graying hair framed her face with pale-blue eyes. She did the best she could to hide the bags under her eyes and the lines on her slightly pudgy face, but there was only so much even her top level make-up artists could do. Fortunately, he had closed the door as he entered the room.

Katherine launched into one of her patented tirades almost the instant Stetson had closed the door. "Now what the fucking hell is going on in Florida? I thought you told me it was all sewed up! Now the cocksuckers at Fox News are reporting it's in a statistical dead heat?" She paused for dramatic effect.

"Well?" She drew out the word for over three seconds. "What the fuck, Don?"

"Katherine," Stetson said carefully, "can we discuss this matter privately?"

"I trust all of my people explicitly, you know that," she said with typical campaign conviction. She glared at him for a full ten count, then she said, "Oh, all right. Susan and Karen, give us a minute. Oh, and I could really use a triple latte and a chocolate-covered, cream-filled donut from the place down the street. You know the one. And I don't fucking care how many calories it has. This stress is killing me!"

The two left the office and closed the door.

"Well, Don?"

After taking a moment to gather his thoughts, Stetson decided against the usual placating intro. Instead, he walked to the special box on Katherine's credenza and pushed the button marked "music." Instantly soft music emanated from the box, with a barely detectable white noise of static designed to prevent any recording of the conversation. This box had been a holdover piece of equipment given to Walter Fontaine when he was directed to give some oversight to the NSA as Vice President. The NSA had repeatedly asked for its return, but Katherine justified hanging onto it despite the high level of classification. She was the leading candidate for President and had the clout to do so. It was a real pain in the ass, Stetson thought, to have gotten the clearances for Susan and himself to maintain and store it.

"Katherine, some of the groups supporting Donnelson down in Florida have published whispers the Afghan widow's story was all fabricated. It's too late for them to publish absolute proof, but the word seems to be getting around among the retirees. It won't matter, though, because let's just say someone I trust has been down there for quite a while, and the special get-out-the-vote projects will insure you get all electoral votes from Florida." After a pause, Stetson continued, "Oh, and we never had this conversation, right?" She paused, then nodded.

Stetson then continued in his most conspiratorial tone, "In the past couple of elections, tens of thousands of voters who may or may not have been legally entitled to vote, found their way to the polls and cast a vote for the correct party. The grass roots party people found not just undocumented workers, but many others, too. My contact - you don't need to know he even exists - will arrange for that number to increase. The flood of new undocumented workers over the past eight years has made it possible to more than double the previous numbers. Let's just say there are other contacts who are similarly active in other key swing states like Illinois, Wisconsin, and Virginia. None of these votes will show up in any poll. Hell, why do you think we fight so hard to ensure a valid ID isn't needed to cast a vote?"

After letting it sink in for a moment, Stetson continued, "My job is to get you elected."

Stetson let his statement hang in the air for several moments. Throughout his explanation to Katherine, Stetson was getting increasingly angry. Whenever he thought about what he and other political advisors did to get their candidates elected, the more soiled he felt. He didn't even want to contemplate the number of federal and state felonies he had committed. Like so many on the political left, he believed strongly the ends justified the means. Rules and laws were there to be bent, or even broken if it got your candidate elected. Getting Katherine elected superseded any other considerations, especially those involving morals. Morals, he thought with passion, were for people without the power to do what needed to be done. What pissed him off were these self-righteous assholes looking down their noses at people like him who gave them the chance at greatness.

"Now listen to me carefully," he said, looking into her eyes with unusual fire. "If you want to be President - the most powerful person in the world - and have the chance to carry out all of your grandiose ideas, stay out of my way and let me get the job done. This shit of screaming for your minions, especially me, stops. Now."

For the first time, Katherine seemed to step back with surprise and just a hint of respect. She buried the latter almost immediately. Stetson had never talked to her this way. After the shock wore off, she instantly showed how she had risen so high in politics. She realized both how important Stetson was to getting her elected and how many skeletons were in her closet. With her newfound respect, she also realized he was probably smart enough to have covered his back, just in case anything bad was to happen to him.

Katherine erased her natural inclination to snap back at Stetson and replaced it with a five-second stare that did not contain hate or rage or any of her normal reactions. Instead, she said, "Let's just say I appreciate everything my supporters do for me."

After a pause, she finished with an uncharacteristically calm and soft statement, "And Don, this conversation never happened." She then turned and walked out of the office.

Upon reflection, Stetson had to consider the conversation to have been the most enjoyable he had experienced with Katherine. At least she hadn't thanked him for both arranging for her election and committing crimes on her behalf. Stetson added his memory of this to one of about a dozen meetings or conversations he could never reveal to anyone. That's why he had stopped drinking ten years earlier. Words seemed to slip over his tongue when he drank.

· · ·

Katherine walked away from the conversation with Don Stetson, feeling the exhilaration racing through her at what he had said. It would happen! She always knew she would do anything necessary to gain the highest level of power, even to the point of selling her soul. Reaching Stetson's so-called gold ring was only the beginning. Once she assumed the office of President, she could command what she wanted and minimize or eliminate those believing they had power over her. Stetson and everyone else were mere tools that would give her the means to power. What she did with the power would be determined after the election. Without thinking, she hummed a strong tune as she walked toward the campaign war room. It was the same tune she always hummed when thinking about imposing her will.

CHAPTER 10
PRESIDENTIAL ELECTION - MINUS EIGHT DAYS

Outside of Beijing, China
1020 Hours Local Time

Premier and General Secretary Song Ren was head of the Communist Party and the undisputed leader within the PRC (People's Republic of China). He sat quietly in his garden on the softly padded stone bench. He wore a collared blue striped shirt and linen trousers. He was tall for a Chinese man at five feet ten inches. His gaunt, clean- shaven face did not show his 67 years of age. He had put aside his tan jacket. With the hot sun out and no wind, it was not needed on this late October day. He sat in a "people's park" in a suburb about an hour outside of downtown Beijing. Several MSS Officers insured no one had access to the well-manicured garden except for General Secretary Song and his family. It was not mere coincidence the park abutted his private residence.

Song practiced his inner calm as MSS General Lao Tung approached across the pathway. Lao was a short, slender man who liked to wear a thin goatee of dark hair. He was young for a leader of the MSS. Rising to his position at only 50 years of age indicated how clever and ruthless he was. It also did not hurt his father had been high in Chairman Mao's Communist Party leadership.

Sitting in the park helped Song collect his thoughts, especially while admiring the late blooming flowers. It put the hundreds of issues facing him and his nation in perspective. High on his list for consideration was whether to replace the beautiful Lu Bai. She was an exquisite creature. Her name meant "person of purity." He presumed she was the best the MSS's special Charm School had to offer. Unfortunately, she had recently thought her opinion mattered or was even desired. She was bright and well-read. She was the best he had experienced from the girls sent from Charm School for his use. He couldn't decide if it was her acrobatic abilities or her creativity in exciting him through touch and visual means that put her above the rest. After consideration, he decided he would not discuss the matter with Lao. Though Lao was one of the few with which he could discuss almost anything, something prevented him from discussing Lu. He would discipline her one more time to remind her of her purpose, and then he would see how she reacted.

Lao bowed low in front of the General Secretary. He then complimented Song on the magnificent job done in designing and maintaining the garden. Lao was well aware they had flown the late blooming flowers in from the south and were receiving warm air treatments from special heating units each evening and throughout the night.

Lao had selected Song's security detail for both their competence and their loyalty to him. The head of the detail reported to him on a weekly basis. He kept Lao advised of everything involving the General Secretary, including with whom he met and what looks or comments were made by anyone in contact with him. These reports also included how many times he voided his bowels per day.

Decorum dictated the conversation should touch on the garden, the weather, and families of each man. Almost immediately after the bare minimum of pleasantries, Song invited Lao to sit on the ornamental stone bench directly across from him. This bench had no soft pad, but Lao would have been both surprised and alarmed if there had been one.

Song opened with the usual question that always opened these encounters. "Lao, when will our renegade province be returned to the People's Republic?" The question referred to when Formosa, the Chinese breakaway island province known in the west as Taiwan, would again come under the complete control of what Song believed was the only true China.

Directly after the Americans had dropped the atomic bombs on Japan and the Japanese surrendered, the civil war between the communists led by Communist Party Chairman Mao Zedong and the nationalists under Chiang Kai-shek began again. This war had been ongoing since 1927; however, it was delayed following the Japanese invasion and war from 1937 to 1945. Major combat between the Communists and Nationalists ended in 1949, with Chairman Mao having driven the Nationalists off-shore to the island province of Formosa/Taiwan, Hainan, and their surrounding islands. Song and every other communist leader had always considered Formosa to be a break-away province which should be returned to their control. But for the American Navy, and a very well trained, equipped, and financed island army, this insult to the Chinese people would have been rectified decades ago.

Lao apologetically admitted there had been no major advances on reacquisition of Taiwan. He had learned not to placate Song with political drivel. The one time he had, the resulting dressing down had made him feel menial, stupid, and vulnerable. It was a feeling not experienced since right after he entered military officer training. Those army experiences had neither the eloquence nor ferocity of the one given him by Song. Song had berated his ancestors by name, going back four generations. Lao had been impressed Song had known his ancestry back that far.

After lowering his eyes with the admission, Lao quietly mentioned there was a positive movement for the relatively near future. Again, he paused for his statement to register with Song.

"Tell me Lao," Song said with more than a hint of curiosity.

"General Secretary, as I have reported previously, it appears Katherine Fontaine will win the American election for President. It is also possible her party will, once again, take control of the American Senate. When this change happens, we will dominate the Americans across the globe."

"Are the Americans aware of our actions to ensure her victory?" Song asked in a very soft voice. Even Song was aware of how sensitive these intelligence activities were and how quickly they could blow up, should they become known.

"No, General Secretary. None of our intelligence operations have been penetrated or discovered."

Lao made this statement knowing the American intelligence people probably knew, at least generally, that the Peoples Republic strongly supported the Fontaine Presidential run. In another of the mystifying actions and inactions by the Americans, nothing was said either publicly or even informally. Lao was confident even if there were the smallest inkling of the operation involving Walter Fontaine, his wife's people would squash it immediately. The fact Fontaine had been serviced by the operative only two days earlier was a powerful sign the operation was continuing successfully.

Lao looked forward to the receipt of the video and sound of the "delightful interrogation" of Walter Fontaine by Su Ling. The image quality of the film was never great, but Lao's wife had previously commented on his performance when he came home the evening after having had a viewing. Lao was a student of all things American. His wife seemed to have the same wisdom shown by former Yankee's manager Billy Martin's third wife when she told reporters, "I don't care where he gets his appetite so long as he eats at home!"

Changing the topic, Lao said, "You will recall your decision to support our continued purchase of U.S. bonds? This policy was begun during the Clinton administration and has continued since then. The Americans are nearly 25 trillion dollars in debt, and we continue to acquire large portions of it. When you envisioned the plan to exploit their vulnerability, my analysts determined it would require an American President and administration just like Fontaine to raise the probability of success. It appears the pieces are falling into place. Your plan will work!"

Lao let the moment and ramifications coalesce into Song's mind. "The Russians have also agreed in principle to supply significant amounts of crude oil to China on short notice. We will very soon be able to drag the Imperialists down far enough economically we can pass them militarily."

Song sat silently for several minutes listening to birds fly and chirp above the garden. The city sounds were never far away, but here, it was possible to escape that world for a time.

"I want you to prepare a Most Secret briefing for the Politburo," Song told Lao. "It is to outline the overall strategy, and it is to give accurate projections of what will happen to the Americans. And Lao, these projections are to be accurate," Song said with special emphasis. "You understand? None of the wishful thinking dung normally coming from your people. We are moving on to great things, including a time when Formosa will no longer be protected by the Americans, but we are also moving much closer to a war no one will win."

Song waved his hand in a gesture, dismissing Lao from his presence. He had many enemies within and outside the Politburo, which acted as the governing body for China. Information given to them was always a risk, but in this case, a necessary one to avoid their interference if not to gain their support. Song had only about fifteen more minutes of meditation before he had to take his motorcade into the city. He would once again manipulate mindless bureaucratic leaders into doing something productive.

Walking away from the garden, Lao's mind strayed to a wild theory advanced by General Hu. Hu was in charge of the joint Special Warfare Division of the MSS and the PLA. He had given this presentation at the Most Secret conference in Shanghai the previous day. Hu had informed the few that were present, "The rest of the world, and particularly the Americans, are unprepared for an Ebola or bird flu type plague. Should such an event happen in the United States just as China is poised to take back Formosa..." Hu let the concept hang in the air, like a struggling butterfly attempting to climb away through the air from a hungry bird. Just before Lao's very nervous aide changed the topic, Hu had noted that the source of the plague attack would have to be conclusively from some other enemy of the US.

CHAPTER 11
ELECTION DAY

Washington, D.C.
Fontaine Campaign Headquarters
2000 Hours EST

Katherine was beside herself. In fact, she was positively giddy. The new poll numbers from two days earlier were compared to the exit polls by Don Stetson's people. The exit polls put her a point or two higher, making her true lead over Donnelson seven and one half percentage points. In a Presidential election, this level of difference was, and would be proclaimed by future political commentators to be a landslide. Stetson hurried into the room and nodded with a neutral expression, but his eyes showed his excitement. No one wanted to jinx the election by beginning to talk like victors, but it was only with the greatest of efforts was this avoided. Katherine was happy she hadn't had to talk to anyone all day. Like everyone in her war room at the Waldorf Astoria in New York City, she was watching the early exit polls with interest, but her mind could only think of the power she would soon wield like a crusader.

"It looks like CNN has all but declared you the winner," Susan Cassel whispered from just behind Katherine. Without thinking, Katherine extended her hand over her shoulder, which Susan took hesitantly. Everyone but Marc Baxter politely found somewhere else to look. Not that everyone didn't suspect there was something going on, especially since Walter was so obviously uninterested in Katherine except for how she could get him onto Air Force One.

Everyone in the room also knew Katherine had been giving exclusives to Marjorie Klein for the past two years, and she and Marjorie had needed to meet regularly–in private–to discuss various political topics, and usually at night. It just wasn't discussed when security personnel observed Marjorie departing Katherine's suite. She always seemed at least somewhat disheveled. Having a job of high stress coupled with long stretches of mind numbing boredom, anything potentially titillating was both fair game and readily expounded upon during the few off-hours they received. These discussions were only among themselves, but somehow many of Katherine's staff learned of those observations. Within the beltway, referring to the Washington, DC area within the circling highway system, the personal and especially the sexual activities among the 'pols' was a standard topic of conversation.

The way Katherine took Susan's hand was like the way she had taken Marjorie's hand in the past. Marjorie was at the doctor's office, however, so Susan seemed to be an adequate replacement.

More and more exit polls continued to show the likelihood of a Fontaine victory. Walter had a strong urge to plan for when he moved into the White House and when he would have strong input into many of the things, the new administration did. This plan included several appointments to positions of trust and influence within the administration. Walter already had a growing list of Chinese businessmen who would be invited to overnight in the Lincoln bedroom at the White House.

Walter also believed it would be beneficial for both his portfolio and his personal requirements to avoid the over-watch of his "goddamned knuckle draggers." He'd do whatever had to be done in order be able to enjoy the talents of Su Ling. Even the thought of their last encounter brought a rush of blood to areas of his body that had forgotten the feeling. The other girls just didn't seem to have that special something Su oozed naturally. The first time he met with his doctor over at Walter Reed, he had to get tough with him to get the little blue Viagra pills directly, without going through a pharmacy. Sonofabitch even tried to kid around with him about what it would be like to fuck a President. Like that would happen!

While the afternoon progressed with agonizingly slow speed, Katherine began to drag. No sleep over the past forty-eight hours was taking its toll. When Susan suggested she lie down for fifteen minutes, she couldn't think of a single reason she shouldn't. All the thoughts of what she would do with the power kept her head in a constant spin.

Susan led her to a chaise lounge in a private room just off the main war room. "Madam, please come in and just lie down for two minutes. It'll do you a world of good." Susan then directed Katherine to the chaise, where she sank onto the surface and laid back. Susan began to gently but firmly knead Katherine's shoulders. In a matter of seconds, Katherine's face went slack, her mouth opened, and she snored loudly. Susan looked down on the older woman, much like her mother probably looked down upon her as a child, and momentarily felt the weird dichotomy in the more dominant role despite Katherine's position as the next President of the United States.

"My God," Susan thought, looking down on the tired, wrinkled face, losing the rigidly sharp-eyed look, and the stress seemed to melt away. "This must be what mothers think when their positively devilish and mischievous children go to sleep. So innocent. And not nearly the flaming bitch she is when awake. What am I going to do when she's actually the President?"

Susan realized her desire to be among the great and to help them wield power unimaginable to her only three years before had led her to do things and become someone alien to what she thought she was. Three years earlier, when she had first joined Katherine in the Attorney General's office, she had felt the raw power in her. It was intoxicating to be around the woman. Even then, it was clear Katherine had aspirations to become President. Susan had been swept along and convinced herself she would do anything to see Katherine in the Oval Office. Besides organizing everything from her campaign to her life, Susan had known she was personally responsible for Katherine's political success. Without her, or someone like her, Katherine would not be elected to any office. Early on, she had seen Katherine was periodically, but regularly meeting Marjorie in intimate settings. Susan was OK with that since it both advanced Katherine's aspirations and put Katherine in a good mood.

About a year earlier, Marjorie had been unavailable to meet with Katherine one evening when she and Susan were working late. Katherine had looked at her in a certain way several times before, but tonight, she caught Susan's eyes and wouldn't allow her to look away. "Dear, please knead my shoulders a little," Katherine said as she took up a straight sitting position in her chair. Susan could never say no to Katherine, so she dutifully took up a position behind Katherine and squeezed her shoulders like she had done many times for her father. After that, she had just gone with the flow.

CHAPTER 12
INAUGURATION - PLUS ONE MONTH

The White House
1100 Hours EST

Marc Baxter was a man of medium height in his early-30s, clean-shaven with short, curly, dark hair and pale blue eyes. For at least the third time, he asked himself if accepting the invitation to join the Fontaine Press Secretary's office had been sheer lunacy. He had just walked back to his office after standing in for his boss, Press Secretary Marjorie Klein, at one of the new President's cabinet meetings. Marjorie had again been "sick," and was reported to be at Walter Reed Hospital undergoing a lengthy series of tests to diagnose the problem. The Chief of Staff had sent her deputy, Towanda Jefferson, to meet with a group of conservative journalists. She was reminding them of the traditional 100 days each President expects from the press, during which they do not criticize the President's initial moves and policies. At least they did not do so with their usual fervor. Several conservative news outlets were blasting virtually everything announced by the Fontaine administration. Baxter sighed silently to himself. It had somehow fallen upon him to represent the Press Secretary at the meeting.

The first thing he noticed was President Fontaine stood up and wandered around the conference room every time someone gave a report she found boring. At the start of the meeting she had acknowledged each of her present cabinet members. Many still came to these weekly meetings while the new administration tried to capitalize on the fervor of the successful election. The previous administrations' Secretary of State, David Cumming, had agreed to continue working for the new administration. The new Secretary of the Treasury was Seth Goldberg, a partner for a major Wall Street investment firm. Dmitry Roskov was the new Secretary of Homeland Security. U.S. Air Force General Roger Tignor was Katherine's new Director of National Intelligence (DNI).

Except for Marjorie, Katherine had neglected to choose either a female or a minority to serve on her cabinet. Lining the wall behind each of the Cabinet members were at least two and often up to four members of their staffs. Despite the centuries of experience represented in the room, it was clear Katherine the Great didn't feel anyone present was much more than an individual minion whose sole purpose was to do her bidding.

Marc couldn't help but also notice only he represented the Press Secretary's office. Fortunately, he was required to respond to only one question by Katherine, which was, "Baxter, where the fuck is Marjorie?" He succinctly informed her Marjorie was at Walter Reed for tests, and her deputy was meeting with the conservative press people. Katherine's initial reaction was not concern for Marjorie's health. Instead, it was a hint of personal anxiety. She then exploded into anger, "Well, this shit has been going on since before the Election! God dammit, SHIIIITTT!!... What the fuck is wrong with her?" This was obviously a rhetorical question. It was also equally obvious Katherine took it as a personal insult Marjorie was not available at her beck and call.

Almost as quickly as the anger had appeared, Katherine calmed herself, followed by looking at Mark as though peering right through him. It was as if he was not worthy of her notice, especially compared to the rest of her minions. She then moved her attention to the next Cabinet member.

Marc had awakened at 3:00 a.m. to prepare a concise, two-minute list of recommendations for press releases addressing all five of the major hot-button issues in this news cycle. Standing in for the Press Secretary, he wanted to make a good impression on everyone present. Instead of demanding to know what the Press Secretary's office was doing about the issues, she ignored them all.

"Madam President," Marc began, trying to inject humility in his voice, "I have prepared…"

Katherine cut him off before he had barely gotten started by glaring at Chief of Staff

Burton "Burt" Combs. "Burt, you can address the press issues?" When Combs nodded without conviction, she redirected her attention to General Tignor.

Unknown to Marc, Katherine had strayed from listening to what was going on in the staff meeting. She now brought her focus back to the meeting.

"General," Katherine began, with the falsetto politeness she sometimes used when addressing the military, "please enlighten us on the latest threats coming from around the globe."

Within thirty seconds of his beginning a list of the top threats, Katherine got up from her chair and walked around the room again. She seemed oblivious, if she was even listening. General Tignor provided a summary of the latest terrorist threats, yet another Office of Personnel Management personnel data hack, Russia's latest moves in Eastern Europe, and the other threats.

This was the fourth such staff meeting Baxter had attended. The first three had been as an observer and feeder of information for Marjorie or Towanda. Katherine had at first seemed to fawn all over Marjorie, giving her the 100 percent attention reserved for very few people. Marc couldn't help but think it might have something to do with Marjorie having come out of the closet several years before. Before the campaign really kicked off, Marjorie had lost her companion of fifteen years to breast cancer. Marjorie was an attractive woman who had both a strong sense of empathy and femininity that seemed to be able to calm Katherine during her loudest outbursts. Marc had heard the rumors among the staff about her connections to Katherine. But since the election, even as Katherine was putting together her cabinet, Marjorie's health and her status with Katherine had been steadily declining. Marjorie suffered from intense headaches and had been called to visit Katherine only infrequently.

Katherine's staff meetings placed the very real question in Marc's mind as he thought, "What nightmare had I gotten myself into?"

CHAPTER 13
INAUGURATION - PLUS ONE MONTH ONE DAY

Outside of Beijing, China
0845 Hours Local Time

General Secretary Song stood by the window overlooking "the People's Garden" while his Secretary and de facto Chief of Staff, Wong Jie, stood and waited the prescribed four steps into the room for Song to notice him. Many years earlier Wong had discovered it to be unnecessary to make a sound or clear his throat to let Song know he was present. Though both were much younger then, the scars from the beating ordered by Song on his bare bottom could still be seen and felt in the privacy of his own apartment. Wong had stood patiently for over ten minutes and was prepared to stand for the rest of the morning.

"Wong," Song said without turning from the window, "tell me your thoughts about the American election of President Fontaine. And not the same thoughts you shared the day after the election, but how you think this election will best serve China."

Song's use of the word 'China' instead of the People's Republic or People's Republic of China particularly pleased Wong. Unlike the so-called learned class, Song made a point to always use the all-encompassing description for all of China. It continued to thrill Wong to hear Song imply China was, or would soon be, one great empire.

"Comrade Secretary," Wong said softly, "as the intelligence reports have been showing for the past two years, election of President Fontaine appears to be the best outcome for our strategies for several reasons." Knowing Song expected this, Wong had said "our strategies," instead of "your strategies," though they were almost entirely because of Song.

"Yes, yes, I know what the reports say." He paused for effect. "What I want now is your opinion of which reasons are correct and how accurate those reasons have proven to be so far." Song made this statement in his deep, rich voice that carried the authority of his office and more.

Wong was somewhat taken aback to have Song make such a demand. Although he did sometimes ask for an opinion, it was expected the opinion would be more like confirming what he thought the General Secretary thought. It was disturbing for Wong to have to answer this demand without having the chance to think about it, but he knew that was precisely what Song wanted.

"Comrade Secretary," Wong continued, "The President continues her apparent policy of dividing the American electorate through creating race inequities in the name of diversity. At the same time, she buys off several of the minority groups through promises of overly generous government programs while cutting military spending. These actions benefit us in two ways. First, it drives up the American debt which allows us to add to what we have already acquired. It also insures her continued power base, which prevents fiscal conservatives from doing anything about it. Recent intelligence reports show her choices for major administrative positions have been assessed to weaken the American military and drain their economic growth capacity. Soon, Comrade Secretary, the United States will be unable to match us militarily in the Pacific Rim or influence the world stage against us. To do so will risk their financial ruin. Our strategy of arranging the American death-by-one-thousand cuts - economically, continues to be effective. The Russian moves in Ukraine ensure the United States will have to divide their attention. Our intelligence regarding American intentions is, shall we say, diverse and reliable."

Wong was careful to avoid mentioning any specific details about Chinese spies that had penetrated the American government. The Americans appeared to continue keeping their heads in the sand concerning the threat of Chinese intelligence penetration. Wong knew of several American intelligence officials who were aware there were likely catastrophic penetrations. Katherine Fontaine and her inner circle were more interested in the contributions made to their various foundations than any actions which might cut them off. The electorate would view serious government penetrations as incompetence. No administration could afford to have such a reputation.

Song's office was swept for bugs twice each day. Wong was one of the few within the highest level who knew about the most sensitive penetrations of the

Americans. Like the MSS director and Song himself, Wong knew just how important it was to speak carefully at all times. This caution applied even when in the General Secretary's own office. All three men had used these types of leaks for their advantage in rising to the pinnacle of their political careers. They did not underestimate their enemies. This high level of discretion was yet another reason Wong had remained with Song so long.

"That said, Comrade Secretary, I believe there is a growing arrogance felt and exhibited by many in the MSS and PLA intelligence groups lumping all the Americans into the same mindset as the Fontaine administration. You have taught me well history is one of the most important indicators of future political actions. The biggest mistake made by the Germans and Japanese during World War II was in believing the United States would not fight or could not afford to fight. Under President Reagan, the Americans again gained the will to stand up to the Soviet Union outspending them nearly to death with the Star Wars program. President Carter may have gotten the Iranian hostages back, but it was the fear by the Iranians of Reagan's impending inauguration that moved it along."

Wong could see Song was becoming impatient with such detail, so he moved ahead quickly.

"Under this President, the American Congress will be divided and polarized. There will be no political will to oppose the critical points in our plan until it is far too late." After only a short pause, Wong continued in a much more serious tone.

"Comrade Secretary, I have hesitated to mention this, but there is one major concern." Song gave Wong the hand gesture he should continue.

"President Fontaine will be tentative about using military force, much preferring to use the American Special Forces and Predator drone strikes to accomplish everything, but socialist-leaning leaders like her seem to escalate to the highest denominator far too quickly. I fear she will threaten, and may even use, the nuclear option as she sees the United States' conventional military power surpassed by our forces. Yes, she will be intimidated by our might, especially when we exert the economic hammer. We must exert this pressure with great subtlety to avoid a radical response."

After a momentary pause, Wong continued, "You have seen the reports of her legendary outbursts and her loss of control under pressure. That is most dangerous when someone has a finger on a nuclear button."

Wong paused before going on but then decided it was enough said and remained silent. Song looked out the window in deep thought. The complexity of his strategy allowed for options along the way, but the goal of complete domination in the Pacific Rim and relative domination and influence throughout the world did not account for a nuclear exchange with the Americans. Much like the Soviets had discovered in the 1960s, a nuclear exchange would likely result in mutually assured destruction. Both the Americans and Soviets came to use this concept to prevent nuclear war. Yes, modern munitions were far less "dirty" than those atomic bombs of the past, with neutron weapons killing humans and leaving most structures standing. However, that much death and destruction in China was not acceptable, mostly because of its indiscriminate nature. In concept it would be very useful, he thought, to remove the less desirable within China, possibly the rioting peasant farmers, and most especially if it could we could blame it on the Americans.

Contemplating further, the thought haunting Song's dreams suddenly came to mind. Might it be better to use a far more radical approach, as had been suggested by General Hu Sengai? Song made a mental note to plan a visit to the large factory near the Special Warfare research facility. A clandestine meeting and briefing could be arranged.

Most uncharacteristically, Song paused for only thirty seconds before dismissing Wong. Wong left the meeting with a feeling of unease, knowing Song was contemplating something very important which he did not wish to share.

CHAPTER 14
INAUGURATION - PLUS ONE MONTH ONE DAY

Lexington, Kentucky
1100 Hours EST

Mike was not looking forward to the arrival of Lauren's younger brother, Marc. First, the generational difference caused problems. He was twelve years younger than Lauren. He was also a liberal son of a bitch who couldn't keep his commie thoughts to himself. He and Kerry DuBois seemed to be birds of a feather. Too bad, Mike thought ruefully. There was no hunting season for liberal idiots!

"Mike," Lauren said as she got ready to head off to another volunteer meeting. "Marc said his plane was scheduled to touch down in Lexington at 3:30 this afternoon. Are you sure you don't mind picking him up and bringing him home? I know you don't like him much, but he is family, and I haven't seen him for over a year."

The smile she saw on Mike's face reminded her of a little boy who was told he has to go to the dentist to have a tooth pulled. He was putting on his "I'm a big boy" face.

"Come on, honey. He really isn't a bad person if you can get by all the delusions he picked up at Columbia."

The look of skepticism on Mike's face was comical, causing Lauren to break into a laugh. "Hey, I raised him. I would have drowned the little twerp myself if he weren't really, deep down, a decent person."

Lauren's parents had both been killed in a car accident when she was 18, and she had helped her aunt Kathy raise Marc.

"Okay, okay. I'll go get him, and I promise to be nice," Mike said with a smile. He really wanted to get along with Marc.

"Remember, Mike," Lauren said, "use the rules you told me you used in dating. Avoid talking about sex, politics, and religion."

Mike walked over to Lauren and tried to give her a big hug. "Off with you," she said. "You don't want to be late."

Mike had wanted to suggest an intimate payback for doing this favor for Lauren. Unfortunately, she didn't seem to have much interest in those types of things lately; he grumbled to himself all the way to the car.

When he got to the airport, he splurged and parked in the short-term parking lot. It was nice to park near the entrance to the building. Walking into the entrance, Mike saw a man in his early 40s that looked suspiciously like Marc. After a full five-second stare, he became convinced the lone man was Marc, or rather a version of Marc who had aged at least ten years since he last saw him. He might not have even recognized him outside the terminal.

Marc brightened upon seeing Mike, and whatever he was thinking about so deeply seemed to have been put aside. "Hi Mike! God, it's good to see a friendly face for a change."

Mike was more than a little surprised. There had never been a lot of love lost between them, with Lauren as the only thing they had in common. "Hell, it's good to see you, too. How are things in Washington?"

At the mention of Washington, Marc's face shut down. He then looked around and quietly said, "Let's keep where I'm from and where I work on the down low until we're in the house or at the car. Can we please?"

The seriousness of Marc's response hit home with Mike, who said, "Sure, Marc. We can do that. How was your flight? Everything on time?"

Marc had only a small carry-on, so they walked straight to the car. On the way, Marc complained about the TSA pat down at Reagan National Airport and about how little real service was provided on the flight out. It was only a regional jet, so the one flight attendant had politely informed everyone on board she was there for insuring their safety, only. They canceled beverage service on the flight when they hit turbulence thirty minutes into the flight.

Mike thought to himself Marc had not lost his propensity to whine.

Entering the truck, Marc opened a small pouch-like bag and inserted his cell phone. He then reached over and touched Mike's arm to stop him from pulling out.

"Mike, thanks a lot for understanding when I first saw you in the terminal. One thing I have learned is there are ears everywhere. If anyone had a clue of what

I really thought about what's happening in Washington, DC I'd be fired and, who knows, maybe even 'disappeared.' That's the term the spooks and military guys use when someone is killed and the body is never found." The earnestness in Marc's tone and on his face struck home with Mike as nothing else could.

"I don't need to, and can't, get into a lot of things with you and Lauren about what I have seen and what I know, but let's just say I thought the last administration was fucked up. Now I'm really getting to be scared shitless."

After a pause for a full fifteen seconds, Marc continued, "Would it be ok if you just told me how you and Lauren are doing and what you've been up to? It may take me a while to decompress and really figure out what I can talk about."

"Sure Marc," Mike said with a look of real concern on his face. "Lauren has been really getting into gardening and has even started raising chickens!" At the look of bewilderment on Marc's face, Mike continued, "No, not for the meat but for the eggs. You know every chicken we have is a pet for your sister. She names them and everything! We've lost two chickens to hawks so far, and your sister had a proper burial for each one. Not sure if she would have survived any suggestion of using a stew pot," Mike said with a grin.

This description brought a grin to Marc, knowing how much of an animal lover Lauren was. "In fact," Mike continued, "I've started using my new favorite curse around the house, 'shit, shit, double shit and chicken shit!'" This bit of humor brought a deep chuckle to each of them and seemed to help Marc come down, at least a little off of his mountain of stress.

Mike continued to share anecdotes about their normal, everyday lives. Almost all of them centered on humor. After a thirty-minute drive, they arrived at Mike's house. Lauren was waiting for them on the front porch. It surprised Mike again to see Marc jump out of the truck, almost before it quit rolling, and trot over to give Lauren a big hug. He may have been used to doing that before he went off to Columbia, but recently he had tried to play the arrogant, Ivy League liberal media representative who was above such things.

"God, it's great to see you, Sis." Mike couldn't help but notice there were tears in Marc's eyes. Lauren's reaction was predictable and immediate.

"You come right inside and wash up. I have dinner waiting for you two." Mike understood at the moment, they needed his presence for emotional support, but he should just stay out of the way.

"Marc, what have they done to you?" Lauren asked herself this question with quiet concern.

Sitting on the bed in Lauren's spare bedroom, Marc let loose as the tears rolled down his cheeks. Something about the feeling of relief outside of what he considered the pressure cooker. Then seeing Mike and his sister seemed to release a torrent of emotion. He had been such a believer and was on top of the world when he was hired by the Fontaine campaign two years earlier. All the talk about change and helping people and sticking it to the money grubbers had really inspired him to believe he had lucked into the best job in the world. Two years of campaigning and seeing everything that went into it had really perplexed him, especially the money. Now, sitting in a normal house in a nice neighborhood of hard-working people, it all came home to him these were the kinds of people held in such disdain by so many of his colleagues.

Marc considered how he was on an adrenalin roller coaster that was thrilling, but he didn't see a way to get off. Gathering himself together, he stood up to go enjoy a wonderful home-cooked dinner.

. . .

Lauren was cleaning up after dinner with Mike's help. Marc went up to the guest room to make some phone calls. It was twenty minutes after the dishes were done that Marc came downstairs.

"My God, Marc," Lauren exclaimed. "What in the hell have they done to you?" Her question was now more of a demand than simple concern.

Marc had declined Mike's offer of bourbon after dinner but accepted a glass of red wine. Self-consciously, Marc checked his cell phone holster noting it was empty and took a deep breath. "Good, I remembered to leave the tether up in my room. Would you mind if we kept our voices down? And would you mind taking your cell phones and putting them in another room?"

The mystified looks on both Mike's and Lauren's faces caused Marc to pause again before taking another deep breath and continuing. "I've had so many security briefings, some of them keep haunting my dreams. But this information isn't even classified since it can be found several places on the Internet. In a nutshell, mine, yours and everyone's cell phones can be turned into open microphones by hackers—either criminal types, you know, the nerdy computer geeks, or those working for foreign governments. I just have to presume someone is listening whenever I have my phone with me. My phone has some special gizmos, but they probably only stop the criminals from listening. They do nothing to prevent any government with the technological capability from listening. Even our own government."

When Mike returned from dropping the phones out on the porch, he looked at Lauren to confirm she was thinking the same thing he was. Apparently, she was.

"Marc," Lauren said cautiously, "don't you think that's a bit, well, you know, far-fetched?"

"You mean paranoid?" Marc said with an ironic chuckle. "I would have thought exactly the same thing before now. I can't talk about any briefings I may or may not have had, but it has been published in many 'open sources' these capabilities are out there."

"Open what?" Lauren asked.

"Open sources are sources of information, like newspapers, other news media, the Internet, university graduate papers, or really any information source that is not classified by the government. Several fictional spy novels I have read talk about these capabilities and even footnote them."

"Look guys," Marc continued, "for the past several months, I haven't really been in what I previously would describe as the real world. Everything I do at work—hell, I can't even bring myself to call things by their real names anymore—lends itself to the buzzword of the day, 'plausible deniability.'"

Uncharacteristically, Marc seemed to have trouble even putting full sentences together. "Specifics of what happens on any given day are classified, so I won't get into those. The Secret Service takes its secrecy and the secrecy of everyone working for the government," Marc gave the finger motions to add quotes to the phrase, 'very seriously.' "By working there, I gave up all privacy. I mean, really, I signed over a dozen forms giving up any right to privacy up to and including how often I go to the restroom, if they ask. To top it off, it's a federal felony if I lie to any of those guys. I never want to lie to a polygraph operator. Let's just say he or she is not your friend!"

Marc's description had been blurted out rapidly. He appeared to have said all he was going to when, after a long pause, he continued, "I can't give specifics, but let me just say the world has gotten a hell of a lot scarier. Oh, and this conversation is never to be repeated."

He then looked around the room as if someone might be listening. "The number of threats easily outnumbers our capability to stop them all." After a pause for effect, he went on, "And the worst part is I don't think..." At this point Marc froze, contemplating what he was about to say. "No, uh, I mean, I took an oath of allegiance."

Marc paused again before Lauren said, "Marc, honey, you need not tell us anything. You know that! We love you and understand you have a job that's just unimaginable for most of us."

"I need to say something, though," he said with a voice hoarse with emotion. "Hypothetically, what would you do if there were suddenly no electric power or water and if that situation were to last for months? What do you think would happen?"

Mike glanced at Lauren who nodded at him before Mike responded, "Well Marc, your sister and I and several of our friends have been thinking about the same thing."

Throughout the rest of the evening, Marc enjoyed the discussion tremendously.

He couldn't remember ever having such a practical talk with anyone that did not involve denigrating someone. Instead, it focused on practical things that didn't manipulate anyone; it just seemed to make good common sense. Throughout, he didn't mention a single liberal slogan or issue.

• • •

On the way to the airport early the next morning, Mike had placed his phone in a freezer bag since it was raining and put it into the bed of his truck. Marc had put his phone back into his little bag, which he called his Faraday. The stress level Marc had shown when arriving at the airport appeared to have been nearly reached again.

"Marc," Mike said with a strong sense of concern, "I just want you to know whatever happens, you always have a place here. And you know, Lauren. We have more than enough of everything for all of us, if you can make it."

Out of the corner of his eye, Mike could see tears rolling down Marc's cheek as he whispered, "Thanks, Mike. You don't know how much that means to me."

CHAPTER 15
INAUGURATION - PLUS TWO MONTHS

The Mountains of Southeast Afghanistan
0830 Hours Local Time

Ahmed was smiling as he walked away from the cave where the person he called the "aid girl" was kept. He had placed second wife Jasmine in charge of insuring the aid girl would properly instruct his twenty-four martyrs in the American language and how to travel and function in the United States and across the world. His second assistant, Abdullah, had been instructed to follow Jasmine's "suggestions." He reported everything to Ahmed after the fact. Abdullah and ten men were given strict orders the aid girl should be imprisoned but not spoiled in any way. Each man knew he would be slowly tortured and then beheaded should the girl escape or should they try to use her as the whore her culture had created. Ahmed did not even consider such actions to be rape. Everyone knew Western females were all whores. In his own mind, Ahmed was certain the Prophet had specifically said raping infidels was proper conduct for a Muslim man.

It had been surprising to him when Jasmine had requested Abdullah beat the girl on her back and buttocks with a leather horse harness. After her capture, the girl had done nothing but explicitly follow instructions and cry. Yet, on the second day Abdullah beat her until she screamed hysterically. Three women were then instructed to clean the girl using the old oil and scrape method where olive oil was rubbed on her naked body and scraped off with a wooden hand scraper. Jasmine had even boasted to him about the marks the beatings had left on her fat little body! The girl had screamed in pain and plaintively cried out for direction in what they wanted of her.

Jasmine had instructed that no one respond to the aid girl until told to do so. Beatings occurred daily for six days before Jasmine herself saw the girl. At first she recoiled in fear from Jasmine, as she did from everyone who came into the alcove of the cave. It was lit by a single candle. Jasmine had brought a lantern, causing the girl to be momentarily blinded by the bright light. Despite the beatings, the girl had at least used the bucket provided for her bodily functions.

"Do you know why you are here?" Jasmine asked the girl in a firm but neutral voice.

The words came tumbling out of the girl. "Oh please! Help me! I have done nothing but help your people and want to harm no one!" She continued to babble about how her only desire was to help all people, including the people of the mountains.

Jasmine remained silent while the girl ran on about how her family would pay money for her release and then begged Jasmine to help her. After almost ten minutes, the girl seemed to run out of words and realized Jasmine was not responding but waiting.

The girl looked into Jasmine's eyes and then dropped her gaze to the floor and waited with bowed head.

"The usual intention with Western whores like you is to alternate between torture and giving the fighters the use of your loins." Jasmine spoke slowly and deliberately while watching the absolute horror spread over the girl's face.

"We know virtually all Western girls over the age of 16 are probably whores who use their bodies for their own delight and to control the brute urges of men." Another long pause followed before Jasmine continued, "The last girl only lasted three days... although the one before lasted over a year before she finally killed herself."

The level of hopelessness showing from the girl's face was just what Jasmine had been expecting. "I have convinced my husband," she said, lingering over the term to let the girl know of the level of power Jasmine had, "that you might be useful in other ways. Is that true? Can you be useful in other ways?"

The girl immediately gushed out a torrent of words all revolving around her willingness to do *anything* to be helpful.

Jasmine continued, "The girl who lasted over a year seemed to think the call of her loins gave her some kind of power over the men who used her. The man she convinced to help her escape was beheaded after three days of torture. For five days she was used, naked and tied to a barrel. Five days with only a few sips of water and beating with a switch every two hours."

Another pause then, "I have asked my husband to consider you a pure one for now. You will not make me regret my request. Will you?"

Again, the girl profusely promised to be good and do nothing but bring honor to everyone around her.

Later that night when Ahmed came to her bed, Jasmine told him of the encounter and gave him assurances the girl would provide the instruction for the chosen twenty-four and would not use her female powers to corrupt any of the men. Ahmed thanked Allah again for giving him his second wife. He had not even considered the possibility the aid girl could have corrupted his fighters.

CHAPTER 16
INAUGURATION - PLUS TWO MONTHS

Outside of Cronin, Kentucky
1930 Hours EDT

Mike and Lauren had Fred Callahan and his wife, Penny, along with Peter Worthington and his wife, Elizabeth, over for dinner. Fred had quickly worked his way up from patrolman to become the well-respected Cronin Chief of Police. He sometimes joined Mike, Jim Carson, and Rollie McDermott at deer camp. Mike had first met Fred years ago when a 17-year-old kid had skidded into Mike's truck at a stoplight during a snowstorm. Fred was on duty as a patrolman at the time. Both Mike and Fred were sympathetic to the kid, who had no father in the picture and was on his way to the drugstore for his mother. Fred decided Mike was his kind of man when Mike had driven the boy to the drugstore and then home. He then arranged for the boy's old clunker to be towed to a nearby shop where it was put back in running condition. Afterwards, Mike kept track of the boy who got a Ph.D. in Diplomacy and International Economics, was a university professor and had just been elected to the state House of Representatives.

Fred considered Mike's actions to be directly responsible for preventing the boy from going bad at an early age. Fred especially liked the fact Mike did these things with no fanfare or recognition.

When Mike first met him, Fred was the only black officer on the small Cronin police force. Back then he was a somewhat non-descript man in his late 30s, of medium build with short black hair. At just over six feet, he seemed to project authority with no intimidation. His wire-framed glasses magnified his wise brown eyes. He and Penny had a son who had just started high school. After their first meeting, it was natural for Mike to invite Fred to dinner. The two couples quickly grew into a close friendship. Now in his early 50s, Fred had gained a paunch and had given up on his male patterned baldness and just shaved his head. Penny, of Korean heritage, seemed to be almost ageless.

Peter Worthington, who was in his mid-50's, owned 235 acres of land abutting Mike and Lauren's 5-acre lot in the back of the neighborhood. Peter was a Professor of Mechanical and Environmental Engineering at the university and, despite his small stature and thinning hair, had a quiet, commanding presence. Unlike most of the academia-types at the university, Peter was politically conservative and was quite successful outside of the academic environment. He was tolerated and even well-liked by most in his department because he brought in ten times as much grant money to the university compared to the rest of the department combined. Besides teaching at the university, he also taught short training courses around the country and the world. Companies paid him to educate their employees on how to use his software, which was the gold standard for meeting environmental concerns involving exotic metal mining and manufacture. Not only had Peter become moderately wealthy, he had the personal satisfaction of teaching miners throughout the third world how to mine and manufacture exotic metals without killing off the surrounding environment.

Mike always found it fascinating how a good, strong conservative could also be environmentally conscious. It kind of reminded him of the liberal viewpoint of hunters. It was hunters and their fees that made it possible for the Department of Fish and Wildlife to function.

With her guests sitting at the table in the Florida room, Lauren walked in with a tray containing wine and beer. Handing Penny her wine, Lauren said, "Penny, I don't think you ever heard the story of how Peter first met Mike." Lauren knew how much Peter loved telling the story, so it was a great conversation starter.

"Well, as I recall," Peter said with a faint smile while looking out the screen door to some distant point, "you and Mike had just moved into your house here and had lived here only about a month or so." Looking at Penny's face and seeing interest, Peter was encouraged to continue. "It was a bright April Saturday afternoon..."

"Not a dark stormy night," Fred said with a chuckle proving to be contagious among the group. After the chuckles calmed down, Peter continued.

"Mike had heard some equipment operating right over there," Peter said, pointing out the window behind Mike's house, "in the woods that flows over onto our property, so he went to investigate. When he found the noise, he also found three men. One was in his 30s and two in their late teens. They were running a rototiller in a clearing there in the woods. Mike knew it was on his property, so he walked right up to them and asked what they were doing. At first he seemed to have scared the bejeezus out of them. Then the older one reached down to the ground and picked up a baseball bat while one of the younger punks pulled out a boot knife."

"I had been out on my 4-wheeler working my way through the woods and had to stop for the call of nature. It was then I heard the rototiller and decided to sneak over and have a look. So I was peeking through the trees and brush when I saw Mike walk into the clearing."

From the outer porch at the grill, Mike chimed in, "And I was damned glad Peter trespassed on my property that day!" His comment brought another chuckle.

"Oh, hell, Mike. I didn't know exactly where the property line was! Anyway, seeing the bat and the knife, I just couldn't help myself and stepped out. I racked one into the chamber of the shotgun and asked if they were foolish enough to bring a bat and a knife to a gunfight." With a chuckle Peter continued, "I never go out of the house without a pistol, and that day I had my Glock Model 20, .45 caliber pistol in a drop holster hanging from my belt, plus the 12gauge pump shotgun I keep in a rack on my 4-wheeler. At the sound of the shotgun those boys took off for the hills, or wherever they came from." Peter softly chuckled again at the memory.

"And you know what the best part of the whole thing was? When we called the Sheriff, the Chief Deputy came out and found their brand new tiller, a spade, and forty marijuana plants. He seized all of it and later returned the tiller to Mike as abandoned property! Brand new tiller the Chief Deputy said had been purchased with cash from a hardware store in Tennessee. No way to identify the buyer. Bastards lost their plants, tiller, and had the fear of God put into them." Peter had a deep belly laugh at the thought of drug dealers losing their things and Mike ending up with a new tiller!

From the grill, Mike chimed in, "And you really pulled my bacon out of the fire, Peter. Can't say it often enough. Thanks!"

"Mike, you know I appreciate the favors you've done for me over the years, and hell, that's what friends are for!" Peter made this last statement with a wide grin.

Everyone was feeling the spirit of friendship on the porch when Fred changed the subject. "At the risk of being a real downer, and before too much beer is involved, what in the hell is going on in Washington? That stupid bitch is cutting the military and raising taxes? What the hell!"

"Yeah, I couldn't believe it either," Peter said in agreement.

Lauren glanced at Penny and Elizabeth and as if on cue, all three women got up and start getting dinner ready in the kitchen. Although all three women agreed with their husbands concerning most things, when talk turned to politics they knew it was best if they gracefully found someplace else to be. None of the three were interested in stereotypical girl talk, so they began talking about political events without the profanity used by their husbands. Elizabeth changed the direction of the conversation by asking how they would manage if power were lost for a long period of time. Their conversation then morphed into considering what canned and long-term food they had stored.

"We were over $18 trillion in debt in 2015, and now we're probably going over $25 trillion soon," Peter said with some disgust. "The Wall Street Journal just reported government loans and guarantees to over fifteen 'green companies' totaling over $23 billion dollars were lost when they went belly up. Think it was just a coincidence each of the company founders was a big Fontaine campaign donor? Each has also walked away from their companies with golden parachutes, just before they went belly up. The bitch's Department of Justice says there's nothing to prosecute since they left the companies over six months before they went belly up, so they violated no bankruptcy laws."

"You mentioned tax increases," Mike said as he finished up with the grill. "I heard Fontaine wants to both cut the military budget and pour more money into green projects, all while ramping up the Environmental Protection Agency to fine and shut down any business dealing with fossil fuels."

"Yeah," Peter continued, "my friends in mining are already drawing up plans for huge layoffs everywhere they have operations in the U.S. Looks like what little mining is left is going overseas. Hell, almost all of the rare metals used in Silicon Valley and the Space Program already come from Russia and China."

They cut the conversation short with the start of dinner, which was their normal mix of great food and hilarious stories from Fred and Peter. Afterward, while enjoying drinks, Peter sat down with Mike and Fred and again turned to the country's situation.

"Boys," Peter said, "I think it's time we start planning on what we're going to do when, not if, things go to shit."

A glance into both men's eyes found nods of agreement. The conversation went on for the next couple of hours and covered who could be trusted under fire and what they could and should do. Mike confided in both men he, Jim Carson, and Rollie McDermott had already begun storing extra food and water. Mike had also dug a well and had set up several solar panels.

Fred mentioned, "Guys, you both may recall my son, Sean knows a few things that might be useful." Sean Callahan was a Major in the U.S. Army. He was an Army Ranger and had seen combat in places he could not talk about.

"Yes," Mike said with feeling. "We can use all the help we can get!"

Chapter 17
Inauguration - Plus Two Months

Washington, D.C.
2015 hours EST

Su Ling was visibly nervous when she knocked on Lisa McIntyre's apartment door. If Sung knew she was there, the beating he had given her after her last meeting with Walter would be mild by comparison. He might even send word back to Shanghai and have something awful done to her family. Despite these possibilities, she was drawn to Lisa and had finally allowed her schedule to open up enough for what Lisa described as a Tuesday wine and cheese party.

Lisa opened the door with a friendly smile that could melt anyone's heart. Su hurried in and spontaneously gave her a big hug. Lisa was surprised but could immediately tell Su desperately needed a hug.

Su whispered into her ear, "I am so glad to see you." Lisa's face bore a strong look of concern and curiosity as she broke the embrace and invited her into the room.

Su plopped onto the couch while Lisa inspected Su's face and demanded, "What happened to you?!" Lisa had seen the puffiness around her left eye and the red partial handprint on the side of her face, which Su had tried to hide with make-up.

Su looked down at the ground and replied, "Nothing."

Lisa didn't hesitate for an instant. "I'm my father's daughter and I know what I see. Who did this to you?"

Su kept looking at the floor then said, "I'm sorry, I must go," and began to get up from the couch.

Lisa moved over to Su's couch. She gently took Su's shoulders and pulled her onto the couch, where she cradled Su in her arms like a child. Su shook with sobs for the next several minutes. Lisa simply held her, making soothing sounds and beginning to wonder who this strange Chinese girl was and why it felt so natural for her to want to act like an older sister to her. She wasn't like some girls who seemed to be constantly taking in strays. But it was something much more. Lisa had recognized both Su's high level of intelligence and her profound decency.

While Su cried herself out she could sense and feel Lisa was possibly the first person she had ever met, she wanted to trust. Finally, she pulled away and tried to get herself together. Lisa got up and grabbed a box of tissues. "When I am in one of those moods, two tissues isn't nearly enough!"

Su grabbed a handful of tissues and wiped off her face, smearing off the makeup in the process. Through her hands, Lisa could see the beginning of a smile creep onto Su's face.

"In fact, I know I'm really in trouble when one box isn't enough!" Lisa made the statement with a full smile on her face. Now a matching smile bloomed onto Su's face. "The time I crashed dad's new car through the window of the hardware store, it took almost a box and a half!"

By now, both girls were giggling and laughing until both had to reach for the tissues—which generated even more laughter. In between gasps, Lisa described the look on an older lady's face as a display stand in the store crashed to the floor.

Finally, both had to look somewhere else in the room other than at one another to keep from spontaneously giggling again. Stomachs and facial muscles were in pain from the spasms. Lisa, without looking at Su, said, "Do you want to talk about it?"

Su responded, "I shouldn't…" She hesitated but looked at the side of Lisa's understanding face and decided to tell just a little.

"My Uncle Sung was angry with me when I didn't do what he wanted me to. If he gets too angry, they will send me home. And he can cause great trouble for my family if he wants to." Through the several years of training she had not only learned to please men, who she had found to be pathetically easy to maneuver, but she had also been trained how to hide her thoughts and feelings. One way was to divert the attention of the other person away from the important information. She used several techniques over the next few minutes, even though she was reluctant to do so. She had already decided they were sisters and felt mildly guilty at the subterfuge.

In Lisa's experience, the male way to deal with any emotional situation was to immediately jump in and fix the problem. Men are hunters, and the first course of action is to go kill it. She had seen her father do so enough times. Fortunately, she was both smart enough and intuitive enough to know it was better to identify the problem and ask Su what she wanted to do about it.

"In this country it's illegal for someone to force someone else to do things. Is he doing anything illegal?"

After only a moment's thought, Su said, "I don't know, but it doesn't matter. He has the power to make my parents and family miserable."

"What does he want you to do?"

Su sat silently for a moment before shaking her head no, showing she would not talk about it. Lisa made the snap judgment it was time to move on to happier subjects.

"Want to see what one of the nerds in my class sent me on Facebook?"

Su seemed to have the capacity to easily click the switch and change to an entirely different subject. She smiled and followed Lisa to her desk and laptop. The Facebook post was really quite artfully done, showing the tremendous, nude body of a man whose private parts were obscured by a university towel. Next to the picture was a button labeled "laundry time." When Lisa clicked on the button, the towel floated off his body and deposited into a laundry hamper. Under the towel the man had on Speedos with a conversation balloon which said, 'I don't have this body, but someday guys like this will call me boss! Are you busy Saturday night?' Again both girls broke into laughter.

After handing Su a glass of wine, Lisa busied herself getting the fondue ready. She had added pasta salad to the menu to go with the cheese fondue cooking on her illegal hotplate. Both women grazed on salad and a few other hors d'oeuvres while they sipped their wine. Su refused a second glass, and Lisa didn't press.

Lisa talked about having to move around while growing up due to her dad's job, although she never got around to saying what he did. She learned at each stop even the advanced classes were slow and boring for her. Entering college at 16, she was socially awkward, but academically bored with all but the most advanced science courses. At 22, she was nearing completion of two Ph.D.'s, one in Chemistry and another in Biology.

Su took in all of Lisa's background, but only said she had grown up on a collective farm outside of Shanghai. In what she considered only a little white lie, she told Lisa she had tested well and had escaped the countryside and gone to college, where she had done well enough to be selected and sent to American University for her Masters and Ph.D. in Biology.

"It is so important I do well to make my parents proud. Many villagers think the pictures I have sent home are fake and I am working in a factory or worse in Shanghai." Su justified this second white lie as a good cover for her, not wanting to disappoint her parents and to explain why she studied so hard she was rarely available.

Lisa asked Su about the subject of her dissertation, and both girls traded the difficulties of trying to satisfy the demands of their professors. In the back of her mind, Lisa recognized Su was just as bright as she was, and she formed a question. Why would Su claim to be having any trouble at all, especially getting away from studies for a simple girls' evening? Lisa was mentoring two other women in the Master's program, working for a professor on a grant project, plus working on two simultaneous dissertations. None of these responsibilities seemed to stress Lisa out.

When Lisa asked Su if she had been invited to work with any professors, Su looked down at the floor and said, "Yes, I have but didn't feel like I had the time to do such things."

Lisa knew in her heart Su was lying but didn't press. Just like the beating she had received from her uncle, it was best to save these topics for another time.

Just before Su walked out the door, both agreed they had had a wonderful time and promised to schedule something else again soon. When Lisa mentioned the upcoming weekend, Su politely declined, saying she was tied up. It was on this awkward answer she left.

Su walked the eight blocks to her apartment deep in thought. Her new friend Lisa made her feel like she had never felt before. Here was someone who had the capacity and the apparent desire to understand her. She also cared. The feelings were not physical, but emotional. Growing up, none of her friends could ever understand the way she could see things they missed. Her parents had been disappointed enough to have had a girl instead of a boy, but had punished her when she kept asking questions about everything. Looking back, this punishment began around the age of seven when they could no longer answer any of her questions. She was just beginning to understand her intelligence had resulted in her emotional isolation, making her an easy target for the MSS.

Could Lisa ever understand what they had trained her to do? Throughout the evening, when she had tried several of the techniques to throw Lisa off a subject,

Lisa had smoothly and expertly recognized her attempt and had politely and almost knowingly let the subject drop. In retrospect, Su realized Lisa had seen just what she was trying to do and had even helped her to do it! This revelation brought Su to a dead stop in front of her apartment building.

After a pause for thought, Su told herself it was good training and worthwhile to continue to develop the friendship with Lisa. But I must exercise caution. Desperate as she was to see the friendship to grow, could she really trust Lisa, even with her life?

CHAPTER 18
INAUGURATION - PLUS TWO MONTHS ONE DAY

The White House
0945 Hours EST

Marc Baxter walked slowly to the weekly meeting with a complete lack of enthusiasm. On top of everything else going on in the Press Secretary's Office, Marjorie was in the hospital with what they were now calling an advanced case of Lyme disease. The tests months ago had been negative, but a specialist had finally determined she had been suffering from Lyme disease for several years, and it had grown tumors in her brain. She now had IV antibiotics dripping into her veins, but it was too soon to determine whether she would recover.

Towanda Jefferson had stepped in as the acting Press Secretary and was stumbling through her duties. Every time she went before the White House Press Corps, she seemed to smile too much, had moments when she froze, and did not articulate her words. She was, however, a stubborn woman and did not react well when Katherine's Chief of Staff had suggested someone else do the press briefings. Marc just shook his head when he thought about how anyone else would have been dumped quietly or otherwise replaced. Towanda was black and was not shy about reminding people who criticized her. Playing the race card had quickly become tired and overused, but continued to be effective.

Despite her shortcomings, Towanda still needed to at least try to prepare to address the many issues of the day. The biggest issues included the loss of all electrical power at the New York Stock Exchange during the trading day, the Wall Street Journal's website homepage temporary shutdown and a nationwide United Airlines computer system malfunction. She should have been at the weekly meeting to gather the information and receive instruction from Katherine on how to handle these issues, but she locked herself in her office, alternating between throwing things against the wall and burying her head in her hands. She had sent Marc to stand in for her and get the needed information.

Unlike the last weekly meeting he had attended, Marc didn't get up at 3 a.m. to prepare. Instead, he had directed his intern to do so and collect all the previous day's hot button topics and prepare recommendations of what to address. When he arrived at 6:15 a.m., he discovered Towanda had done nothing to address the issues of the major malfunctions in three different industries. He quickly pulled all the related major news stories and noted the FBI Director had announced late the previous evening there did not appear to be any connection between the three incidents. Marc's intern was in a complete panic, having dropped all other issues to pull information on the topic. Marc immediately redirected her to write a blurb on each of the other four priority issues. The issues included the Military appropriations bill, the Supreme Court ruling to be announced later that day concerning health care legislation, yet another country leaving the European Union's monetary system, and the Senate Confirmation of one of Katherine's lower-level appointments.

Marc arrived in the meeting room trailed by his administrative assistant, John Butler. He noticed all the major players were present. It appeared most of the Cabinet members were in attendance. Each had only one administrative assistant. He was ten minutes early, and everyone else had arrived even earlier.

"Marc," said Katherine's Chief of Staff, Burton 'Burt' Combs, "please ask your assistant to wait outside." With raised eyebrows, Marc nodded at John, who turned around and left with a visibly annoyed expression. "And where the hell is Towanda?"

Before Marc could answer, Burt continued, "No wait, she's in her office?" At Marc's nod, Burt picked up the phone and dialed Towanda's secretary's number. "Marsha, I don't care what she said. Put her on the phone. Now."

After a pause, Burt continued into the phone, "Towanda, Katherine wants you here right now. I don't care what else you think you need to do, drop it and *please* make your presence here." He abruptly hung up the phone.

"Marc," Burt said with some reluctance, "are you prepared to present on the three hot-button issues?"

"You mean, sir, the stock exchange, UAL, and The Wall Street?" When Burt nodded, Marc said, "I have put some things together sir, but I wouldn't say I am prepared."

Burt nodded before saying, "That'll be good enough." After a brief pause he continued, "Oh, and before the President gets in, I want to remind everyone that like all the weekly meetings, this one is classified Top Secret and all the other initials you can think of." After a pause for it to sink in, Combs continued, "It will become obvious, but there are to be absolutely no leaks from this briefing. Understood?"

Everyone nodded. The CIA Director had an approving but sad smile on his face.

Everyone stood up when Katherine walked into the room only five minutes late. Towanda had slipped in just before she arrived. Silence dominated the room until the Secret Service agent closed the door and took up his station.

Katherine looked like she had been involved in a train wreck. Her normally coiffed hair was out of place, the bags under her eyes were twice their normal size, and her anger seemed to be either contained or spent. She walked around the table and, without fanfare, plopped down into her chair. She sat there for a full fifteen seconds before noticing everyone else continuing to stand. "Oh, sit down," she said with almost her usual annoyance.

"Mr. Pittson, please brief everyone on what you told me at 1 a.m. this morning," Katherine said with a neutral voice. Katherine rarely used anyone's first name. CIA Director Bradley Pittson, a tall, hawkish-faced man with gray hair in his early 60s, said, "At 10 p.m. last evening, my Chief of Station contacted me in Beijing. He had just been visited by a high-ranking member of the MSS. This MSS official was delivering a message with the full knowledge of Chinese Communist Party General Secretary Song. The message purported to be a sincere apology for actions by an illegal group of Chinese hackers who had bragged of having shut down electrical power at the New York Stock Exchange, the Wall Street Journal computers, and the United Airlines computers. Song wanted to assure the United States the hackers had been identified, detained, and would be appropriately handled. When the Chief of Station demanded access to the hackers and their computers, he was informed that would not be possible and not to ask again. It was the wish of General Secretary Song the matter be completely closed at this point."

A barrage of questions erupted before Katherine cut them off with a commanding shout of "Quiet!" She then continued in her most venomous tone, "Mr. Pittson, please tell us what the bastard really meant."

"Madam President, there is no doubt this is a very clear message, and frankly, a threat by the General Secretary he can shut down critical computer systems in the U.S. whenever he wants to." After a pause, Pittson continued, "The NSA and my people at the CIA have been warning of just such vulnerability for over ten years."

"Sit Down, Pittson." Katherine said quietly and with considerably less feeling than previously expressed. Pittson sat down without hiding the annoyance he felt at her rudeness.

"Rostov," Katherine nodded to the Homeland Security Director, "are we really that vulnerable?"

Dmitriy Roskov, the short but stout son of Russian immigrants, sported a neat, dark van dyke beard and mustache. He had been the Chicago Police Commissioner before they brought him on board with the Fontaine administration. He was recommended by a number of well-funded donors and other political hacks in Chicago. Despite playing the political game well, Roskov had both backbone and character.

"Madam President, this warning by the General Secretary is just that, a warning. Are we that vulnerable? In a word, hell yes. As Mr. Pittson just stated, it has been known by our government for over a decade our continued reliance on technology was a double-edged sword and any computer connected to other than a completely closed system can be hacked."

"What do you mean, closed system?" Katherine asked.

"A closed system, in the computer world, means there is no connection to any computer outside of the secure system itself. For example, if there were ten computers in the system, none of them would have any connection, including any Internet connection, to any other computer. Nor would there be any modem access into the system from the outside. Our Top Secret Systems and most of our Secret systems are closed systems. Unfortunately, a closed system is, by definition, a limited system. It is limited to only input of data from an authorized user at an authorized closed system terminal. That data has to come from somewhere, likely another computer system, so there are strict rules for handling and inputting data to insure against an outside infection."

"Yes, yes. Go on about our vulnerability."

"Madam President, what we have just seen happen at the direct action of the Chinese could rightly be considered an act of war." Roskov let it sink in for everyone in the room.

"General," Katherine said while looking intently and almost threateningly at DNI Roger Tignor, "please tell everyone what we can do about this situation."

"Madam President," Tignor began.

"And please cut the usual bullshit," Katherine interrupted, "and just lay out the options."

Showing the strain of the obvious insult but containing it as only a professional soldier can, Tignor continued, "We have four major options. Yes, yes, there are sub-options but four main ones. First, we could launch a retaliatory strike against China."

Gasps were heard around the room as the true gravity of the situation seemed to hit home. "This strike," Tignor continued, "could range from a simple missile strike up to a full-blown nuclear strike. Assessments coming out of the Army War College show that today, we could probably win, but at a devastating cost."

After a pause, he continued, "Even a minimal military strike would likely lead to escalation to at least the invasion of Taiwan by the PRC."

"Option two?" Katherine interjected to cut off Tignor's propensity for storytelling.

"Option two," Tignor continued, "is a surgical cyber or on-the-ground espionage attack, which is best addressed by you, Donald, or you, Bradley," Tignor said, looking directly at NSA director Donald Clayborn and CIA Director Pittson.

"No, we'll get into details in a minute," Katherine said, interrupting again.

"Option three?"

"Option three is to threaten major trade sanctions. Without the American market for Chinese products, the Chinese economy would likely collapse. Such threats, if carried out, would be nearly catastrophic for the U.S. economy as well, considering our huge dependence on Chinese imports. It would also likely result in the PRC demanding immediate repayment of all our debts they have purchased, which totals in the trillions of dollars."

Several people sitting at the table began asking questions of Tignor at once, prompting Katherine to say, "Enough!" This statement brought silence from people who are not normally silenced by anyone.

"And option four?"

Tignor continued, "We do nothing overtly or covertly. Instead, you direct David," referring to Secretary of State David Cummin, "to demand a meeting with the Chinese Foreign Minister to first, demand they turn over those responsible along with their computers and then feel them out and determine what their game really is."

Virtually everyone at the table had already determined what the game was and, with varying degrees of discomfort, realized with this Commander-in-Chief, almost all effective responses were off the table.

"How effective would a - what did you call it - a surgical cyber-attack be against the Chinese?" Katherine asked, looking directly into the eyes of Clayborn, a short, chubby, nerdy looking man with thick horned rim glasses and a round, clean-shaven face.

"Very effective, Madam President," Clayborn said with confidence. "Now this information is all classified as high as it gets, you all know." Marc thought with gallows humor how everything the NSA did was considered to be the highest of the high in terms of sensitivity.

"We could take out a majority of their military nets and even a large part of their space program. But," and he paused for effect, "anything we do beyond annoyance attacks are assessed to result in escalation to similar strikes against us from China and possibly war. We have all just seen what they can do while trying to remain subtle."

"So we can either go to war with China or send David over there to find out what the hell they want. Is that about it?" After a ten second pause, "Come on people, I want some indication of agreement from every one of you." Looking around the room at each person present, even including Marc, all nodded their head in agreement.

"David, you heard the consensus in the room. How soon can you leave?"

David rapidly stood up and said, "See here, Madam President!" In that moment, the astute gentleman in his 60s realized to do what he wanted to do, which was to stomp out after telling Katherine the Great to go screw herself, was not a viable option. He could say the words to Katherine, but he could not abandon his country in such a time of need. Nor would she accept plausible alternatives. He could see only one answer was acceptable to her.

After a deep breath, he said, "I would demand the Chinese Foreign Minister come to Washington, D.C., however they would likely ignore or delay any answer indefinitely. I would also demand their ambassador come to my office to express our outrage, but that too would likely result in silence."

Taking a big sigh, David said, "It will take several hours for diplomatic arrangements to be made. I will depart from Washington for the West Coast within the next two hours and, barring a major snafu, I should be able to meet with the Chinese Foreign Minister in about twenty-four hours."

Having said the words, Cummin also realized what a loss of the Chinese concept of "face" it was for him to take these actions, but he also realized Katherine would accept no other answer.

"Good. Do it," Katherine said. She then abruptly stood up and briskly walked out of the room without another word. Chief of Staff Burt Combs looked around the room at everyone present and decided additional words or explanations would not be beneficial.

"Thank you for your time, everyone. Please keep me advised of any further developments," Combs said, closing the meeting.

CHAPTER 19
INAUGURATION - PLUS TWO MONTHS ONE DAY

The White House
1145 Hours EST

Katherine walked purposefully into the Oval Office following the full cabinet meeting in which she had just dispatched David Cummin to Beijing. She masked her surprise to find the tall, black man sitting on what she thought of as 'her couch.' Without missing a beat, she said, "I take it you've heard the news, Eli?"

Sitting on her couch was one of the wealthiest and most powerful men in the world. Eli Fredericks, wearing a black $30,000 Armani suit, was the son of two very liberal college professors at Grambling State University, one white and one black. He was not an unattractive man, but she always had trouble looking into his pale green, almost lifeless eyes.

Despite graduating from Princeton University, Eli initially found it difficult to get work. He finally settled for a job as a traveling salesman for a food wholesaler. That job did not work out well. He felt unappreciated and believed accepting such a demeaning position was entirely because of his race. While at Princeton, he had become closely involved with several black activists from New York and Philadelphia. Having a belligerent attitude toward everyone who was white and privileged caused him to have few friends outside of the civil rights movement.

It was after receiving advice from his white mother, the woman with whom Fredericks had a love/hate relationship, he moved toward the power he would later acquire. Seeing her son rebelling against the establishment, she called him home to Ruston, Louisiana and made him sit in a chair in her home office, which was decorated with photographs of all the great civil rights leaders of the time.

"Eli, do you know why Dr. King was such a great man?" Eli sat silently with a bored expression, waiting for her to continue.

After a full minute and with an angry voice Eli replied, "No Sylvia, why don't you tell me?" Eli had been raised to call everyone, even his parents, by their given name and not anything more endearing.

With a critical, professorial look, she continued, "Dr. King realized there was power to be had in the world, but not through violence. Acquisition of power must be acquired more subtly. Do you remember seeing all the white people marching along with Dr. King? He didn't attract white people by preaching hate and war. But he attracted people of many cultures. Do you agree?"

"Of course! Everyone knows that," Eli responded with some disgust, as if she were wasting her time.

"Eli, what I see you doing is raging and beating your head against the wall trying to fight 'whitey' while not understanding where you're going or what you truly want to do. How has all this hate been working for you?"

She looked sternly into his eyes, which he refused to lower. "The truth is, one more angry black man shouting against the world accomplishes nothing except to make you very unhappy. Wouldn't it be better to figure out how the world really works, then use that knowledge to build wealth and power? Then you could use that power to make the changes you want. In college, you didn't move a beer keg without directing power. If you were smart, you figured out how to get someone else to help you, or move it for you. Your father is making small changes by educating black and white students about the terrible things the capitalists are doing to the world. For you, with first wealth and then power, you can change the entire world."

She made this pronouncement with a starry look in her eyes, but it resonated with Fredericks in ways she never comprehended. Play the game, accumulate power, and then change the world!

The next day, Fredericks took the suit his mother had bought for him for his graduation and drove the car his parents had given him to Shreveport, Louisiana to see the President of Hightower Holdings. Steve Hightower had been in love with Sylvia before she gently dumped him for Eli's father years ago. Despite her marriage, Sylvia had maintained a secret "friends with benefits" relationship with Hightower. One of the many benefits they shared was two hours of heated sex on the occasional Sunday morning while Eli's father played golf. Steve was happy to do her a favor.

Eli was hired by Hightower, who taught him finance, but more importantly he learned the basics of hedge funds and currency manipulation. Over the next twenty years he gained the kind of wealth his mother could not even comprehend. He had hardly noticed when both his parents were killed in a drunk driving accident. By the time Katherine was running for office, Eli made a point of insuring the Fontaine Foundation was generously funded through shell companies, many of which were from outside the United States. He also founded and funded the political action committee, or PAC, called America Always Forward, which had supported Katherine's election. During the campaign, Don Stetson had used these funding sources well, particularly in swing states.

"The news?" Eli asked in response to Katherine's inquiry.

"About the Chinese shutting down the stock exchange, The Wall Street Journal website, and the airline's computer systems?"

"Oh yes, I'm well aware of that," Eli said. "Have they contacted you yet with demands?"

This time Katherine could not mask her surprise. "How in the hell did you know that?"

"Katherine, it doesn't take a genius to see their work and figure out it was a less than subtle message they have the U.S. by the balls. So what do they want?"

Fredericks had no official place in the government, nor did he hold any type of clearance, but this was irrelevant to Katherine. In the past, she had been mildly concerned about violating stupid classification laws, but now she was above all of that. At her first briefing before becoming President, one of the few things she remembered was she was the top authority to classify or declassify anything.

"The bastards had the audacity to come see a CIA prick in Beijing and apologize for what their own fucking hackers had done and to reassure him they were all over it. It was nothing but a veiled threat to show us they could shut us down any time they want. Can you believe that shit?"

"Well, can they? And what can the NSA and CIA do about it?" Fredericks was speaking quietly, but firmly. Even though Katherine had banned the Secret Service detail members from her office, they and other staff were always lurking just outside the doors.

"My so-called expert advisors gave me choices from small actions that will probably lead to war to out and out launching of missiles. I will not start a nuclear war with China!" Katherine's voice was raising into a near shout. Fredericks was already calculating how he should move money to best optimize the profit to be gained from the situation.

"What are you planning to do about this situation?" Fredericks made the question sound reasonable and calming. It had the desired effect.

"Cummin is on his way to see the Chinese Foreign Minister to find out what the fuck is going on. That reminds me. I need to make sure the Navy doesn't do something stupid like send carriers into the Pacific or something." She walked to her desk and picked up the phone to her Chief of Staff. "Burt, make sure the Joint Chief's Chairman is told I said no naval or air operations are to take place which could be interpreted as remotely hostile to the Chinese until I say otherwise. Got it?"

"Yes, Burt, I said stand down on anything ongoing anywhere in the Pacific Rim fitting that description. Questions should be directed to me. Okay, good."

"Fucking knuckle draggers could cause all kinds of shit just trying to show who's got the biggest dick!" This crass comment brought a smile from Fredericks.

"I always admire how you grasp these types of situations and the men who blunder into them," Fredericks said. Katherine allowed herself a small smile at the compliment, despite her deeply buried fear and loathing of the man.

In some ways, she was aware she had sold out to someone who could very well be the devil. However, for the chance to become President, there was nothing she would not have done. It even surprised her she didn't see more of Eli with demands which would garner more money and power. He had poured tens of millions into several of the foundations supporting her. She knew there was truly no such thing as a free lunch.

"So tell me, Eli, what is your assessment of what the Chinese are doing and what they plan to do?"

Eli thought for only a moment before saying, "Katherine, you know I have some good contacts all over the world. They have all assured me China only wants to dominate their own sphere."

"Which is?" said Katherine.

"The Pacific Rim all the way down through Australia."

"What about Africa," asked Katherine? It surprised Eli she even knew about the Chinese designs on the whole African continent.

"Yes, I guess you should include Africa, mostly for the raw natural resources."

CHAPTER 20
INAUGURATION - PLUS TWO MONTHS THREE DAYS

U.S. Embassy, Beijing, China
1600 Hours Local Time

Cummin sat on the bed in the VIP suite in the U.S. Embassy in Beijing. He had the look of a pasty, medium-sized academic with male patterned baldness who had not seen the sun in a long time. His finely tailored clothing was rumpled and had the residue of a soup spill from earlier in the day. Although he sorely wanted to put his head in his hands, with immense effort, he managed to just sit placidly while his mind reeled. He could not show this reaction under the presumption the Chinese MSS had managed to get a video bug into his suite. After the previous, newly built U.S. Embassy had to be torn down and rebuilt, even the vaunted NSA had not guaranteed the security of the entire Embassy. Their only guarantees against foreign surveillance extended to what was euphemistically called the Secure Working Environment.

The so-called negotiations were not going well and, in the back of Cummin's mind, he thanked the founding fathers of the United States for having the wisdom to provide the chance to replace a President every four years. At the orders of this President, he had just emasculated the United States by going hat in hand, to ask what the Chinese planned to do with their newly demonstrated power. In meeting directly with Chinese Foreign Minister Gong in Beijing, the United States' reputation, known to the Chinese as face, had been severely diminished. He was also aware the only way to regain face would have to wait until the next President was elected and showed some balls.

Cummin had been the Secretary of State for the previous administration. He had periodically been overruled in pursuing America's policies, but only after the

President and Cabinet had at least listened to his well-reasoned arguments. He was understanding more and more how British Prime Minister Neville Chamberlain must have felt. Chamberlain was forever known to history as the man to prove conclusively a policy of appeasement toward Adolf Hitler's Germany did not and would not work.

Cummin next experienced a flashback to his third grade class. He had been small for his age and a bully named Carl, who went by the name Duke, constantly picked on him, particularly at recess on the playground. Complaining to his teacher earned him a punch in the stomach before he got onto the school bus to go home that afternoon. Duke reminded him not to say a word lest he face the consequences. It was when his equally geeky buddy Ben started karate lessons the next school year he saw his way out from under Duke's threat. He pleaded with his parents until they allowed him to take karate classes.

Two months after he had begun karate training, Duke had grabbed Ben by the shirt in the far corner of the playground. Duke's face changed quickly when Ben used a wrist lock and took him to the ground. When one of Duke's cronies tried to step in, Cummin had kicked him in the head using a roundhouse kick, which landed him on the ground crying next to Duke. After that, grade school turned out to be only boring.

Funny, Cummin thought. He hadn't thought of that lesson since beginning junior high school. His parents had ensured he had their more attentive power and influence to protect him the rest of his formative years. Having power handed to him had made him very soft.

Why had he forgotten for all those years? Cummin asked himself. Short of war, there was no going back on the weakness displayed by President Fontaine's ordered actions.

. . .

General Secretary Song sat quietly in his Beijing office. MSS General Lao and Foreign Minister Gong Xi had just left after giving their report concerning Gong's meeting with American Secretary of State Cummin. If he had not enjoyed pulling the wings off of insects as a child, Song could have even had some sympathy for Cummin. Although Lao had predicted such a weak response from the Americans, Song was still shocked to have seen it come to pass. He had expected the Chinese Ambassador to be summoned to the American State Department with at least a stern demand the hackers be turned over. Instead, President Fontaine had sent Cummin, with tail between his legs, all the way to China to plead with Gong.

Song had asked Lao to remain behind after Gong left. Lao broke into a large smile as soon as the door closed. "It is as I predicted. Fontaine does not understand what is coming."

"We should take the steps previously discussed to make sure her mind continues to be distracted," said Song.

"That may not even be necessary," said Lao. "I have just been informed the Russians are planning to step up their support of the Ukrainian separatists with the addition of both artillery and up to 5,000 special troops in the non-uniforms of separatists. Her eyes will soon be focused firmly away from the Pacific Rim."

"Keep me informed and delay further computer attacks until we see how this operation develops. Oil import negotiations with Moscow continue?"

"Yes, General Secretary," Lao said with a somewhat smaller smile. The Russians were proving to be shrewd negotiators in the details.

"I want weekly reports on how the negotiations are going."

"As you wish, General Secretary," Lao said with a nod. He then departed at the wave of Song's hand.

CHAPTER 21
INAUGURATION - PLUS TEN WEEKS

Washington, DC
2100 Hours EST

When Walter entered the hotel room, he found Su Ling lounging on the couch dressed in a red, skin-tight turtleneck top and black stretch pants. The ensemble highlighted her legs, which ended in black open-toed stilettos with a large shiny chrome buckle. The whole package perfectly showcased her perfect, petite feet finished with cherry red toenails. She had been crying and held a tissue in her hand, although her makeup was not smeared. She smelled of his favorite French perfume.

Walter had planned to break things off with Su after he had enjoyed her talents one last time. The Chinese subtle announcement to the CIA Station Chief in Beijing had placed literally everything Chinese related into a "stay away" status. He had intended to gently but firmly chastise Su for what her government was doing and use it as an excuse to walk away from both Su and Mr. Sung. He had worked himself up for over two hours to be prepared for this meeting.

"My dear Su, what is troubling you so?" Walter asked this question in his most soothing voice, cultured over the decades to show seemingly genuine concern.

He walked across the room and sat down next to her. She immediately fell into his arms and lap and sobbed uncontrollably. She had learned in training; it was only necessary to think of something horrendous happening in your life to let such emotions flow naturally. Her thought was how many more times she would have to fake enjoyment while having sex with this old, fat, ugly man. Sex for her was no longer an intimate act. It was merely a tool to influence men.

Four and a half years earlier, Su had arrived at what she later learned was the MSS Charm School. Within an hour of arrival, she found herself sitting in a chair, wearing only a short, baby-doll dress and no underwear facing the headmistress. The dress was made of red silk and had slits cut in the front exposing her breasts. The headmistress had informed her on the first day that as part of her training, she would be sexually available to anyone at the school. Refusal or hesitation on her part would result in immediate punishment. She would only be punished twice.

The first time they punished her had been on the first day when she was escorted from the headmistress's office to her room. A man in his late 30s with dark hair and cold, black eyes from an Eastern European country had stopped her in the hallway just outside of her room. While the female escort, also dressed as she was, stood aside, the man pushed her roughly against the wall while fondling her breasts. Her reaction was to strike the man in the face. He didn't even blink at the blow, but grabbed her wrist and twisted it behind her back while grabbing a handful of her hair. With the help of the other girl, she was dragged down the hall to one of what turned out to be several rooms scattered throughout the Charm School and literally shackled in irons suspended from the ceiling. The restraints caused her to stand on her tiptoes.

Only that first time did she allow her spirit to show and looked with challenge into the man's eyes. What she saw was neither anger nor pity. He looked at her with the disgust someone would have at a dog that refused to heel. After only a moment, he ripped her dress from her body, leaving her dangling naked from the restraints. He then walked to the wall and took down a whip she later learned was a cat-o'-nine-tails. He told her to remain perfectly still as he walked around behind her. When she tried to turn to follow him with her eyes, he moved to the wall and cranked a winch type machine, which raised her completely off the floor. "Do as you are told, or it will always get worse," he said with a bored tone to his voice.

Dangling from the restraints, Su could feel her shoulders ache while the restraints dug into her wrists. She later learned both the whip and the restraints were specially designed to avoid leaving permanent scars.

She didn't notice until later that under the restraints was a linoleum floor, which was highly polished and easy to clean. For the first three cracks of the whip on her back and bottom she was able to remain quiet; however, as the blows kept coming, she cried out. After what seemed like hours but was probably only a few minutes, the man stopped beating her and waited patiently in front of her for the sobs to stop.

"You have experienced what every girl experiences when she arrives here. You have a choice and think carefully before you answer." He paused before continuing, "You can learn to do exactly what you are told, and I mean exactly and with the appropriate amount of enthusiasm, or you will be whipped and punished in many unpleasant ways until you do. If you decide to see how long you can endure, your body will be buried without even a marker, and your family will be told you were killed trying to steal from another girl."

The man let her think about what he had said for a full minute.

"Now, will you joyfully receive my sexual favor?" He asked this question in a bored, accented voice.

Still dazed and in serious pain from the beating and the restraints, Su said, "wh-, what? How could you?"

"Wrong answer," the man said with bored indifference. He then walked behind her and began beating her again. During this beating, he continued until she hung limply from the restraints, having fainted.

Su regained consciousness and realized what she had hoped was a nightmare was, in fact, reality. The man was standing in front of her with an empty bucket, and she felt freezing water running down her body. Looking down, she realized some of the water was pink from her blood. She had also lost control of her bladder and bowels.

"Ahhhh, you are back with me again. Do you remember our last conversation?"

Su immediately recalled having been aghast at the man's blatant question. She also recalled his response to her answer.

"Well, let me ask you again," and the man asked the same question.

"Oh, yes, I simply cannot wait to feel you raping me while I hang helplessly."

Almost with resignation, the man said, "I will tell you only one more time since you are apparently a slow learner. The only way girls leave this place is by complete obedience and learning what is needed to help China." He then walked out of the room, leaving her hanging from the restraints, which had been lowered so she was standing in her own excrement.

Over the next two days, she remained hanging from the restraints. Another girl had come into the room twice daily to clean up the floor and give her some water to drink. The girl refused to talk to her, despite her desperate pleas. Finally, at the end of the second day, the girl whispered to her, "You bring this punishment on yourself, you fool!" She then left with some disgust showing on her face.

On the third day, the man returned to the room and, without a word, walked to the wall where he put on black, insulated gloves and picked up what looked like the jumper her father used to start his tractor.

The man paused and then said, "I last said I would not ask you the same question again. I will ask a different question." He paused for effect.

"Tell me, girl, do I need to use these?"

Su's answer was immediate and concise. "Oh no, master. I will delight to pleasure you in the most pleasing way possible." Finishing the statement, she smiled and was mildly surprised to see the man couldn't help but smile as well.

· · ·

Su let her sniffling cries end while snuggled up in Walter's lap. She could feel his excitement grow, but decided to change the subject. In her most child-like voice, Su said, "Mr. Sung told me you not want see me again."

She sniffed and muffled another sob. "He say you no pleased with me, and I should leave."

With a sniff and tears in her eyes, she looked into Walter's eyes and asked, "Is, is true?"

"Of course not, my dear," Walter said with his most winning smile. "If you want me, I will make sure to find time to visit with you. In fact," Walter said as an afterthought, "I brought you something!" He brought out a flat jewelry case containing a silver sapphire necklace.

Su squealed with delight and threw herself onto him. She then went into the bathroom, only to return wearing the necklace and nothing else but a smile. That night there was very little intelligence gained from Walter, but it overcame all of his hesitation at future meetings with her.

The after effects of her intense sensuality were beyond anything Walter had ever encountered, even in sex-crazed Washington, D.C. Normally an intelligent man, the spell Su cast upon him superseded any level of rational thought. After all, he had always done whatever he wanted and usually when he wanted. At this level, rules didn't apply to him. At least as long as he was careful.

CHAPTER 22
INAUGURATION - PLUS TEN WEEKS

Outside of Cronin, Kentucky
1900 Hours EST

Peter Worthington noticed that over the past several weeks Mike had really begun to shine in the leadership role of their little community. He took some satisfaction in knowing he had gently been pushing Mike toward doing just that, especially when it became apparent Katherine Fontaine might win the presidency. He was, however, a little surprised how naturally Mike was growing into the role. Since first meeting him in the would-be marijuana patch in what Mike called his "back forty," Peter could tell Mike was both very competent and had a way with most people. "Hell, he's instantly likeable," Peter thought to himself. Mike was also someone who got things done. He even seemed to have the same personality traits found in the CEO's of top companies, including the mining companies Peter had been trying to save from environmental bankruptcy.

These thoughts came to Peter as he sat in Mike's family room with Fred and Sean Callahan, Jim Carson, and Rollie McDermott. Lauren and Elizabeth were listening nearby in the kitchen.

"Guys, thanks for coming over," Mike said without fanfare. In the back of his mind, Mike was very impressed with the other five men in the room for several reasons. Despite the cooler full of iced beer over by the sink and multiple bottles of liquor, none of them had made any move to begin with the booze.

"Before we get started, feel free to help yourself to the bar." Glancing at each of the men, he instantly received the unspoken message relaxation would come after the important portions of the meeting were done. "Maybe in a little while," said Rollie, to which the others all nodded.

"Fred, thanks for inviting Sean. And Sean, it goes without saying how much we all appreciate your being here." Sean Callahan, who was a man of few words, merely gave a friendly nod.

Fred and Penny had named Sean for his Irish-born great grandfather. Grandpa Sean had violated the norms of the time by marrying young Sean's black great grandmother almost right off the boat from Ireland. At six feet tall, clean-shaven with closely cropped black hair and the build of an NBA point guard, Sean projected quiet confidence and command found in many military leaders. Unusual for a black man, he had the same striking hazel eyes as his great grandfather.

"You all know why we're here. But to reiterate, it comes down to the fact that none of us believes things are going well with the country's security and think it possible, no, I'd say it's probable things will go quickly downhill when a triggering event happens," Mike said. "Before the meeting, I asked if each of you would mind talking about areas where you have expertise."

"Sean," Mike said turning to the younger Callahan, "you probably have the most to say, but we all understand if any of our questions are touching on areas we shouldn't, you'll let us know, and we'll shut up. Is that OK?"

"I don't think it will be a problem," Sean said with a deep voice. Mike always wondered where the deep voice came from, since Fred had nearly a tenor level voice. Possibly from his mom's side? Mike knew Sean was probably the most dangerous man he had ever encountered. Instead of looking like it, he just displayed a calm confidence that, from a distance, made him look almost ordinary. The cords on his forearms did, however, appear to resemble steel cables.

"Rather than put Sean on the spot, I've asked Peter to sum up the threats we're likely to face. We'll address what we should do about them after everyone has spoken. Is that OK with everyone?" Nods all around gave the floor to Peter.

"We've talked about threats individually, but this is the first time I've sat down and lined them out," Peter said softly. "To tell you the truth, it scares the hell out of me. When Mike asked me to sum up the threats in ten minutes, I thought it would be pretty easy. Boy, was I wrong! Fortunately, you guys have a good understanding of history and geography. You know, those bits of knowledge the vast majority of people don't think are important?"

The resulting chuckle was a momentary mood lightener, but with a hint of resignation. Few people seemed to know much about history or cared to know. Of those, even fewer fully understood why history was important. The concept that, "those that fail to learn from history are doomed to repeat it," was like a foreign language.

"Let's hit the worst ones first and work our way down. I wish I could say they are in ascending order of likelihood, but I'll just leave it alone for a minute. I'll skip things like a huge meteor striking the earth that would just wipe everyone out. We can't do anything about those, anyway. The same goes for a full scale nuclear war. The worst scenario I can think of would be a global biological warfare attack. For instance, if the Russians have weaponized smallpox," he glanced at Sean who returned the glance with no reaction, "or any of the antibiotic resistant or weaponized strains of bacteria which could be spread through the air, with better than half the population killed or incapacitated, society as we know it would cease to exist. Our infrastructure, including utilities, food shipments, and almost everything else would pretty much collapse. If you want to lose sleep for the next several nights, feel free to borrow my copy of BIOHAZARD by Ken Alibek. He was one of the heads of the Soviet bio-warfare program who defected and wrote a book. Since that book was written, the world has added nanotechnology to the mix to ramp up the potential effects."

"Besides the massive bio attack, the next worst scenario I could think of," Peter continued, "would be a massive EMP, or electro-magnetic pulse. As you know, that could come in the form of either a massive solar storm or from high altitude nuclear detonations. I think the last time the sun put out such a huge pulse was in the 1800s, before we were so dependent on everything electronic. The idiot in North Korea or the zealots in Iran could really mess us up with a high level nuclear detonation. Sean, got any idea how much of the U.S. the North Koreans could paralyze with what they have access to?"

Sean paused for only a moment before responding, "Let's just say for speculation now that they've flown a so-called satellite delivery rocket over San Diego during the last Super Bowl, they could strike all the lower forty-eight states with an EMP." Sean's words sank in and each one present considered the implications on their friends and family.

Peter continued, "Another threat is a terrorist group or an enemy country could attack our power grid. Such an attack could focus on just one junction point or several. Because of the way they structure the grid, one junction point taken out could snowball and shut down power for most of the country. That could come in the form of blowing up certain grid nerve centers or through computer attack on the computers controlling all or part of the system. Each of you recall the day when the airline, stock exchange, and on-line newspaper all went down on the same day? What if such a thing happened to our power grid?"

Each of the men had already considered the loss of electric power, but only a couple had thought of losing the entire power grid.

"What you probably don't know, is if several of the command structures of the grid were to go, or several transformers were to be destroyed, it would literally take more than a year to get replacements, if we could get them at all. Most aren't even made in the U.S." Peter paused for effect, even though all present were already way ahead of him.

"Next comes natural disasters. What if a massive hurricane hit the East Coast or drove inland from the Gulf 'a la hurricane Katrina?' We also tend to forget about the potential for earthquakes. Some disaster movies depict the devastation of a massive earthquake on the San Andreas Fault line in California. What if the New Madrid fault line around Western Tennessee, Arkansas, and Missouri let loose? The effects on commerce and the economy would dwarf even the catastrophic destruction of the earthquake itself. The entire center of the country would be unstable causing transportation nightmares. Jim, maybe you can elaborate on the economic effects later?"

Jim Carson nodded.

"There are a bunch of other, smaller possibilities such as natural pandemics, ice storms, and major weather events affecting whole regions of the country. Economic depressions, race riots, even a bio attack on our agricultural sector are possible. I think for a lot of things, state and local governments are pretty well prepared. Right, Fred?"

"Yes, we've gotten a hell of a lot more prepared since 9/11 than we used to be," Fred said. "I've been on the Governor's task force for emergency preparedness for the past six years. The bio attack preparations have been mostly made at the national level, courtesy of the wonderfully efficient organization known as FEMA."

The chuckles around the room were again somewhat restrained. "And I don't think we need to prepare for everything." Everyone nodded thoughtfully, but without comment.

Mike appreciated Peter's assessment, particularly how concisely he had delivered it. "Thanks, Peter. I'm reminded of what it must have been like for the original residents of Fort Boonesborough here in Kentucky. In Daniel Boone's day, they had to first and foremost worry about how they would find food, either by growing it or killing it. Next they had to worry about everything from diseases to Indian attacks to snowstorms coming out of nowhere. What I see in this room is the same kind of spirit. What I will want to see going forward is how we will instill that kind of spirit into the likes of our neighbors, including people like Kerry DuBois who have grown up with the attitude someone else will always take care of them, even when they don't take care of themselves."

Everyone else glanced around the room and, with a simple visual acknowledgement, they all seemed to come to the same conclusion. They wanted Mike in charge if or when they needed to deal with this crisis. Mike's air of command and quiet confidence seemed to flow naturally. He didn't have to order anyone to do anything. He merely asked, and everyone seemed to just want to do it.

"I seem to recall families had lots of kids back in Daniel's time to help make up for the fact life sometimes ended quickly and brutally," Rollie McDermott interjected. "And folks didn't live all that long, anyway."

Jim Carson piped in, "At least they were tough, or they would have stayed in Europe and not come to America. Now it seems like the country is filled with people who want nothing more than government handouts."

General nods around the room showed agreement.

"If it does hit the fan," Mike said with some resignation, "we'll have to deal with all of them, even in our own neighborhood. Now what I think we need to do among this core group is quickly and efficiently begin planning to gather supplies and equipment for the most obvious threats. Next, we need to motivate the neighborhood to be more self-sufficient and not rely totally on the government. Initially, I think people should plan for at least two weeks of supplies for themselves and their families."

"What about getting them to put back six months of stuff instead of only two weeks?" Rollie said.

"Personally," Mike said, "I'd like to see everyone get enough for two years, but you know how people are. They'll say, 'Oh it'll never happen,' or 'the government will surely step in and take care of us.' Hell, Kerry will probably be at my door demanding I give him half of what I have, even if he has put back enough for his own family."

After a pause for chuckling, Jim Carson added, "Yeah, and he'll find himself staring down the barrel of your .40 caliber Glock!"

Peter interjected, "That brings up another question of whether we plan to motivate just those in our neighborhood or more people?"

"Good question," Mike said, "and that'll lead to a whole host of other questions. Please hold on to it for now, and I think it'll get answered in a few minutes."

Peter nodded understandingly.

"Jim," Mike said, looking over at Jim Carson, "please fill us in on more details about financial threats?"

"Sure, Mike. I get lots of financial data besides the accounting stuff I handle with my business."

They all knew Jim had made a small fortune in the stock market and seemed to spend most of his waking moments, when he wasn't handling the accounting for his clients, watching and strategizing his money. "It looks like there are about five or six major triggers that could run us into serious economic problems. The biggest one is our $25 trillion dollar national debt. Next would be the occurrence of financial crashes involving bubbles, such as the bubble that would burst if commercial real estate values were to fall, kind of like what the bursting housing bubble did to the market in 2008. Other events in the U.S. could trigger a crash as well, but each of them would have similar effects for us."

"Next," Jim continued, "we should carefully watch what other countries are doing. For instance, China is a huge importer of oil. No matter what the environmentalists say, this world currently runs on oil. What would happen if China suddenly stopped importing? The oil market glut would force oil prices world-wide to plummet, much more than the drop we've been seeing so far. I will not take up time with details now, but there would be a crippling recession all over the world. It would stomp on the Chinese economy, too, but to screw up the U.S., they may do it."

Looking around, Jim could see everyone but Peter had an interested, but quizzical look on their face.

Mike interjected, "So what do you think is the likelihood of this economic crisis happening, and when could it begin?"

Jim continued, "Guys, as I just said, five or six different major triggers could have a devastating effect on our economy. Another six or eight minor triggers can trip one or more of the major ones. If that happens, it will make most people terrified. People get really stupid when they're afraid. Just look how everyone reacts when a little snow storm is predicted. Multiply that by a thousand. Frankly, this Fontaine administration should scare everyone."

"I wish I could say the oil threat was the only problem, but it's not," Jim said with resignation. "Peter, what you mentioned about the power grid would trigger a separate and equally bad hit on the economy. The result is not just turning off the lights in our homes, but also shutting down everything from running water to deliveries of food to grocery stores. Just as important would be an inability to even get gas for your own car or truck, not to mention martial law."

Again Mike jumped in, "Let's hold off and let Fred and Sean talk about that issue."

"Ok," said Jim, "but other actions which could have big effects include even a small bio attack on our agriculture which could cut off part of our food production and hit us hard economically. An attack could be directed at our transportation system, or even a simple suicide bombing would mess things up. The thought is enough to keep us all awake at night, but the one I'm even more concerned about is the country's debt crisis. Hell, this country will soon borrow again to drive up the national debt to over $25 trillion dollars! To most people, these are numbers that are incomprehensible, so they just ignore it. In economic terms, we're living in a house of cards with literally dozens of factors which could bring it all down."

After another long pause for effect and a long drink out of his bottle of water, Jim continued, "Mike, guys, I don't see how we can avoid a massive economic tragedy for much more than a few more months or up to a year at the outside. The moves this administration is making have lit the fuse. I just don't know how long the fuse is."

The pronouncement, given in a soft but passionate voice, hit everyone in the room hard. Mike didn't let the feeling linger, however. "OK, thanks, Jim. Knowing what we're facing is the first step in overcoming it."

Mike then looked over at Peter, "Peter, who is that investment banker you go to who has made you so much money?"

Peter paused for just a moment before saying, "Scott Shelby."

"Can you trust him? I mean *really* trust him?" Mike asked.

"Yes, Mike, I think I can. In fact, we've had several conversations along similar lines to what I'm hearing tonight."

"Good. Can you set up a meeting with me, you, Jim, and Scott ASAP?"

"Sure," Peter said with a spreading smile on his face. "Are you going where I think you're going with this line of thought?"

"Contingencies," Mike said with a rueful smile. "You know me. I always like to hope and pray for the best but plan for the worst."

"Hey, Mike," Peter said, "how about if I teleconference in our buddy Hugh McIntyre? Like Sean, he probably can't say much, but he has some good sources of information, especially since he lives and works in Washington, D.C."

"Sure," said Mike. "He will be a good addition. Even though his parents are gone, he grew up in Cronin. In fact, when you call, see if he has any plans to come this way for a visit."

"On that note, let's take a break and visit an adult beverage. I know I'm ready. But I know everyone's got to get home this evening, so let's grab and be right back here."

Mike headed up to the bathroom where he cleared his mind for the rest of the meeting.

• • • •

After only five minutes, during which time Lauren brought in a tray of mixed healthy snacks, venison summer sausage, and cheese and crackers, all five rallied back in Mike's family room. Lauren and Elizabeth then sat down to join the meeting. From the kitchen, they had been listening with interest. All the men appreciated their presence and valued their opinions. Mike knew Elizabeth had been keeping Peter out of trouble, personally and economically, for decades.

"Guys, I asked Fred to give us a little talk on what local, state and federal governments would do in the event a disaster or other horrendous event occurred. Fred, the floor is yours."

"Thanks, Mike. Before I go on, it probably goes without saying, but I will rely on the discretion of everyone here to ensure nothing said gets repeated outside this room."

Fred got several curious looks. "I say that because I want to talk from both the head and heart and don't want to deal with repercussions from the Mayor or anyone else. If I didn't mention it, I couldn't lay out the unvarnished truth. Understand?"

Everyone nodded their agreement.

"FEMA puts out disaster plans. The State has one and even a countywide disaster plan has been written, all of which go into effect once a disaster happens and someone in authority announces the plan is in effect. For what you're talking about here, I think you'll need to give some real consideration to several things happening in no specific order of likelihood. First, you'll likely see the government putting out a whole list of mandates to include rationing. They will probably call out the National Guard and even attempt to restrict the sales of so-called national security items or anything the federal government thinks it needs to maintain itself. A continuity of government, or COOP, plan will go into effect. There will probably be measures implemented to control the population by prohibiting protests, communications, and restricting travel. They could also restrict purchases of what the government thinks it needs to function, like fuel. With this government, I could even see some sort of Executive Order dealing with the sale of guns and ammo. These actions could be in conjunction with a declaration of martial law. Sean, anything to add?"

"Dad, I can neither confirm nor deny there are contingency plans for institution of martial law or even institution of a Presidential Executive Order. If they did it on a national level, it would have to be done by the President or his or her designee."

Everyone present knew to read between the lines.

Sean said, "Just for shits and giggles, let me hand out an excerpt from a Presidential Executive Order signed in 2012 dealing with federal authority during emergencies. This EO has the effect of law, without having gone through the bothersome process of requiring to be debated, much less passed, by Congress. In essence, it gives the President the ability to grant various federal government agency heads complete power to operate everything under their mandate as they see fit. An example would be the Secretary of Energy having these powers over everything relating to energy. This EO means he can suspend contracts and take absolute control of gasoline sales and distribution, home heating oil sales, and distribution. Everything energy touches, he has absolute authority."

After each person had a few minutes to read and think it, Rollie said, "That sounds like it covers just about everything."

Fred added, "Basically, if the President invokes martial law, all the things you take for granted today would be out the window. Under martial law, the Constitution is suspended, meaning all of our rights are suspended. A military governor can be appointed, or any group designated by the President, like the FBI, can take control of literally everything. They could seize weapons, foodstuffs, or anything. It all falls under the heading of desperate times call for desperate measures." He continued, "You all remember what happened in New Orleans after hurricane Katrina? The idiots seized weapons from everyone, leaving people defenseless."

Sean said, "Under the Executive Order, the President probably doesn't have the ability to suspend the Constitution. Unfortunately, if there is a big enough emergency for her to do so, it's unlikely there will be much opportunity for a court challenge. Practically speaking, this EO would give her the ability to do pretty much whatever she wanted to."

Everyone in the family room sat in stunned silence. Lauren seemed to be more horrified than the rest.

Fred broke the momentary silence. "As police chief of Cronin, I'm about as far down the ladder of power during an emergency as you can get. But, at least, I will be in the position to move around and learn what is going on. Through the Emergency Management Task Force, I've got good contacts within the state, so from the local level we will at least be informed."

"Sean, how do you think something like a long-term loss of power would go down," Mike asked quietly.

"OK, if power goes out across the country by whatever means, there will probably be a period of twelve to twenty-four hours where everyone runs around in semi-panic. Contingency plans will kick in, so they would declare martial law whenever Fontaine gets her act together. All National Guard and military reservists would be called to active duty immediately, and National Guard generals would politely listen to their respective governors briefly before opening up classified contingency plans and orders. Movement outside of a specific area or town will be immediately restricted except for critical industries, such as food and energy and particularly fossil fuels. State and local departments of Emergency Management would be co-opted to begin collection of and distribution of essential items such as food and medicines under the watchful eye of the National Guard. This arrangement will work out fairly well for the first couple of months, until supplies run low, and then official and unofficial 'gathering' of unavailable items will begin. It'll probably be during that three to six-month period after martial law is declared some acts of rebellion to the restrictions will justify the arrest of anyone bucking the government's orders. Next, a sweep of identified agitators will begin. Things are expected to get ugly pretty quickly."

"So for a neighborhood like ours, who might be at least semi-prepared for a crisis, our biggest threat might be from our own National Guard gatherers?" Mike frowned as he asked the question.

"From my viewpoint, when things get bad, you're either going to deal with armed brigands brought out by anarchy, or the official brigands that start 'gathering' by specific orders under martial law. At least the first year after a disaster will be dangerous and unpleasant for everyone."

Mike continued, "Sean, are there contingency plans to seize guns under martial law?"

Sean looked at the floor, "I really can't say, Mike." For everyone there, it was enough. The pall hanging over the room was heavy.

"Hey, guys," Mike said with a genuinely cheerful voice. "As most of you already know, I'm working on some ways to deal with most of the threats brought up today."

Peter observed the mood in the room slowly lift, and even the lights in the room seemed to brighten a little. Mike continued. "I used to admire JFK and that quote about, 'It's not what your country can do for you, but what you can do for your country.' I know with the kind of people in this room, we will get through this mess. If anyone disagrees, please feel free to go your own way."

Mike looked each man in the eye, one at a time, for a full ten seconds. None looked away, and all nodded to him and gave him a smile and a thumbs up.

CHAPTER 23
INAUGURATION - PLUS TEN WEEKS TWO DAYS

Outside of Cronin, Kentucky
1800 Hours EST

Kerry DuBois sat on Jim Webb's back deck, sipping the beer Jim had just handed to him. It never occurred to Kerry to thank Jim for the beer. After all, he was bringing ideas to Jim for consideration. Therefore, Jim owed him the beer.

"Jim," Kerry said with his most learned and reasonable tone of voice, "have you heard anything about Mike Broehm and some friends calling a special neighborhood meeting for the next week? My wife apparently talked to Karen, who talked to Mike's wife, Lauren. The meeting has something to do with some prepper bullshit and ordering everyone to stock up for some imagined catastrophe. Are you aware of anything like this?" Kerry watched Jim closely, looking to detect any lies.

For his part, Jim watched Kerry watch him. This observation gave him a mixture of amusement and annoyance. He was more than a bit put off not to receive even a thank you when he offered Kerry the beer. Kerry had just interrupted his after dinner relaxation. It was one of those early March days in Kentucky that had spiked to almost 70 degrees with blue skies.

He agreed with many of Kerry's wild ideas about helping people. He was a lifelong union man, and the shop steward of the International Brotherhood of Electrical Workers. He had learned about reaching out to others and getting others to help since he was old enough to hold wire cutters. He hated all this trickle-down economics crap that seemed to make the rich richer and left the poor with nothing. He had heard all he needed to know about this stuff at union meetings for over twenty years. It was like he had once heard the professor say at the local community college, "The rich will keep their thumb on you. They make sure to make tons of money off the backs of the working man."

That's why he was proud to join the union. Unions stood up against the rich industrialists and moneygrubbers who got their money off *his* labors.

There were some unsettling things he had learned and observed only since becoming a union steward. Most he had not known while working on the line or in the electronics shop. An example was how large a percentage of their union dues went to political contributions. It struck him a little odd that the union leadership didn't want anyone outside leadership, and trusted stewards, to know about these contributions. But hell, they seemed to know what they were doing. The last contract had seen a five percent raise across the board!

"Jim," Kerry continued, "I don't have money to be buying a bunch of stuff the government will give us for free, even if something like an ice storm or other minor problem arises. Between FEMA and the Governor sending out the National Guard, we'll have everything we need, anyway. I mean, isn't that why we pay taxes?"

After a pause, Kerry asked, "Jim, you don't have a big stock of stuff in your basement, do you?"

Jim looked up at the sky for a moment, contemplating what might be in his basement. "No, not really. I've got a few days' worth of canned goods, maybe. With four boys and a wife who loves her own cooking, that won't last long at all."

Jim couldn't put his finger on it, but for some reason he didn't want to tell Kerry he had already stocked up on staples such as pasta, canned goods, and even bottled water.

Jim continued, "Kerry, haven't you heard the commercials on TV and the radio? They're talking all the time about how everyone should have three days of stuff, things like flashlights and batteries. Seems like it would probably be a good idea to be ready for an emergency." After another thoughtful pause, Jim asked, "Well, Kerry, what do you have stored away for an ice storm or something like the dry hurricane that passed through year before last?"

A Gulf hurricane had passed through Kentucky and, without ever shedding a drop of rain, had knocked down power lines with straight-line winds causing three days of no power in the neighborhood.

"Me?" Kerry asked with faux innocence and a shifty look. "I don't have enough food to last over two days."

This statement annoyed Jim since he had seen Kerry at Sam's Club frequently helping his wife wheel around at least two loaded carts.

Kerry then said, "If things get bad, I keep two five-gallon gas cans in the garage and plan to drive to somewhere that has power! If nothing else, there's always going to be free food at whatever shelter they set up in Cronin."

Jim was proud of his union affiliation and always voted democratic, which put him in contact with Kerry more than he liked. Tonight, however, he was becoming very tired of Kerry. He recalled Kerry's ready excuses whenever there was work to be done.

"Look, Kerry, I need to be into the plant by 5:00 a.m. tomorrow, so I will call it a night."

Kerry began to respond with a request for another beer, but Jim had already gotten up from the deck chair and walked toward the door. "Well, Jim, don't miss the meeting next week. I'm going to need your support to keep these prepper nuts from scaring our wives and costing us money!"

Jim's response was a wave of his hand as he closed the sliding glass door.

The Mountains of Southeast Afghanistan
1415 Hours Local Time

Ahmed looked carefully over the edge of the rock ledge at the advancing Afghan Army fifteen-man patrol. It was moving down the slope at the far end of the valley, more than a full kilometer and a half from his position. With one of his prized possessions, a pair of Swarovski binoculars, he could make out their pathetic attempt at stealth. They were following a trail left by his four best fighters that dipped into this valley and moved away toward a distant village. He was initially concerned, because the leader of the group showed what looked like competence in the field. This expertise had caused him and his fighters to scan the skies for one of the American's tactical drones, just in case they were supporting the Afghan patrol.

Under the new American bitch President, Ahmed thought with some pleasure, drone use and American Special Forces support for the Afghan troops had almost ceased to exist. This lack of patrols had emboldened Ahmed to expand his raids and ambushes on the Afghans and had expanded both his cache of weapons and materials. Whatever the Afghan troops had, he eventually took.

Watching the patrol, thoughts of the aid girl distracted Ahmed. Over the past several weeks, she had lost much of the plumpness she had when captured. She had also requested the acquisition of children's books in English to be used in teaching his martyrs the language and culture of the Great Satan. Jasmine had ordered her beaten again, but only for a few minutes, as a punishment for her attempt to corrupt the martyrs. This reminder ensured the aid girl would not use the materials for this purpose. Jasmine had even commented to him the aid girl could be attractive if she were to paint herself up. When he didn't understand, Jasmine had said, "Painted like the whores of the West did in their movies and television." Ahmed nodded, having seen two movies made in America, and he remembered how the women looked.

For only a moment or two each day, Ahmed caught himself imagining what the aid girl might look like in slave silks. These thoughts lead to his taking Jasmine to his blankets, out of turn from his other two wives and even though she was pregnant. He was uncertain, but Jasmine might even like it when he did so, taking it as a point of pride. Pride, however, is forbidden.

Ahmed, leader of over 200 fighters and indirect leader to possibly thousands, did not even recognize when his second wife manipulated him.

At least the training for his twenty-four martyrs continued. One of his older fighters had told him the smartest of the martyrs would be capable of moving around the U.S. soon. It would take at least six to nine months for the slower martyrs to be trusted to pass through security checkpoints in Europe and Mexico.

Ahmed also considered Jasmine's brother, Ali al-Hadiz, would come in just a few months. Jasmine had assured Ahmed as a Ph.D. in Pharmacy, he could analyze the great infidel-killing disease. Ahmed was not so naïve as to believe Cho would give him anything that would hurt China. That is why Allah had given him Jasmine and her brother Ali, to ensure all of Allah's will was done.

CHAPTER 24
INAUGURATION - PLUS TEN WEEKS THREE DAYS

The White House
1730 Hours EST

Late in the afternoon, Katherine endured the photo op with the women's college softball national champions. On the plus side, several of the girls were attractive and had very firm, athletic bodies. Most seemed to look at her with near reverence, the epitome of a role model. While leaving the photo op, she informed Susan she would be needed in her residence directly after the scheduled dinner with the Minority Leader in the House of Representatives. The Minority Leader was a loyal party member, but he had other agendas. Katherine expected him to badger her to throw more support into green projects. On the other hand, he would want her to stop downsizing the military.

The meeting with the Minority Leader had not gone quite as she expected. Walking toward her private sitting room, Katherine thought he had sounded like the opposition party with his insistence the military not suffer further cuts. He had even voiced concerns about the White House-backed spending bills, which would increase the deficit another $1.5 trillion over the next year. The man didn't seem to grasp the facts. Despite over two decades of deficit spending and a national debt over $25 trillion, the economy continued to move along with nary a hiccup. Well, there had been the 2008 so called "bubble crash," but the economy had bounced back as it always did. If there were another crash, her investment advisor had told her she was well protected. The economy would just have to bounce back once again. The damned wealthy would just have to cough up more of their fair share. She made a mental note to have her speechwriters include something about the rich not paying their fair share in her next speech. Keeping the masses divided was critical to maintaining control.

Katherine shook off the annoyance of the Minority Leader and thought to herself how it really felt to be the most powerful person in the world. God, the thrill of all that power, she thought. In almost the same instant, she began to think of the huge number of people who wanted nothing more than to take that power away or at least stop almost everything she set out to do. They were just jealous; she thought. Vacationing in Martha's Vineyard, flying everywhere in Air force One, ordering generals around like the servants they were, all caused this level of jealousy. There were so very few she could trust. Fortunately, at least most now knew to fear her. In fact, watching them squirm was becoming one of her favorite past times. She had ruined the careers of over 200 people the last time she tallied it up, but her enemies list continued to grow. Let the word get around. They will learn not to mess with her!

Entering the Presidential suite on the top floor, she didn't even notice her Secret Service protection detail had dutifully stopped by the elevator. The first thing she had done upon moving into the White House was to set strict limits for her personal privacy. She had the head of her detail demoted and reassigned when the man had become too insistent that agents must be only seconds away from her at all times. "As if I will let the bastards listen to everything I do and say," she thought wryly.

She had changed almost everything in the Presidential bedroom suite. It still had the masculine feel of the most powerful person in the world with a few feminine touches. She couldn't care less the cost of doing so would have covered the cost of living for twenty-five average American families for a year. Her minions handled details like that. No, she reminded herself, they are my "people." Yeah, right, she thought with a smile.

Walking in, she saw Susan stand from a chair in the sitting room. She marched straight to Susan and fell into her arms in a strong embrace. Susan made cooing sounds she craved so much while she held the President closely and firmly. A few seconds later, Katherine found herself in Susan's arms on the couch. Susan seemed to know when to make soothing sounds or just be quiet and hold her even better than Marjorie had. Her tensions lost just a little of their edge. She looked up into Susan's eyes and eagerly kissed her with a demanding passion. Almost an hour later, lying in bed with a feeling of euphoria, she heard the door close as Susan left.

Susan's walk down the hall led her past the two Secret Service agents dutifully guarding the top of the stairs, well away from the Presidential Bedroom suite. Although she looked closely into the faces of each man, she did not detect the smirk she expected. Both professionally nodded their heads to her in polite acknowledgement. They refrained from speaking in keeping with their training. She felt grateful for their presence and their discretion. She had tried to put herself back together. On the inside, she was conflicted by feelings of self-derision. Those were balanced against a personal pride of having given the most powerful woman, no person, in the world, a much-needed release. Her stride picked up, and she perked up for her forty-five minute ride to her apartment on the North side. Maybe she could get four hours sleep before she was back in her office early in the morning.

• • •

Susan left the Presidential Suite just as Walter arrived in the White House grounds. He was back from a meeting with several businessmen described by conservative reporters as his "cronies." He walked into what had previously been named the "Queen's Bedroom." He had renamed it the "Gold Bedroom." Privately, his Secret Service detail had dubbed it the "Queen's Bitch's Bedroom," or QBB. When he overheard them referring to the QBB, they told him it stood for Quality by Barton. Barton was a high end furniture company that had donated the furniture. After donating the furniture to the White House, Barton had received large orders from twelve different green energy company CEO's. Coincidentally, green energy companies had received government contracts and/or grants from the U.S. Departments of Energy (DOE), Environmental Protection Agency (EPA), and the U.S. Department of Defense (DOD).

Walter smiled happily, looking at the beautifully handmade furniture and decorations in the room. He thought, "What goes around comes around." Another favorite platitude jumping immediately to mind was, "You scratch my back, and I'll scratch yours." This line of thought lead him to remember how wonderful it had felt two days earlier when Su scratched his back, both before and after she did all the other amazing things.

"My God," he thought as he felt his body reacting to the thought of Su's talents, "I wonder where she learned to be so incredible in every way? I've had hundreds of girls who never made me feel the way she does." He immediately thought, "Every woman should be taught those kinds of things. Hell, there ought to be a school every girl should have to go to learn to keep a man happy!"

He climbed into his king bed with its silky sheets, thinking briefly about how he would have to arrange for another meeting with Su. That caused him to remember he had placed the "burner phone" or prepaid cell phone in his jacket pocket in the laundry hamper. Mr. Sung had given him the phone as a confidential means of contact to arrange meetings with Su. He got up to retrieve it before some over-diligent maid decided it was a security breach.

CHAPTER 25
INAUGURATION - PLUS TEN WEEKS FOUR DAYS

The White House
0830 Hours EST

The morning after Susan's latest 'therapy session' with the President, Marc Baxter sat in the White House canteen by himself, watching CNN. His coffee sat untouched on the table. Back in his office, he had twelve news programs going at the same time. They included eight domestic, and four foreign news channels. His favorite was the BBC or British Broadcasting Company channel. He knew Katherine the Great liked to watch CNN, so he spent more time than was appropriate making sure he missed nothing on that channel. He had a note on Towanda's desk asking for five more interns plus a dozen more special news summary services. Towanda was dragging her feet. The Secret Service had already complained about the large number of young volunteers that were cleared for access to the White House, and Towanda had proven she didn't like confrontation. She was so far out of her depth she was literally floundering.

Susan walked into the canteen looking like she had been run over by a truck. Her eyes displayed twice their normal puffiness, her hair was a mess, and she had an overall dazed look. After getting her coffee, she noticed Marc. She then joined him at his table.

Marc didn't know why, but Susan and several other staffers within the White House seemed to view him as someone in whom they could confide. Even though Susan was fifteen years his senior, she seemed to gravitate to him more frequently over the past four weeks. Whether it was his journalistic training or something about his personality, Marc just had an ability to be a good listener.

All the security briefings he endured when getting his security clearances had really put the fear of God in him to keep his mouth shut. The briefings had definitely not done the same to a majority of the White House staff. Marc knew about several of Towanda's personal 'friends' in the press who made sure she received tickets to all the best events. She also had a large, low-rent apartment three blocks from the White House. Then she mysteriously won a new car in a raffle in which she had likely not even purchased a ticket. The press ensured one of their own did not receive the kind of scrutiny directed at most in the White House.

"God, Susan," Marc said with concern in his voice. "What happened to you?"

Susan responded almost automatically, "What, do I look all that bad?" She quickly followed by looking directly at Marc and saying, "I'm sorry, Marc. Short night and all the crap going on around here really wiped me out." She then lowered her voice and said, "Marc, I don't know how the President does it. My God, the pressure!"

"Well, at least she has someone like you to help her get through the pile that is always landing on her desk," Marc said reassuringly. In between responsibilities during his usual twelve to fourteen-hour days, Marc had thought about everything he was seeing around him. He still felt the administration was trying to move in the right direction and help those who needed it most, but just the beginnings of doubt had crept into his head. It was not, however, anything he could share with anyone else.

Softly, Susan responded, "You don't know the half of it." Looking around the room to ensure no one was listening, she continued, "You wouldn't believe the steel cords running across the woman's neck and shoulders. And with Marjorie down, she has no one but me to lean on and hold on to."

Just as the sentence left her lips, she flashed a quick look of panic into Marc's eyes. He responded by his usual calm acceptance and small nod, letting her know the secret was safe with him. The look of fear drained from her face, replaced by one of deep, emotional appreciation. "Thank you, Marc," Susan said with sincerity.

"I meant it," Marc said. "She's very lucky to have you to help her through whatever comes down. We all need someone we can depend on, especially here."

Marc didn't know it then, but his relationship with Susan would become his best window to know what was really going on in the White House. Eventually, it would save his life. Marc would often meet with Susan and exchange observations on the country and the world. Then Susan asked to see his apartment. It was small, but it was located only five blocks from the White House. With no discussion, Susan began to sleep over at Marc's place to save commuting time. After only a few nights in Marc's bed, she felt she could really confide in Marc. It was there she confessed to the lesbian relationship she had with Katherine and how soiled, but honored she was to fulfill that role. Marc even came to agree with her it was, in fact, the patriotic thing to do. It was there, too, Marc learned the meaning of the term 'cougar.'

Washington, D.C.
1600 Hours

Su's call to Lisa was motivated by her successfully convincing Walter he wanted to continue seeing her. Uncle Sung had debriefed her following her last meeting with Walter two days earlier. He even gave her a backhanded compliment. It was quickly followed by his usual leering comments about her artful use of her body. She knew how important this MSS operation was. She also believed the only reason Sung had not demanded sexual favors for himself was his fear doing so would become known to his superiors.

Su had dutifully bowed her head when Sung had reminded her the well-being of her parents was contingent on her continued meetings with Walter. He reinforced the threat by describing, in grisly detail, what he had done to the family members of a traitorous minor diplomat. He said similar things would happen to her parents if she were unsuccessful in keeping Walter coming back for more. What was worse, Sung appeared to have enjoyed both describing and exercising his sadistic tendencies.

The girls met with a hug at Lisa's apartment door. Continuing the norm, the first ten minutes of conversation consisted of a rapid-fire catch-up of what both were doing at school and in their lives. That ten minutes was sufficient was a testament to the efficiency in which each could give the update. They had discovered each could almost finish sentences for the other, just following the free flow of thought.

After the catch-up period wound to a conclusion, Lisa offered wine and was very surprised when Su accepted. Su admitted she did not know much about wine. She enjoyed it very much, but did not want it to interfere with her studies. Lisa was not ready to confront Su on this blatant lie, so she described various types of wines and asked which Su thought she would like best. It was finally decided that one month later Su would come over for a real wine tasting.

CHAPTER 26
INAUGURATION - PLUS FOUR MONTHS

Washington, D.C.
2110 Hours EST

John Levy, the Secret Service agent leading Walter Fontaine's security detail, was tiring of his protectee's increasingly foul moods. Until the last month or so, Walter had been fairly easy, except for when he would sneak out on one of his adventurous escapes. The detail had called them his cathouse outings. When he reappeared, he seemed to have the contented look of someone who had just been laid. John had reported the disappearance the first time. His supervisor told him it had better not happen again, or he would end up assigned to guard a nuclear silo. Walter told him very bad things would happen to him if he ever reported another disappearance. After that, Walter had used the covert signal of brushing an index finger across the side of his nose to let the detail know when he would be on his own for a few hours.

The no-win situation left the Secret Service with a "fuck it" attitude concerning these excursions.

For the past month, there had been no excursions. This dry spell reinforced the validity of cathouse outings to describe the disappearances. Walter's mood also seemed to confirm it.

It was almost with relief when the detail saw Walter give the cathouse outing signal as he walked out the back door of Smith and Wallenski's restaurant. John had posted the extra agent detailed for the evening on the rear entrance of the restaurant. He had strict instructions to get a license plate, but not to be seen if Walter walked out that way. He reported back only a partial plate on the Hyundai Sonata that had picked Walter up behind the restaurant. The plate had been smeared with mud, some of which had dried and had fallen off. The team then settled in to wait outside the front of the restaurant.

The driver of the Hyundai had stopped a half a block from the small luxury hotel. He had also given Walter a hat and thick, horn-rimmed glasses with uncorrected lenses as a disguise. Mr. Sung was waiting for him at the elevator and pressed the button for the eighth floor. He then said, "810" and handed him the plastic, credit card-sized room key. Walter nodded and watched the doors close on Mr. Sung.

Sliding the key into the door lock of room 810, Walter couldn't help but notice the bulge in his pants. God, but it seemed like it had been forever since he had seen Su. Entering the room he could hear soft music. He had to walk down a short hallway into the suite's main sitting area. Lounging gracefully on the couch, wearing a red silk dress, was Su. Her dress was short and form-fitting. Nestled between her breasts was the necklace he had given her. The plunging neckline of the dress wonderfully displayed it. She jumped up from the couch and threw herself into his arms for a big hug and kiss while subtly grinding against him with her belly.

He tried to lead her toward the bedroom of the suite when she stopped him and dropped to her knees and opened his pants. He took less than fifteen seconds. After his shuddering climax, he fell backward into the chair, closed his eyes and sighed with satisfaction.

"Wait here, my darling. I think you need much more," Su said in her heavily accented China-doll voice. There would be even more sensual and satisfying things to come. She then walked into the bathroom. He could hear water running briefly before she returned with a large terrycloth robe for him. While he undressed and put on the robe, she prepared his favorite single malt scotch on the rocks and brought it to him. Another deep sigh of satisfaction followed his messy slurp.

"It has been so long, my darling. Please tell me everything that keep you away from me." They captured the scene on hidden digital video recorders while Walter described first one crisis and then another. He talked about almost everything going on in the White House. He was hesitant to bring up the computer hacking threat that had almost denied him Su's company going forward. She gave him her guileless smile when he complained about how much of a pain in the ass it was to communicate while in the White House. There was satisfaction in his voice when he announced he had prevailed on Katherine to use one of his friends to set up a private Email server. He had agreed, upon pain of Katherine emasculating him with a dull butter knife, he would never scan and send out anything with classification markings on it. "Hell, even I know that'll get me in trouble. My buddy Preston says it's easy to remove headers or footers on any document, anyway. Should work out ok. Katherine even wants to use it to avoid all the Presidential historical document preservation crap."

With a twinkle in his eye, Walter changed the subject. "Baby, what was the new thing you said you wanted to show me?" Su rose from the couch, grabbed his hand and lead him into the bathroom shower. A rubber stool sat in the middle of the shower stall between two opposing shower heads. "You such a dirty boy," Su said sweetly. "I just wash you all over."

The White House
1000 Hours EST

The morning briefing began on time for a change. Katherine even entered the room without a scowl. She was pleasant when she asked General Tignor's representative to touch on the highlights of the document in the briefing book. Marc Baxter had left an exhausted Susan Cassel sleeping in his apartment. Susan had virtually collapsed when she got there and fell asleep in less than two minutes. She had called in sick to the White House switchboard the night before, with Katherine's blessing. It ensured no one would look for her that day. She now used Marc's place as a convenient crash pad when her duties kept her up late. Marc marveled at the amount of clothing she could pack into her briefcase. Security personnel at the White House never even questioned the constant presence of the clothes, since it was common for many of the staff members to be kept overnight with no notice.

Tina was the primary assistant and scheduler for Chief of Staff Burt Combs and the President. She had already informed Katherine she had a light schedule. The only item was a four-hour block of time set aside for her to review drafts of her upcoming speech. The speech concerned the need to scale back military expenditures yet again for another stimulus plan. Fortunately, the last stimulus plan had resulted in a positive jolt to the economy. The Dow Jones industrial stock index jumped up almost 600 points. She was even considering having her first press conference in over three months, maybe even without a teleprompter, though she wasn't sure. There had been no press conferences after the first disastrous one following her inauguration and announcement of her cabinet picks.

That was probably one of the few things Towanda had done right. She had convinced her friends in the press to back off for at least the first sixty days, if not the normally afforded 100 days, of a new Presidency. It never occurred to Katherine to wonder what Towanda had to give up for the accommodation.

Katherine's almost jovial mood continued throughout the morning meeting until near the end. Defense Secretary Carlton Hathaway's chief aid, U.S. Air Force Colonel Francis X. Gallagher, had asked to brief last, which was only slightly out of order during a routine morning briefing. He had also requested all the other intelligence briefers refrain from mentioning his primary topic until after he briefed the President.

"Madam President," Colonel Gallagher began, "satellite imagery confirms the Chinese are building an additional three islands in the Spratly Island area of the South China Sea. The Australian Minister for Foreign Affairs contacted Defense Minister Hathaway directly after receiving no response from Secretary of State Cummin."

Katherine recalled Cummin's response when, two days earlier, she ordered him to avoid contacts by anyone from Australia over the Chinese island building mess. Cummin had argued, "Madam President. My job is to speak to the foreign ministers of other countries, especially those of our closest allies. If you no longer want me to do my job, feel free to ask for my resignation."

Katherine said, "I won't ask for or accept your resignation at this time." She then broke the secure telephone connection. Cummin was a good soldier and had made no more fuss over the incident, so she considered the matter resolved. And now, she thought with growing anger, the damned Aussies had gone around Cummin's back to Hathaway.

Gallagher continued, "Madam President, the Aussies are most concerned about not just the six islands the Chinese have already created by dredging material from the sea floor and dumping it onto living reefs, or the three additional islands they are trying to build now, but also about the U.S. apparent acquiescence to their demanding all shipping within 200 nautical miles get their permission to enter the control zone. The U.S. has never honored more than the internationally recognized twelve-mile territorial limit, and a reef destroying man-made island is not, in Secretary Hathaway's opinion, even sovereign territory…"

"Enough," Katherine made the statement with fervor in her voice. "All you soldiers want to do is send a battleship or bigger gun to show who has the biggest dick, spinning up a confrontation. I will not allow some macho sonofabitch drag this country into war with China." Katherine's voice continued to rise, and the veins stood out on her forehead. "I am in charge here, and the order stands—no ships, planes, or even surf boarders are to challenge the Chinese concerning those islands. Do you understand me?"

She made this last question with a tone indicating emasculation would happen should there be disobedience. Could these cretins not see the delicate nuance and balance needed to deal with the Chinese? Like so many other things, these people were just too stupid to understand the complexities, she thought coldly.

Calmly, and with dignity, Gallagher responded, "Yes, both the Defense Secretary and I are clear on your orders, Madam President. Secretary Hathaway also wished me to inform you an additional six senior officers have resigned in protest over the current China policy. One from the Marine Corps, two from the Army, and one each from the Air Force, Navy, and Coast Guard."

"So what you're telling me, you sorry little prick, is they are jumping ship," Katherine said, directing all of her displeasure on Colonel Gallagher. "If you want to resign, I will accept it right here, right now." Her stare bored into Gallagher's eyes with blatant malice and contempt.

"Madam President," Gallagher said with a steady voice, "I am sworn to protect my country from all enemies, foreign and domestic. Until relieved of duty, I intend to continue to honor that pledge."

"Get out." Katherine gave this order with a low, gravelly voice quietly displaying her hatred and contempt. Looking around the room and in the same voice, she continued, "All of you get the fuck out!"

In an orderly fashion, everyone in the room quickly gathered up their papers and left the briefing room. Katherine sat for a full three minutes thinking about how it appeared literally everyone around her was both stupid and actively working to doom the country. With a start, she thought of one thing she could do and picked up the phone to dial the operator. "Get me Burt Combs," she commanded into the receiver.

"Katherine?" Burt asked into the phone. "I just heard and will be right down." He had sent his assistant to help run the morning briefing while he handled another crisis dealing with Secretary of State Cummin. On the way down, Burt considered it had only been four months, and he had regretted leaving the Senate seat from the second week after taking over as Katherine's Chief of Staff. He had taken the job out of a sense of duty when Katherine had met with him personally to recruit him for the job. Having dealt with the prior Chiefs of Staff, he knew it was a thankless, miserable job. It had its benefits in terms of wielding real power in the Cabinet. What he had not counted on was working for Katherine and all it entailed. He had a thick skin and didn't expect thanks from anyone. However, her meddling in everything from staffing decisions to how the Pentagon was run had resulted in his spending eighteen hours of every day putting out fires and smoothing over the outrage of far too many. He had thought the Chief of Staff was supposed to be the hard-assed bastard, not the President.

Upon entering the room, Burt found Katherine staring at the seal of the President of the United States, hanging from the unused podium standing in the corner. "Madam President," Burt said gently as he took a seat at the table, "I have informed Hathaway to fire that goddamned Colonel and have his office contents sent to Pentagon Security. There they will be sifted through carefully. He might eventually get his personal belongings returned to him. You won't have to deal with that kind of insubordination again. I promise." Burt hoped he wasn't also sealing his own demise.

In an eerily calm voice, Katherine said, "Thank you, Burt. I know I can always count on you."

After pausing for several seconds, she lifted her index finger to prevent Burt from saying what he was about to say. She continued. "There are beginning to be far fewer people I can trust these days." Turning to face him and looking him in the eyes she said, "I want to know I will always be able to count on you. Can I, Burt?" Before he could answer, she followed with, "Can I really count on you, Burt?"

Putting all the hundreds of fires aside for the moment, Burt returned Katherine's stare and said, "Yes, Madam President, you can really count on me. Always." In his mind Burt mentally added to himself, "And I will always do what is right for my country." The conviction Burt placed into both the spoken and unspoken pledge seemed to satisfy Katherine. He could see how desperately she needed that support.

"Now, what are we going to do about these rats abandoning ship? It has to look bad, and the press will probably have a field day."

Burt considered for only a moment before saying, "Madam President, have your press office come up with a new line of releases congratulating the retiring, not resigning, senior military officials without naming them. Then follow with an appropriate statement, something like your new administration continues to assess the new, better direction you are taking the country. In the process, you have found a few senior officials from the previous administration who are not compatible with our goals. You appreciate their past contributions to their country, but you believe we need new blood to steer the country forward, or something like that."

Katherine's mood seemed to brighten a little to a look of mere gloom. "Yes, Burt, I like it! Why don't you get Baxter on it right away? The boy seems to be the only one in the Press office who doesn't have his head up his ass or someone else's. And better yet, he doesn't blame his race to cover up his incompetence." Burt had spoken with Katherine on two separate occasions about dumping Towanda, but had to back off both times. Something about fears of "black lives matter," protests.

Katherine got to her feet and walked out of the room with no further acknowledgement of Burt.

Ten minutes later, Burt stopped into Marc Baxter's office. Having done so many of the duties of the acting Press Secretary, he and Marc were on a first name basis.

"Hey Marc," Burt said with more cheer in his voice than he felt. "I've got a new challenge for you." Seeing the wince on Marc's face, he followed with "And I will see you get the five interns you wanted, but it may take a month or two."

Marc's face showed cautious interest, all without a word in response.

"The President wants a new press campaign complimenting the retiring generals and admirals while at the same time suggesting they were from the prior administration and did not fit into this administration's march to progress. Hmmm, I like that phrase. Maybe use it as a new slogan for Katherine's administration–March to Progress."

"Burt, you mean the six generals who resigned in protest?"

"No, Marc, they retired after learning they didn't fit in with the direction this administration is taking us. Really do it up right. Have Towanda stroke the press friends who keep giving her all that free shit."

At Marc's quizzical look, Burt continued, "Yeah, the security people told me about all the things she's been adding to her apartment, a new car, etc. Makes her look like she's been bribed, but then again, who in Washington hasn't?" Marc's neutral face hid the shocked outrage he felt at both Burt's flippant attitude and the fact he was probably right for ninety plus percent of the administration.

"That'll take me two or three days to get together and move it out, Burt. I won't be able to handle morning briefings or keep tabs on the hot button topics while I'm working on it."

"Ok, if anyone asks, particularly Towanda, tell her I told you to have your assistant, what's his name, Butler?"

"John Butler," Marc offered.

"Yeah, John. Have John take over what you were doing and get this project out. I'm sure you'll have time to go over his work to make sure he's getting it right before the morning meetings. How soon can you get me an outline of the strategy?"

"Barring any real crises, I should be able to get you at least a draft of the plan by close of business."

"Good!" Burt said with his first real feeling of hope. "That should do it."

"Burt?" Marc said as Burt was walking out the doorway of his pod.

"Yeah, what Marc?" Burt was clearly distracted and somewhat annoyed at Marc's delaying him.

"You know at least one or two of the generals or admirals will probably be on the Sunday morning talk shows, and more may give interviews to the conservative radio talk show hosts. Got a plan for that?"

"I'll handle it, Marc. But thanks for the heads up. I had forgotten that angle." Burt hurried off to his office to call Defense Secretary Hathaway. He strongly suggested Hathaway put a muzzle on his generals. Part of Hathaway's appeal for his position as Secretary of Defense was the way he had been able to stick it to enemies, and those who protested his programs while he was Director of the Environmental Protection Agency. After all his years in Washington, D.C. politics, Burt was no longer amazed at how poorly veiled threats to regulate and inspect a business to death usually resulted in their complying with whatever you wanted. Hathaway would find a way to at least shut the generals down before they could further damage the President's reputation.

Marc sat in his office beginning to draw out the minor press campaign. He couldn't help but think about how his job really had little to do with sharing the truth or the facts with the American people. Instead, it was about 95% spin to present whatever image made Katherine and her policies look good. Wryly, he had to admit that was the job for which he was hired. It was ironic how similar the activities in the Presidential Press Office were to the examples of yellow journalism denounced in history books in high school. He had gotten his first taste of reporting the correct spin in the journalism classes at Columbia. Curious, he thought. He hadn't noticed it then.

CHAPTER 27
INAUGURATION - PLUS FOUR MONTHS

Outside of Cronin, Kentucky
1900 Hours EST

Mike called the special meeting of the neighborhood association to order. The association President wasn't available. The meeting was held in the fellowship hall of a church down the street from the neighborhood. It surprised him to see there were almost 100 people present, more even than at the chili cook-off. No one had brought their kids. The mood of most everyone seemed to be fairly good. There was a combination of a social atmosphere coupled with what appeared to be genuine interest in emergency preparedness.

Mike opened the meeting with, "First, let me thank each of you for coming. This is a subject I think is important. All of us need to begin not just thinking about it, but doing something about it. By the way, Josh and Emma," Mike said with just a hint of a smile, "who is looking after those six kids of yours?"

At neighborhood functions, Mike and the guys had gently kidded Josh he needed to learn about the birds and the bees. "Heck, Mike," Josh said with a big smile, "they're used to being alone for a couple of hours at a time. How do you think we got Meghan, Jimmy, and little Scotty made?" There were jovial laughs all around.

With a big smile, Mike continued in his heavy Kentucky drawl, "Well, now that we finally have Josh all 'edjumicated' in where babies come from," followed by a big pause for effect, "let's get started on why we're here. Most of you know him, but for those who don't, I'd like to introduce neighbor and Cronin Chief of Police Fred Callahan. He's got some information I think we should all hear."

"Thanks, Mike," Fred said with deference in his voice. "Everyone here should already know it continues to be a dangerous world out there, with everything from winter storms and ice storms, hurricanes and fires, to terrorist wackos. Just ask Bowling Green, down in Western Kentucky, if you don't think terrorists might be living among us right now. You all remember the two Iraqi-born terrorists Mohamad Shareef Hammadi and Waad Alwan were arrested there. They plotted to ship money, guns, grenades, and shoulder-fired missiles from Bowling Green to al-Qaida in Iraq in 2010 and 2011. Both guys were in the U.S. on refugee status. Also, since 2012, the federal government has quietly brought over 100,000 Syrian refugees into the U.S. and dumped them on unsuspecting communities."

"In 1993," Fred Continued, "the federal government created the Community Emergency Response Team program, or CERT teams, to help address many of the emergencies we all face. Here, let me pass around what's on the FEMA website." He handed out a stack of one page information sheets.

"In a nutshell, all this information means is there is a system in place to help interested communities get organized, trained, and prepared to help themselves when government agencies, such as fire, police, and medical support aren't available."

"Isn't that what the police department, fire department, EMS, and shoot, even the National Guard are for?" The question came from Kerry DuBois, who had come into the back of the church meeting room.

"Oh, hello Kerry," Fred said. "Didn't see you come in." Kerry gave Fred a scowl when he was identified by name to everyone present. He had wanted to snipe anonymously.

"That's a great question. Yes, government agencies including all of those and more have the responsibility to provide help in cases of emergency. They can and they do, but sometimes there are situations that overwhelm resources. What we're here to do today is talk about some things each one of us can do to help ourselves when other services aren't available." Most in the room nodded their heads at what was simply good sense.

"So you're sayin' we should all spend thousands of dollars to hoard stuff in case of the apocalypse," Kerry said with a snide tone and country drawl to his voice.

"No, Kerry, I haven't really said anything of the kind. In fact, I haven't had a chance to say much at all yet. Do you mind if I continue?"

"Well, I know what you're gonna say, tellin' all of us we should go out and buy food and guns and ammunition and hoard it for some imagined catastrophe." Kerry had everyone's attention and was enjoying the stage, so much so the words kept pouring out. "In fact, I talked to some friends at the state who have contacts at FEMA and other federal agencies and even the Fontaine administration. What they're tellin' me is even if something really bad happens, they'll just declare martial law and send the military out to gather what's needed to distribute to people in need. In fact, they'll want to know where all the stores of food and stuff are so when things get scarce, they can come get yours."

The final words had tumbled out of his mouth before his brain registered he might have said more than he should have.

"So let me get this straight, Kerry," said Jim Webb from his seat in the audience. "If we have prepared for our families in case of emergency, you're going to tell outsiders where they can come steal food and other supplies to be handed out to whoever they see fit?" The question hung in the air while everyone present who had not turned to look at Kerry now did so.

"I, I didn't say steal. I mean, I said redistribute...." All of Kerry's arguments seemed to die in his throat as he fearfully looked around the room of people. The mood of the room toward him was definitely unfriendly and moving toward openly hostile. "You people just have no compassion for others!" Kerry shouted, backing away and nearly running out of the room.

Everyone in the room sat in silence, considering what had just been said. Jim Webb was especially troubled by Kerry's whiny description of what some of his friends in the state capitol had said.

Mike stood up and seized the moment. "Fred, I'm sure we all have some important questions, but would you please comment on how emergencies have been handled in the past?"

"Yeah, thanks Mike." Fred seemed relieved to have everyone's thoughts redirected. "In the past, we have used a pretty effective system in this state to handle emergencies. Heck, when the 2012 tornados went through West Liberty and other places in Eastern Kentucky, the outpouring of help from all over Kentucky and even from outside the state was amazing. It showed how the good people in Kentucky pull together in times of crisis. For now, I think we should best begin our preparations for the things we've seen in the past." There were general nods of agreement around the room as everyone seemed to settle down following Kerry's agitation.

"To start, I suggest as many as possible take the CERT informational courses. In addition, Mike has a handout of what each family should try to put back in case of emergency. It's based upon what FEMA recommends and covers a wide range of situations. They say three days is the minimum, but I think a good starting point is two weeks. And talk to your doctors about getting at least a thirty-day supply of whatever medicines your family might need. Remember, folks, these suggestions are all voluntary, but I know I don't want to be a burden to my friends and neighbors should an emergency come our way."

The rest of the meeting centered on practical questions and suggestions about what types of things to acquire. There were also suggestions on where to get the best price and what other things could be done to prepare. The critical need for a family communication plan, in case all communications like telephones were lost, was also emphasized.

Fred also asked, "In an emergency, does everyone in your family know where to go and what to do if they aren't home and, for some reason, could not go home?"

To end the meeting, Mike said, "Thank you for coming. I like to think I wouldn't live in my home or have a car without insurance, as if the mortgage company and my bank would let me." The laughs were quick to follow. "So I'm looking at these things as hazard insurance that doesn't cost much. It really gives me some peace of mind. And what the heck, it's all stuff we will be needing and using, anyway."

After the meeting broke up, Jim stopped both Mike and Fred for a quiet discussion. "Fred, was Kerry right? Could the National Guard really come seize food and anything else some idiot politician thought they needed? And if so, what would it take to allow such a thing?"

Both Mike and Fred liked Jim despite their friendly disagreements about his vehement support for the union. Jim had always been a worker. He also showed his character by both his support for his church and support for anyone he encountered who needed help. They also knew him to be a man of his word.

"Jim," Fred said softly, "can we keep this conversation between us for now?"

At Jim's nod, Fred continued, "I will not sugarcoat it for you, so here it is. Some folks a whole lot smarter than me think there's a financial crisis looming. They'll make the market crash of 2008 and even the depression of the 1930s seem very mild. They think the moves made by the Fontaine administration may not be the only cause, but they are speeding up the process. There are also some serious threats economically from China and Russia. To top it off, the terrorist threat to our economy is also very real."

Jim looked at Mike, who nodded his agreement.

"What we want to do here is get people started preparing for things so we don't have anyone starving should things go into the toilet. Like Mike said, if it doesn't happen, it's just good insurance."

"You know more than you're telling me," Jim said while boring into Fred's eyes.

"Well, yes," said Fred, "I do know more. I just can't say because it's considered law enforcement sensitive. It all tracks along the same line. For me personally, it's more important for people to prepare without causing them to panic."

"How about the National Guard taking our stuff?" Jim asked quietly, but with a strong dose of concern.

"You know my son, Sean, does a lot of sneaky Pete stuff for the military. I asked him the same question. He told me under declared martial law, they can do just about whatever they want. Constitutional or any other kinds of rights are out the window."

The enormity of the statement was not lost on Jim.

Fred continued, "If they declare martial law or only use authority under a Presidential Executive Order, they can and will have nothing to hold them accountable. Now don't get me wrong, I think the Executive Order issued in 2012 was issued only to be used in case of something catastrophic. I hope the President was thinking about what is best for everyone in the country. During World War II, there was a lot of rationing, and people had to deal with it. I'm just tryin' to plan for myself and help others do what is best for them and their families. I do have some concerns about what certain people might do. Like, for instance, what might Kerry and his friends do if they were to gain authority under emergency powers?"

"Yeah, that worries me, too," said Jim with a thoughtful look.

CHAPTER 28
INAUGURATION - PLUS FOUR MONTHS

Washington, D.C.
2030 Hours EST

Lisa McIntyre was mildly disappointed when Su canceled the get together at her apartment. Further disappointment came when Su said she didn't know when it could be rescheduled. That was one thing Lisa had learned about bright people like herself and Su. They could not be rushed. Therefore, she reconciled herself to be patient, but to keep letting Su know she was available.

Outside of Beijing, China
0915 Hours Local Time the Next Day

General Secretary Song sat on an ornately carved stone bench and reflected for a few minutes in the People's Garden outside of his country home. Several months earlier, the simple stone bench and pad had been replaced by an ornate one with a silk cushion. It was a gift from General Hu. With the food riots, crumbling economy, and other pressures, it was a great luxury to take even fifteen minutes to hear the birds sing. Song had informed his Chief of Staff, Wong Jie, General Lao of the MSS, was to be admitted to the garden in fifteen minutes. Wong withdrew while Song disciplined himself to enjoy the sound of the birds. He emptied his mind for a full ten minutes. From experience, he knew answers came to him during such times of meditation.

Within seconds of the expiration of ten minutes, Song's mind snapped to alertness. Outwardly, there was no difference in his appearance. His eyes remained closed, and his posture and breathing were unchanged from the slow, relaxed demeanor associated with a Buddhist monk. A marathon runner would envy his heart rate and blood pressure. In this state, Song could instantly see the answers to many complex issues facing both himself and China.

On cue, Lao walked out of the house and into the garden. Song could hear his slippered feet making only the slightest of sounds with each step on the ground-up shells making up the pathway to Song's bench. Lao stood silently and waited. Lao's head was bowed, and he was prepared to wait for however long it took for the General Secretary to acknowledge him. Song silently relished that Lao was a true professional who, unlike the impetuous youth of China, understood the importance of decorum and tradition.

Song was also aware Lao was the only man in the world who could arrange for Song to die, either painfully or quickly, with no sign of what truly killed him. Song could likewise order Lao's death at any time. Both men knew and appreciated the power and talents of the other.

Song's eyes slowly opened, looking at Lao's bowed head. "Lao," Song acknowledged his MSS Director with a voice nearly a full an octave lower than the average Chinese man. He then made a hand gesture to the bench opposing his own. Song departed from decorum and launched into his first question, without the normal pleasantries. "Lao, when will our renegade province be returned to the People's Republic?"

If Lao thought his partial smile and positive answer would surprise the General Secretary, he was mistaken. Song had other sources of information besides those provided by his Ministry of State Security Chief.

"General Secretary," Lao began, "there has been significant progress on that issue." Song's lack of surprise or any reaction at all caused Lao to pause momentarily. He then continued, "Both the hacking demonstration to the Americans and our island building, which creates sovereign Chinese Territory in the Spratly Islands, has shocked and intimidated the Americans. Through sensitive sources, we know the American President has ordered no confrontation occur with any of our forces. The Spratly Islands are uninhabited. They also have good fishing grounds and are rich in oil, natural gas, and other natural resources. Two weeks ago, a Green Watch protestors' boat, filled with environmentalists, was swamped by one of our cruisers. They were then rescued by the same cruiser. They are receiving appropriate handling in our military jail while they receive a thorough medical examination."

Lao's smile told Song the protesters were very roughly handled and would be medically examined, to include rough body cavity probing. This treatment would ensure against future on-site protests. Song was surprised this group of protesters had not learned from all the warnings circulated within environmentalists' ranks prior to the Beijing Olympics. Most had avoided confronting the People's Republic of China, at least within China's borders. They had a strong fear of its jails, and security forces.

Lao continued, "You have ordered yet another practice ship-to-shore assault exercise, with five division-sized elements for May and December. This will allow for the option to take Formosa in December while maintaining the element of surprise. The potential for provocation has been diminished by your moves in the Spratly Islands and the hacking attacks. Reaction to both by the Americans has been as predicted. Without the Americans to lead them, the rest of the countries in the area have made only muted protests."

Song nodded silently to Lao's news, none of which was new to him. Song responded by unexpectedly getting up from his bench and gesturing to Lao to walk with him. A slight widening of the eyes was the only sign by Lao of his surprise at this new action.

In a soft, barely recognizable voice Song said, "Lao, tell me the current status of General Hu's special project." Lao handled contacts with Hu and made those contacts only face to face.

"Hu's project made a breakthrough two days ago," Lao whispered. "Right after you last toured the operation, the facility was placed on quarantine lockdown, with families told a new, highly infectious disease had been discovered and everyone would be in complete quarantine for at least a ten-month period. My Special Branch people have formed a buffer to provide for what little communications are needed by Hu's team for materials and necessities."

"And the breakthrough?" Song asked again in a nearly indistinct voice.

"Ten criminals have been exposed to the virus, five of whom had been immunized with five different vaccines. Four unvaccinated criminals have contracted the virus and are near death. Four of the five who were vaccinated also contracted the virus. Of the ten test subjects, two are apparently unaffected. One who was vaccinated has developed antibodies to the virus. Hu believes the vaccination received by the survivor shows an effective vaccine. The other has no symptoms or any sign in blood tests of exposure. Hu believes this last test subject has some type of natural immunity to the virus." Lao paused to allow for Song to absorb the news.

"How soon will the vaccine be validated, and how soon can it be mass produced?"

Lao responded, "Hu advised me the vaccine should be validated through a five-year trial." At Song's sharp glance, Lao quickly continued, "However, when pressed, he said they could validate a mostly effective vaccine in as little as two weeks. Amounts of the virus suitable for the proposed operation are ready and available. Production of the vaccine for 500 million doses will require at least four to six months and possibly up to one year and will require massive resources. This project can all be done with your new program to offer flu shots to the Chinese people."

Lao stopped and glanced into the face of General Secretary Song. "You have not given me instructions on how many and who should receive a vaccine dose. I would suggest these issues be determined near the time of vaccination to avoid any of the curious within the medical field learning too much, too soon. I will presume to exclude the logical trouble makers from receipt of the vaccine, including the rioting leaders on collective farms and certain minority groups such as Muslims."

"Hu's statement to me was the virus has nearly a 90 percent mortality rate. Can you confirm it, Comrade Lao?"

"That is in line with what my people tell me. They are closely watching Hu. Hu plans to do a complete workup on the one criminal who avoided the disease altogether by her presumed natural immunities. He thinks she may fall into the one in 10,000,000 category."

Lao determined he would redouble efforts to more thoroughly go through her background. If that did not present a reason for her immunities, he would instruct her severe interrogation. It might be possible her dissident group had somehow immunized her against the virus.

"Lao, see that the vaccine production does not see the usual delays, and also see that the appropriate people get the vaccine in the order of their importance to me. Understood?"

With a bow, Lao responded, "Yes, General Secretary."

CHAPTER 29
INAUGURATION - PLUS SIX MONTHS

The Mike Broehm Residence
Outside of Cronin, Kentucky
1130 Hours EDT

Lauren Broehm was proud of herself. She had single-handedly organized an effort within the neighborhood to expand the number and size of gardens. She now believed the neighborhood was nearly self-sufficient for food production. In anticipation of a good vegetable yield, she had found a stockpile of quart mason jars totaling in the thousands at the auction of an old farm way out in the country. There were enough jars to store everything the neighborhood could produce, and harvest for several years. It surprised her that many of the men jumped in to help. They made completing tasks such as using the new heavy-duty tillers and hauling around the large bags of seeds so much easier. About three quarters of her neighbors had purchased the more expensive heirloom seeds. Lauren knew most of the seeds for sale in stores are hybrids, which do not allow the plants to reproduce themselves from season to season.

Lauren had also noticed some changes in her husband. With Peter Worthington's encouragement, Mike had really taken charge in the neighborhood and had seemed to earn a great deal of respect within the county. When Mike had anything to say, people listened. By-products from Mike's changes for her were even better. He used to duck chores and other boring responsibilities, but lately he had been giving attention to the small things. Now if only he would cut back on the evening beers and the unhealthy things he ate, maybe he could drop some weight. Damn, she thought, especially since she had gone through menopause. It was tough to get interested in even a good man covered in all that blubber. If only he would power-walk with her or join a gym. She now ate like a bird just to keep her tummy bulge under control. No amount of exercise seemed to matter. But Mike didn't seem to care about his weight and had even snapped at her when she mentioned it.

There were other ways Mike had surprised her. In mid-April, he came home and asked if she would want to get a rooster for her chickens. She knew how much he hated the constant noise and crowing they made, so instead of producing their own chicks, they had always purchased them. They now had a very noisy neighborhood with half a dozen chicken coops and four roosters. Their crowing was annoying, but at least the noise seemed to drive Kerry DuBois crazy. So crazy, in fact, he was rarely even seen around the neighborhood.

It was a hot, early Summer day. Mike had been out in the heat all morning hanging bird screening for the blueberry plants. After a quick stop in the house for lunch, he had gone right back out to build runs for the chickens. The owls had gotten two of them before he started locking them up for the night in their coop. Just the week before, Lauren had seen a hawk swoop down and kill one. For a woman who loved birds and animals of all kinds, she had murder in her eyes before he suggested building hawk-proof runs made of chicken wire.

Mike and Lauren walked in together from the 90-degree heat. Mike was coated in sweat while Lauren had a fine sheen of perspiration from having just admired Mike's chicken-run handiwork. All Lauren could think about was how much she wanted to be anywhere but downwind from her husband. She wondered why heavy people seemed to have worse body odor. Just inside the door, Mike suddenly grabbed her and tried to give her a big hug and kiss. She squirmed out of his arms and said, "Honey, you need a shower!" While trying unsuccessfully to hide the hurt look in his eyes, Mike said playfully, "Care to join me?"

"No, that's ok. I want to get in a load of laundry before getting cleaned up." She turned and walked away toward the laundry room, leaving Mike standing there totally frustrated. After she walked away, he muttered under his breath, "damned cold fish." He couldn't think of a time, even before menopause, she had wanted to be held by him.

CHAPTER 30
INAUGURATION - PLUS SIX MONTHS ONE DAY

Beijing, China
0820 Hours Local Time

General Secretary Song had just gone through his mind-clearing exercise and was sitting quietly in his office. Two weeks earlier, after months of cautious and sometimes heated negotiation, agreement was reached with the Russians. They were to provide significant oil deliveries to China for a six-month period. During that time, China would temporarily stop all oil importation from the rest of the world. China was the world's largest importer of oil. This move would cause world oil prices to plummet, according to his chief economic advisor, who had left his office just twenty minutes earlier. The first half of his plan would begin in sixty to ninety days, causing a worldwide economic slump. The Americans will be pushed into a recession.

The second half of Song's plan was contingent on whether the first half worked. If the first half of the plan was not sufficient, his finance ministry would begin dumping U.S. bonds on the market until the market collapsed.

Song made sure his personal investment portfolio would only drop slightly. His two grandsons would eventually be very wealthy men. And unlike the computer hacking activities which had shut down the three targets in the United States several months earlier, this move was calculated to avoid the likelihood of provocations leading to war. It would dramatically weaken the Americans, both in their economic power and their status in the world. It was also one step closer to preventing the United States from coming to the aid of Formosa when he brought them back into the new Chinese empire.

Frankfort, Kentucky
1930 Hours EDT

Kerry DuBois had carefully gathered the four men in the private office and meeting room above the Pen and Ink Saloon in Frankfort, Kentucky. Like him, three were men who stayed in the background of state politics but had developed friends and a power base inside the highest levels of state government.

John Chapman was a tall, heavier man with black, wiry hair and black plastic glasses. He had been the Lieutenant Governor in the previous administration and had contacts in most of the important parts of government. They were important because of their significant budgets, which included the National Guard. John had been a community organizer in Louisville before he was discovered and catapulted into office by Jerry "The Tank" Monahan.

Tank, a hulking brute of a man, had won his fortune by extortion activities targeting Eastern Kentucky coal companies in the 1970s. He followed those successful activities by getting into marijuana production in the same area. Although never in the United Mine Workers Union, he had made more than a comfortable living, ensuring all the mines used union labor. This activity usually resulted in collecting money from both the union and the coal company. Unfortunately for him, the marijuana investments earned him six years in federal prison, after which he went mostly legit. During his time behind bars, his moneyman had more than doubled his offshore investments, which allowed him to begin quietly investing in businesses and state politicians.

Mickey Blondiac, known to everyone as Blondi, had been a classmate of Kerry's at UC Berkeley. Through Kerry's connections, Blondi had been coaxed out of California to Central Kentucky three years earlier to fill the newly created position of political analyst at the largest local newspaper. After he was caught in a very compromising sexual position with his California editor's boyfriend, Blondi decided it was probably safer and healthier to take Kerry's advice and see what Kentucky offered. With the large university presence in Lexington, and an openly gay mayor, it didn't seem like a bad place to move. Naturally, his work at the paper led him to learn about the various levels of corruption throughout the state, but also insured he would have extra money for the very nice apartment near the university. Hell, at Berkeley, he had learned journalistic ethics were never to impede marching toward a more progressive society.

Freddy Dobson was different from the other four gathered at the Pen and Ink. He was the son of wealthy East Coast parents who thought he needed to learn responsibility. He had partied his way through life. At 28 years old, he was shipped off to the family horse farm outside of Paris, Kentucky, to learn how to manage a business. At first, the farm manager made his life a living hell. The abuse stopped when Freddy learned the manager's gambling debts had resulted in his embezzling money from the farm. Although Freddy made a big deal of it to the manager, a small $60,000 withdrawal from the trust fund his grandparents had established for him had taken care of the debt. In return the manager was motivated to give his father barely believable reports on Freddy's progress. Although boring until then, life had gotten much more interesting when he had met Kerry and the others at a fundraiser.

"Gentlemen," Kerry said as each man was served their second drink of choice by a beautiful blonde in tight, black pants and a low-cut top. These clothes showed off her tight butt and overly ample breasts. Kerry said the word with some regret since it was the signal for the girl named Gina, or Tina, or something like that, to leave. Five sets of eyes tracked her gliding stride across the room. Five sets admired her firm, round bottom displaying the faint lines of her thong. Blondi admired both her grace and the lovely cut of her clothing, thinking if he ever decided to try girls again, she might be worth the exploration.

With an audible sigh and an adjustment to his groin, Kerry continued, "God, but that's a nice piece of ass." Solemnly, all five men raised their glasses in a silent toast and acknowledgement to the truth of the statement.

Shaking his head to clear her from his mind, Kerry said, "I asked you here out of great concern for our Commonwealth." Grins popped onto each face, except for Freddy who really didn't care enough to see the irony in Kerry's statement. "If those rich bastards don't start paying their fair share, and things keep going into the toilet with inflation and the economy, I'm hearing things could get bad around here. Are you hearing anything, John?"

"Yeah, the governor has a task force made up of the deputies from each department," John said. "The National Guard is studying many disaster situations. FEMA has been sending out warnings and there have been classified military briefings sent to our National Guard commander and staff. There is major concern on what the feds will do if the NRA hotheads keep bitching about the government taking their guns from their cold, dead fingers and if social order were to break down. Folks in the Governor's office are already talking about what happens when they institute martial law."

In his typical, firm and deep voice, Tank interjected, "I've been buying up a bunch of warehouses all around Frankfort, which I'm happy to lease to the state for only a small profit. You know, just in case you fellas need to store food or anything." The smile on his face matched the poorly disguised glee in his words.

John continued, "I'll see some contracts are drawn up. Can you get me a list of what you have and where they are? I'll also have to clue the National Guard they may have to provide security for each of these locations once they collect essential materials and foodstuffs. I'm told emergency fuel stocks are already stored and available. It's in the plan to seize all available fuel storage tanks as well. Our boys and girls in the National Guard will be busy."

Freddy asked the question that had been forming in each of their minds. "Do you think the military boys will do what they're ordered to do?" There was a pause as each man pondered the question.

"I happen to know the National Guard commanding general will do what he's told, if he wants to keep his job, his wife, and probably his family," Blondi said with confidence. Everyone but Kerry looked at Blondi with undisguised surprise. Kerry had made it a point to quiz everyone for whatever dirt they knew and this was news to him.

"Yeah," said Blondi, "he has a bit of a pill problem that has been kept under the rug. He'll do what he's ordered to do." After a pause, Blondi continued, "And none of you better think you can use that information for your own benefit. Those in the know have big plans, and take it from me, you best not mess around with them." Blondi had delivered this pronouncement softly, but each man knew he meant it.

"All right then," said Kerry. "Just so we're all on the same sheet of music."

CHAPTER 31
INAUGURATION - PLUS SIX MONTHS ONE DAY

Washington, D.C.
2200 Hours EDT

Walter's heart rate and breathing had quickened once again. He was riding in the car provided by Mr. Sung to meet with Su Ling for the first time in almost a month. He had enjoyed the company of two regular girls in the interim. After Su, normal girls just seemed to be boring. He couldn't resist when Su's note had said simply, "Would like to show you something special." His imagination ran the spectrum from how she had once shown him an amazing feat with a vibrator to what he would do if she tried to introduce something weird like bestiality. Walking into the back service entrance of the hotel, he had just decided he would not screw a goat or any other creature, but if she wanted to do anything of that nature... well, he'd just have to wait and see.

Entering her suite, Walter heard oriental music softly playing in the background. Su, wearing aqua colored stretch pants, gracefully rose from the couch. His eyes almost missed the fact she was wearing no underwear. Her pearl colored, close-fitting silk blouse featured, rather than hid, her breasts and nipples. Her air and just the way she moved was like no other woman he had ever experienced. She slid into his arms for a warm embrace and sensual kiss. His erection pressed, almost painfully, into her soft belly.

"Oh, Walter," Su cooed softly. "It has been much too long." Her right hand moved to cup his face while her left expertly adjusted his package to a more comfortable position.

"How did she know to do that," he wondered. Like everything Su did, it pleased him.

"I need you *so much*," Su whispered with just the right amount of sincerity in her China doll voice, "but first, please sit in this chair and let me rub shoulders. You so tense, I fear you break!" She helped him out of his sport coat and led him by the hand to the overstuffed chair before taking up her station behind.

"Oh, you muscles so hard," she said as she kneaded his shoulder and neck muscles. "You have so many worries?" That and a few skillful benign questions opened the floodgates for Walter to complain about everything that had happened over the past two months. He now cared as little for the classified nature of what he said as he had cared about such things while he was in office. After a full fifteen minutes, Walter had talked himself out.

He grabbed her hands, "Now, what was so special that you wanted to show me?" His voice was husky. His arousal demanded attention.

"You let me put mask on?" She asked sweetly. "I show you very special." Before Walter could object, she fastened a sleeping mask to cover his eyes. She lightly scratched fingernails down one arm as she glided around the chair. She opened his shirt and lightly pinched his nipples. "You like this?" She asked as she alternated between pinching and rubbing his chest.

"Oh, yes, I… Oh!" Walter exclaimed as she lightly tortured his nipples. The pain registered, and he noticed his sensual reaction. Between deep breaths and with a firm voice, she said, "You been bad boy. You come to bed now and do what I say." The next hour involved pain and pleasure unlike anything he had ever experienced.

Walter left the room in somewhat of a haze. He didn't look forward to taking off the BandAids Su had put on his nipples, but after some thought, he realized how sensitive his nipples were against his shirt and how much he appreciated Su providing them. He'd have to remember to ask one of the detail members to get him a box of BandAids for later.

Beijing, China
1230 Hours Local Time the Next Day

General Hu reviewed the reports on production of the viral vaccine. There were already over one-quarter billion doses of the red vaccine and they had been shipped out to military bases and the main manufacturing cities, including Beijing and Shanghai. Another 500 million would be ready within two months. An additional one billion doses of simple flu vaccine would be ready by November.

A simple color code was provided to medical personnel. Red would be dispensed to police, the army, all intelligence organs, and high-ranking communist party officials. It gave them priority. Green would be dispensed to professionals, trained factory workers, or others in the middle class. Yellow vials were to be given to the masses, farmers, and a majority of people in Hong Kong, even if they were professionals. The explanation given, should anyone ask, was different formulas of the flu vaccine were tailored to those with differing diets. A peasant diet only required the yellow vaccine.

In reality, Hu thought with some satisfaction, both red and green formulas were the same, with full potency in protecting against the most virulent virus ever to be spread across the globe. He would insure Lao sent the yellow vaccine, which was essentially only a regular flu vaccine, to the group responsible for spreading the disease. By the time the weaponized bird flu and Ebola virus swept the world, only the most desirable Chinese people would be immune.

CHAPTER 32
INAUGURATION - SIX MONTHS FOUR DAYS

Washington, D.C.
1800 Hours EDT

Three days after her last encounter with Walter, Su Ling met Lisa for wine, cheese, and a movie. Lisa had promised over the phone Su would love the movie. When Su arrived, Lisa was already on her second glass of wine. This time, Su insisted she would bring dinner, so she had Chinese takeout food from a high-end Chinese restaurant. Following their established routine, both girls began bantering back and forth about everything from their classes to the boys in their classes. Once again, Lisa shared various texts, tweets, and Facebook posts she had received. Su claimed she did not use social media.

Su then asked, "You said you moved around a lot as a child because of your dad. Was he in the military?"

Lisa paused for a moment, but upon seeing Su's eyes narrow, she launched into the explanation. "No, and please forgive me for hesitating, but I didn't want to frighten you. My dad works for the FBI chasing terrorists."

Displaying complete self-control, Su had no reaction. Lisa continued, "Yeah, dad is a lawyer who decided sitting in, as he described them, dusty law libraries all the time or writing briefs would be incredibly boring. At least that's the speech he gave me when I asked him about following in his footsteps and going to law school. He then joined the FBI and moved us around a lot while he was climbing the bureau corporate ladder."

After a pause which Su declined to fill, Lisa asked, "Su, do you know what the FBI is and does?"

Su met Lisa's open, questioning face with a steady stare. Yes, she was very well aware of what the FBI did and knew if they caught her having sex with the husband of the President, she would either disappear or wish she had merely disappeared. "Not exactly. Are they like the Chinese Ministry of State Security?"

"No," Lisa laughed, "Dad has told me a little about the MSS and the KGB, which is now called the SVR. The FBI is governed by the U.S. constitution, and all agents are sworn to protect each person's civil rights. Even the worst criminals are handled justly, and the FBI protects their individual rights. I believe him when he says that were it not for the FBI, state and local government officials would trample everyone's rights. He says for the espionage cases, it's the people who agree to help the U.S. that were working for other countries who are considered the most valuable. They have relocated whole families to the U.S. when a family member helped the FBI crack a big espionage case."

Looking closely at Su, Lisa continued, "Su, I haven't mentioned to Dad anything about you and won't without your permission. That is, of course, presuming you're not some crazy suicide bomber or running a terrorist network. Are you?"

Su shook her head, and the beginning of a smile showed. Lisa said, "We're practically sisters after all." Lisa came over to the couch where Su was sitting, and they embraced. "I have to say, the way your uncle treats you, I'd love to ask my dad to give him a rough time. I can guarantee after a visit from my father, your uncle would definitely behave himself."

Su's reaction was immediate. "Oh, please don't do or say anything. Your father might be well intentioned, but only harm could come of it. Please promise me you won't mention anything about me to your dad."

Lisa agreed not to say anything to anyone, but in her mind, she finished the promise with, for now. She then put in her copy of the classic John Wayne western McClintock. It was her favorite movie with the fiery Maureen O'Hara and John "The Duke" Wayne in his typical persona. Su appeared to enjoy some portions, including the scene where John Wayne tracks O'Hara through the town to give her a sound spanking. But Su seemed distracted for most of the movie and left soon after it ended.

Lisa didn't know what to think about Su's reaction to learning her dad was in the FBI. She had tried to make it clear he focused on terrorists and not on Chinese nationals, but for some reason Su, as bright as she is, couldn't seem to grasp the concept the FBI was actually here to help foreigners, too. She wondered if that was the last she would see of Su. She hoped it was not the case.

· · ·

Walking back to her apartment, the shock of what Lisa had said was finally beginning to wear off. Both her training and her heart told her she could trust Lisa to keep her word. The FBI! How stupid could she be? Of all the girls in Washington, D.C. she could become friends with, it had to be the daughter of an MSS, no make that an FBI agent. Intellectually, she knew the difference between the MSS and the FBI. During the latter stages of her training, she received extensive briefings concerning what appeared to be foolish restrictions on the FBI's abilities to investigate foreigners. Foreigners having any rights at all was amazing. They trained her to know their weaknesses and avoid detection.

It was not until the next morning when she awoke two hours early she began to believe providence might have given her the smallest glimmer of hope of escaping her current situation. She would visit the public library and use a computer to look up everything she could find about defectors and double agents.

CHAPTER 33
INAUGURATION - PLUS SIX MONTHS FOUR DAYS

The White House
2230 Hours EDT

The President lay on her couch in the Presidential suite face down with only her panties on and her bra undone. Susan Cassel was rubbing her back, neck, and shoulders in ways Katherine had previously allowed only Marjorie to do. Susan wasn't Marjorie, but since Marjorie still had a near-permanent IV dripping antibiotics into her vein and reportedly looked like death warmed over, Susan would have to do. Her hands were warm, and she genuinely seemed to try to rub the right places. It always took Katherine's hand to direct her to the more sensual parts of her body before Susan would, almost with resignation, stroke her like a lover. She had never asked, but she vaguely thought Susan probably preferred men. That thought was fleeting, however, as first Susan's fingers and then her tongue found just the right spots, bringing a gasp from her followed with a sigh.

The ringing of the telephone in the Presidential suite brought Katherine up from between Susan's legs with a string of curses. "Fucking sons of bitches!" She fumed as she reached over for the phone.

"What?!"

"Madam President, please forgive me for dis…"

"What the hell do you want, General?" Not exactly the way one should address the Director of National Intelligence, but with her mood completely shattered by the call, she didn't care. General Roger Tignor had not been subjected to such disrespect since making Captain in the Marine Corps in the early 1980s. After the Fontaine administration had taken over, it was becoming nearly routine.

Without preamble, the General said, "Madam President approximately thirty minutes ago, an unknown number of terrorists attacked the guards at the U.S. Embassy in Manila. They killed several members of the Marine guard detachment. It appears several hostages have been taken, and they seized at least a portion of the Embassy. Information is very sketchy, however, I spoke to the Chairman of the Joint Chiefs of Staff. He has agreed to authorize movement of available naval and marine forces toward the area, and intelligence collection from all available assets is targeted on the Philippines."

"Well, General, why don't you just," after a pause, "no never mind." Katherine had been about to say, "Why don't you just bomb the whole embassy. Isn't that what you cretins do?" Fortunately, she found restraint before making that faux pas.

"What exactly do you mean you have deployed naval and marine forces? And why was this action taken without my authorization, General?" The edge to Katherine's voice was venomous.

"Madam President, the USS Ronald Reagan carrier group was already in the general area and has a 900 man compliment of Marines. I requested these movements to give you as many options as possible to address what is a volatile and fluid situation." General Tignor exerted significant control over his inclination to treat this novice President like a first-year cadet at Annapolis.

"I like options, General, but do not release our forces over foreign soil without my personal authorization. Am I clear?"

"Yes, Madam President, you are perfectly clear. I would also like to advise you the Marine Detachment at the embassy consists of over twenty-five men."

"Do you mean men and women, General, or are there no women assigned there?" Katherine asked with an edge to her voice.

"I don't know if there are any women in the detachment, Madam President, but I will verify that for you." The rage had been building in General Tignor and now spiked upward dramatically. Marines had died, an embassy had been attacked, and this bitch wanted to lecture him for using the word *men* to describe Marines!

"Unless there are more deaths, General, just keep my Chief of Staff up to speed on what's happening."

"Yes, Madam President." General Tignor broke the connection. Per protocol, one never hung up on the President, waiting instead for the President to end the contact. The General broke protocol to avoid saying things he would later regret.

Katherine didn't seem to notice the General had disconnected because she had already punched a button for another line to the White House Switchboard. "Get me Pittson," she said before the operator could say the obligatory, "Yes, Madam President?" The operator was quick thinking and merely responded, "Please hold one, Madam President."

"Madam President, this is Bradley Pittson, and the line is secure."

"Pittson, why weren't you the one to call me first and tell me the Embassy in Manila had been attacked?"

There was dead silence on the line for a three count before Pittson responded, "I'll need to call you back in five minutes, Madam President."

"No, you will meet me in the situation room in thirty minutes with a briefing in hand and someone knowledgeable to deliver it that can tell me what the hell is going on!" She slammed down the phone.

Susan Cassel waited patiently at the door to Katherine's bedroom. She was fully dressed and had somehow put herself together to include even a touch of fresh makeup while Katherine was on the phone. "Some raghead motherfuckers have just attacked the Manila Embassy, killing some Marines and appear to have taken some hostages. I just spoke with Tignor and Pittson, but see what you can find out and report to me in twenty-five minutes outside the situation room. You know what I want, right?"

Susan nodded and walked from the Presidential suite.

Twenty-five minutes later, Susan muttered into Katherine's ear as they walked toward the door of the situation room, "Six Marines dead, four contractors dead, unknown Filipino security forces dead or injured, and three Embassy hostages taken. They are holed up in the armored gate entrance building to the Embassy."

Katherine walked purposefully into the White House Situation Room. The ranking military non-commissioned officer, or NCO, called the military personnel in the room to attention.

"Oh, sit down!" The President snapped out this order as she walked toward the large screen situation board. This LED board covered the entire wall of the mid-sized amphitheater. CIA Director Pittson was waiting for the President in the center of the room.

Katherine gave him a one word order. "Report!"

"Madam President, on the situation board at the lower right is my head analyst for the Far East via secure teleconferencing. Go ahead, Mark."

"Madam President, although the details are still sketchy, here is what we have. At approximately 1300 hours' local time, two suicide bombers approached the main entrance to the U.S. Embassy in Manila by walking down and crossing the congested four-lane highway in front of the Embassy. One approached each side of the Embassy entrance, where they detonated their explosive vests. Several rocket-propelled grenades were fired into the guard building from across the street. Approximately twenty to thirty terrorists then assaulted the building, gaining entrance to the Embassy grounds. Several more rocket-propelled grenades were fired at the main Embassy building, killing the on-duty Marine Detachment and allowing the terrorists entrance to the building. Responding Marines prevented much penetration into the main building; however, three embassy personnel were taken hostage by the terrorists. When the group of terrorists retreated across the grounds back to the main-entrance guard building, fire by the Marine Detachment and responding Filipino security forces shot and killed all but six of the terrorists. They are currently in the main gate guard building with their hostages. Ambassador Tuttle is in contact with the commander of the PNP[4] and the situation appears to be static at the moment."

"Who are they?" The President interjected the question as Mark took a breath.

"Madam President, at this time we don't know. The Islamic terrorist organization active on the Philippine island of Mindanao..."

Katherine cut him off again to say, "You mean the *terrorist organization*, without qualifiers, don't you, Mr. Analyst?" Katherine was following in the footsteps of a prior President by publicly denying Islam as a religion was involved in terrorism.

Mark, who was near retirement responded, "I mean the terrorist organization that happens to be made up entirely of radical Islamists has contacted the usual channels to claim responsibility. However, closely held sources of the PNP have confirmed they are *not* responsible or involved in this attack. In fact, their leadership is extremely pissed off some other group could pull off such a coup in their own backyard."

---

[4] Philippine National Police

Katherine turned her back on the teleconference camera and motioned Pittson to her side. "I want him fired and out of there within the next two hours." She uttered these orders almost with no feeling at all.

After only a moment's hesitation, Pittson said, "Madam President, I can't do that. I can reassign him, maybe even demote him, but if I'm not mistaken, he is civil service *and* an employee on veteran's status. His appeal would be immediate and publicly very messy."

"Goddamn you!" Katherine shouted at Pittson at the top of her lungs. It was just after midnight. With all the other roadblocks she had endured throughout the day, she refused to tolerate some minion telling her what she could not do one more time. "Don't you *ever* tell me what I can't do, not ever again!" This time he was showered with her spit as she shouted in his face from a range of eighteen inches. She turned on her heel and departed the situation room, trailed by Susan.

Everyone in the situation room froze to watch the Presidential meltdown. For five seconds after Katherine's departure, no one moved or spoke. Then Burt Combs, who had come in quietly right after Mark's briefing, said in a firm voice, "Ok people, I want each section to come up with a contingency reaction plan and meet in the conference room in two hours. General?" Burt looked at Roger Tignor. "Please get me everything you have regarding our treaties and overall relations with the Philippines. Also, what needs to happen should we want to handle this situation ourselves? Oh, and coordinate with State. Brad?" Burt looked into Pittson's eyes with some sympathy. "Get me a report on whatever you can get in the next ninety minutes, would you please?" Pittson nodded.

"OK, people, let's get to work!"

About to leave the situation room, General Tignor stopped Burt for a few words. "Burt, just so you know, we have a great relationship with the Filipinos. We can really do about whatever we want to, with their permission. But I don't think you should tell her. Also, the Filipinos have been fighting a hot war, on and off, with the Islamists for decades. They are tough and know how to handle such situations. And finally, just so you know, the Ronald Reagan carrier task force is steaming by the most direct route to Manila harbor. They should be nearing the Spratly Islands and will pass within about seventy-five miles of the closest Chinese operation and within ninety-five miles of the nearest Chinese airfield."

Burt took a deep breath and said, "Let's just hope there are no incidents and General, don't let me see another of these *better to ask for forgiveness than permission* situations again. Ok?"

General Tignor nodded his understanding, but said, "You know I can't promise, Burt."

Burt nodded, then turned to head to his office. He had been enjoying a late dinner with his wife five blocks from the White House when he got the call. She had smiled at him and said, "I'm just going to finish this lovely dessert and my wine. Please ask your driver to call a limo for my ride home, will you dear?" He wondered why she put up with him for all of these years.

CHAPTER 34
INAUGURATION - PLUS SIX MONTHS FIVE DAYS

The Mountains of Southeast Afghanistan
1300 Hours Local Time

Ali al-Hadiz met his sister Jasmine's husband, Ahmed, with very mixed feelings. The meeting had gone well, and Ali felt the stirrings in his heart one gets when in the presence of an inspiring leader. Ahmed had no formal education, but he had that invisible mantle of leadership Allah placed on only a few. He fell under Ahmed's spell almost immediately. Ahmed soon determined Ali was someone he could trust. Two days into the visit, Ahmed called Ali in for a private talk. "God is great," Ahmed said in greeting.

Ali responded, "God is great."

Ahmed said, "How do you find living in the country of the Great Satan Infidels?"

"They have many wondrous things, for which they give no praise to Allah. The things they do cause one to avoid ever leaving home, except for work or study. A month ago, their Infidel police even arrested a friend of mine for having properly beaten his wife. Some policewoman even convinced the wife to say what he had done. The depravity in which they live is nearly indescribable."

"If you were granted a chance by Allah the Merciful to do something to change the world, would you do so?"

Ali's eyes brightened with near zealot-like fervor. "Of course I would. Tell me, what can be done?"

Ahmed then described what the Chinese infidel Cho had told him. He could not give specifics other than Cho had said his men would have to be infected with a virus just before they traveled to their final destination. "You have learned the science of the Infidels. If this Chinese Infidel delivers this chance into our hands, there will be something about it which will protect his people from its effects. Is there anything you can do to insure they, too, will be infected?"

Ali's eyes took on even a more feverish shine. "Yes, yes! My research has involved using nanotechnology to increase the power of vaccines! I can make it work in reverse." Suddenly his face showed strong disappointment. "Unfortunately, I would need a fully functioning laboratory to do what is needed. The equipment alone would cost hundreds of thousands of dollars." Ali bowed his head in despair.

"You make a list of everything you would need. Everything. I will see that it is available." Ahmed was already thinking about the hundreds of thousands he had accumulated through sales of the Chinese Infidel's plastic explosives to other groups and the special sponsorship he received from a member of the Saudi royal family. The rest was just details to be handled by his lieutenant.

Washington, D.C.
2300 Hours EST

Susan Cassel had nearly ripped Marc's clothes off when they finally got back to his apartment. Whatever she had been doing with the President during those late nights, Marc thought, it had not been very satisfying for her. She had not told him exactly what she did for or with the President. Since Marc had no time to date anyone with his work schedule, he just appreciated having her as a friend with benefits. It was mutually beneficial since both could talk freely with each other without fear of violating security rules.

The past five days they only had periodic catnaps as the Philippines crisis played out 8,000 miles from Washington, D.C. Marc had read somewhere that during the highest times of stress and danger, there were biological imperatives driving people to have sex just to perpetuate the species. One of his fraternity brothers had said, "Stress makes you horny, dude!" After a frantic fifteen minutes of near mindless sex, he and Susan slept for almost sixteen hours before they were then rudely awakened by someone pounding on Marc's door.

The doorman of Marc's apartment building had an urgent message from Towanda directing Marc to call in right away. Through his blurry mind, he realized his and Susan's cell phone batteries had died, and he had no landline in his apartment. He waited a few minutes for the charger to bring his phone back to life before calling.

"Where have you been?" Towanda screamed through the cell phone at him.

"Passed out on my bed, Towanda. How are you?"

"Don't give me your patronizing shit, white boy. Just get yo' ass cleaned up and get in here. There's been another school shooting. This time in Chicago."

"Ok," Marc said. "Should be there within the hour."

"Make it twenty minutes," Towanda said and hung up.

Susan had a pillow over her eyes. With some dread, she asked, "Now what?"

"Towanda says there's been a school shooting in Chicago. And I was just dreaming about my head floating between two of the softest white clouds." Marc grinned at the thought of waking up with his head nestled between Susan's breasts. A pillow came flying his way as he stepped into his small bathroom for a quick shower.

On his way to the White House, Marc reflected on the events of the past five days. After thirty-eight hours of negotiations, forced on the Philippine government at the insistence of Katherine, the FBI's Hostage Rescue Team had stormed the small security building at the main entrance and killed the terrorists. Unfortunately, two of the three hostages had also died, and three HRT members were wounded, one critically. The CIA could only say, with medium confidence, the terror cell that attacked the embassy had not been affiliated with any of the known Islamic groups. This new group seemed to have originated in the Middle Eastern country of Yemen. Marc knew since the fall of the Yemeni government in 2014, that country had become a breeding ground for terrorist groups. It was like Afghanistan before 2001. Some of these groups were in contact with Islamic extremist groups that had been fighting the Philippine government for decades. Based on his personal visits to CIA Headquarters in Langley, Virginia and NSA Headquarters at Fort Meade in Maryland, Marc guessed it would be months or even years before the origins of the attackers in the Philippines were determined. Unless they struck again.

Katherine had made a speech condemning the attack, and vowing all involved would face American justice. Following what had become her usual script, she read her speech off the teleprompter and declined to answer questions.

Damage control for the Press Office had been enormous. After two straight days in her White House Press Office, Towanda had gone home and refused to answer her telephone for thirty-six hours. The dust had cleared a little, late on the fourth day, when Towanda reappeared. The next day she had given Marc the rest of the day and following day off.

Arriving at the White House, Marc had to carefully maneuver past a group picketing for gun control. Walking into the Press Office, Towanda saw him coming and ordered him into hers. "The President wants you to spin up a campaign to support a complete ban on all assault rifles."

Marc looked at her skeptically before saying, "Coming out of the shower, I heard on the news the shooting in Chicago involved only a handgun. Is that right?"

"Who gives a shit?" Towanda said with enthusiasm he had rarely seen from her. "Nobody needs an assault rifle, anyway. In fact, nobody needs a gun, period." Towanda had grown up in Chicago and had witnessed her share of shootings. "With this new shooting, added to all the other mass shootings, we can finally push for more gun control and, hopefully, to outlaw them all together. That's what I want and, more importantly, that's what the President wants. She's giving a speech during prime time tonight to strike while the iron is hot. Oh, and by the way, there is a combined cabinet meeting and staff meeting at 3:00 p.m. Be there and be prepared to say how she can get what she wants on gun control. You're the wizard from the campaign, and she seems to think you can get milk from a rock or something. Now get out."

Towanda had stopped looking at him and instead was pretending to be concentrating on the papers on her desk.

Still somewhat numb from the past five days, and even a little groggy from sixteen hours of sleep, Marc almost stumbled to his office and closed the door. It was nearly noon, and he decided a sandwich and an energy drink from the canteen was just what he needed to wake up. His stomach was still a little queasy from all the energy drinks he had consumed over the previous few days, so he would be sure to eat the sandwich first before sipping more go-juice.

Sitting down with his sandwich and drink, Marc saw the Chief of Staff walk in and order. Two minutes later, Burt sat down across from Marc without ceremony.

"Sorry Towanda had to call you in, Marc." Marc appreciated his sympathy and was amazed. The Chief of Staff was supposed to be the hard ass of the White House Staff. Lately, he had been very obvious in his attempts to build bridges and give some caring leadership to the staff which was so lacking in this White House.

"She brief you on what the President wants?" Marc nodded as he chewed stoically on his sandwich. Burt then said, "I think you should reach out to Don Stetson on this project and draft him to help run it through. Thoughts?"

Marc was momentarily shocked to be asked for his opinion. This type of solicitation just didn't happen from someone with the experience of the Chief of Staff. "Burt, I'm not in the NRA or anything, and I'm not a lawyer, but isn't that what the Second Amendment is all about?"

"Marc, you know Katherine is a lawyer, or was. She thinks there's a way around everything. She also feels strongly every death by gun in this country is an abomination." After a pause, Burt looked closely at Marc as he said, "You agree, don't you?"

Almost automatically, Marc responded by rote, "Of course I do, Burt."

Burt nodded and continued. "What Katherine wants is something similar to what you did with the Afghan widows. You know, play all the angles and make it a real top-notch campaign. Save the children and everyone else from those demon guns."

Nodding, he gave Burt a look saying he was deeply contemplating the best route for the campaign. In his head, Marc silently thought about the whole Afghan widows' campaign. After the fact, the credibility of that campaign fell apart. Hell, according to several respected publications, over half of the so-called widows had not even been from Afghanistan. In the last six months Marc had become a very suspicious man. Manipulation was everywhere. He could even believe one or more of the larger terrorist organizations had ginned up the whole thing just to get Katherine Fontaine elected. He knew these organizations hated Donnelson, so it was plausible and even likely they would do anything to avoid a Donnelson presidency. Marc shared none of these thoughts, but said, "Sure, Burt, I can draw up the campaign. What is the goal, exactly?"

"The goal I think Katherine has decided on, is to maybe set up an Australian-type mandatory gun buyback. You know how they raised taxes a little and forced almost everyone to turn in their guns back in the 1990s and 2003? They pay the owners for their guns, but at least they were destroyed. We'll start like the Aussies did and ban the assault rifles and hell, rifles in general first. That didn't help their crime rate, so they banned the handguns in 2003. Try to draw out an outline and then schedule time with my secretary. Maybe the day after tomorrow we can sit down and iron out the wrinkles. Is it doable?"

"Is Towanda back now? You know, really back?" Marc's question was asked without malice or emotion, but only as a practical issue since they had drafted him to be the acting Press Secretary when Towanda had her recent meltdown.

"Yeah," Burt sighed, "I think she's back, but have your assistant quietly keep an eye on her. You know, just in case. If he sees problems, let me know. Well, got to go."

Burt got up and left. Marc hadn't even seen Burt eat his sandwich, but his plate held only a few crumbs and a piece of crust. Magic, Marc thought momentarily. He then quickly changed gears in his head to think about his new assignment.

Walking back to his office, Burt found himself feeling just a little guilty. He had not told Marc all the reasons Katherine wanted guns removed from society. He was, however, a master at getting people to do what he wanted. If Marc knew of Katherine's true intentions, he might not be so willing to do the campaign. Burt still had his own doubts after the meeting with a certain radical Senator and two of Katherine's deep-pocket donors.

Last week Katherine insisted he join her at the donor's summer house on Martha's Vineyard. The substantive conversation started after dinner. Drinks were served, and Katherine described the potential for a serious upheaval in the United States. She focused on how the right-wing radical loons could keep her from taking care of the American people. If the time came, martial law would have to be declared. But there were so many guns floating around the country she believed anarchy would prevail. Therefore, it was critical to devise ways to ensure our government had the ability to maintain control. This control was for the good of all the people, and especially the children. All agreed, maintaining social order was paramount. Katherine insisted having the ability to enforce potentially unpopular policies called for whatever measures were necessary. Getting guns out of the hands of these anarchists was a critical first step. The discussion then turned to just how they might accomplish this protective action.

Walking into his office, Burt briefly considered the origin of Katherine's plans and wondered if her many private meetings with Eli Fredericks had anything to do with it. Shaking his head, he turned to the long list of other tasks on his plate. He would tackle those things over which he had control and let the rest handle themselves.

Marc spent the next ten minutes trying every telephone number he had or could think of for Don Stetson. It appeared Stetson had dropped off the face of the earth. Marc then picked up the phone and called the chief switchboard operator. "Helen, would you please track down Don Stetson for me? I've tried these numbers and can't seem to find him."

Marc gave her the numbers he had already tried. He also knew Helen had an amazing ability to find people. Most people in the Fontaine administration seemed to view everyone below their pay grade to be mere minions. Marc made it a point to get to know the names of everyone he ran into in the White House. He found simply calling someone by their name and treating them with respect seemed to motivate them to help him. It had occurred to him he had learned about the simple courtesies from his sister, Lauren. Hmmm, he thought, treat people with respect and they do more for you. What a concept!

Just before the 3:00 p.m. cabinet and staff meeting, Marc's general outline for the campaign was coming together when his phone rang. "Marc," said Helen, "I found Don Stetson, but he wasn't happy to hear from me. He agreed to call you in two hours. He said his phone battery was about to die, and he was in the middle of a trout stream somewhere out West. He'll call back when he gets to his charger."

"Thank you, Helen. I owe you another one."

"Oh, I think we're almost even now. I still owe you for that delightful beverage you brought me." Marc had obtained two quart jars of raspberry moonshine during his last trip back to see his sister, Lauren, a few months ago. After trying some, he had given the second one to Helen. She had quietly thanked him multiple times. Lauren's husband, Mike, had gotten the moonshine from an anonymous friend in Eastern Kentucky.

Later in the evening, as Marc was cleaning up his desk to head for home, Don Stetson returned his call. "How're they hanging, kid? Oh, and is this call to thank me or cuss me out for having brought you into the asylum?"

Chuckling to himself, Marc thought he actually wanted to both thank and cuss Stetson. "No, Don. I've been given the task by my boss to develop a new campaign to eradicate guns from America. After the mass shootings and all the people killed by guns in this country, the President wants a PR campaign to take advantage of the Chicago school shooting today. Burt suggested I call you and ask for your help."

Marc was aware gun control was probably the only issue that could tempt Don to do anything else for the Fontaine administration. His daughter had been killed by a stray bullet from a drug gang shootout in Chicago fourteen years earlier. Don had immediately jumped into a leadership role in the Chicago based anti-gun organization, Stop Guns Now.

Don gave no response. Marc knew he was reliving the loss of his daughter. He was also building some of the passion he felt concerning removing all guns from the world.

Marc waited patiently for Don to consider his answer. Finally, he said, "OK, Marc, I'm in. But only for this campaign, and I will not be pulled into the other shit this administration wants to do. Got it?"

"Sure, Don. I can work with that. How soon can you come out here?"

"Have the travel office arrange for a flight out of Boise to Chicago. After at least a four-hour layover to get my shit together, get me on a flight to Washington National."

Like most associated with the Fontaine administration, Don refused to call the Reagan National Airport by its current name. Even after all these years, the hate for President Ronald Reagan was still strong.

"Ok, Don, will do," said Marc. "I'll ask Helen to reach out to you when the travel office has the tickets."

"Yeah, and Marc?" Don asked, "Where did you find that woman? She's a bulldog!" He said with admiration and no small amount of awe concerning Helen.

"I don't know, Don, but I'm proud to call her my friend, so please be nice to her."

"Like I told you during the campaign, Marc, she's the kind of person you should always be nice to." Don then broke the connection.

CHAPTER 35
INAUGURATION - PLUS SIX MONTHS SIX DAYS

Washington, D.C.
0800 Hours EST

Su Ling sat alone in her apartment, staring at the little spider crawling across her ceiling. She thought again about the rush of fear she had felt when Lisa had told her father was in the FBI. It was much like the rush of fear she had felt when the European man at Charm School had beaten her. The fear only subsided when she had determined that with absolute obedience, she could control herself and survive. When survival became the end goal, the rest became easy. Whatever it took to please the masters in her life, she would do.

For the first two weeks at Charm School, they raped Su at least three times a day. She learned there were at least twenty-five different men whose job seemed to be to perform rapes. During the first weeks, no matter what sexual activity was demanded, she was told she performed poorly. Every little action on her part was done improperly or without the necessary enthusiasm.

After the first two weeks, the swelling had gone down, and she could sit without pain. It was then the real schooling began. Over the next six months, she learned literally hundreds of ways to please a man sexually. Each one had a different name. After three months, Geisha-trained Japanese women taught her how to be seductive yet vulnerable, with an air of elegance.

Next, they trained her in techniques from the Indian sex manual called the Kama Sutra. Kama was the Hindu god of love. Looking back, she giggled a little at the many times she felt like a pretzel. Near the end of her training, an instructor had told her she had developed a reputation at the school.

The staff found it remarkable she could perform nearly all the positions described in the Kama Sutra. She had also developed an amazing ability to manipulate even the male instructors at the school. They viewed her abilities with near reverence.

At the beginning of the seventh month, Su saw a dramatic shift in her training. The training in giving sexual gratification took up only half of each day and sometimes involved other women. Soon the nature of the training changed from giving simple sexual pleasures to exploring the seemingly endless list of sexual perversions. At first they shocked her by involving animals. Then her training moved more toward inflicting pain to go along with the pleasure of sex. Spanking, whipping, severe pinching of all parts of her body were shown to her as entryways to sexual ecstasy. Sex toys of hot and cold, along with over fifty types of vibrators were introduced, and they required her to master their use. They provided all of this training throughout the afternoon and evening of each day. There were no days off.

Su's mornings were consumed with what were essentially psychology classes for her and twenty-six other girls. They learned from a odd mix of people: university professors, specialists in psychological warfare from the military, and three separate Madams from whorehouses in Europe and the United States. Each contributed information as to the inner workings of a man's head and how it was directly connected to his genitals.

With a start, Su realized the spider on the ceiling had disappeared, and she had made no progress on what she would do about Lisa's father. In her heart, she believed Lisa would be true to her word and not say anything about her new friend. But where did this new dynamic leave her friendship? Was it possible this apparent bad luck could be her chance to escape slavery? Even if it was a small chance, was it worth the risk?

Decision-making had never been hard for Su, as she had learned so quickly at Charm School. She picked up her burner phone and called Lisa. Lisa was surprised and happy to hear from her. They agreed they would meet over the weekend at the university library before proceeding to dinner. Su then reserved a private study room at the library.

Fort Carson, Colorado
1115 Hours MDT

Major Sean Callahan sat thinking in his office on the Fort Carson, Colorado U.S. Army post. Over his ten-year military career, he had experienced what anyone would have to call a lot of weird stuff. Wherever his 10th Special Forces Group unit of Green Berets was sent, it was always classified and always a situation that could go to hell quickly. Even worse, outside of the special operations community and those supporting them, there would be no one to pull their fat out of the fire. The risk was all part of occupying the top of the elite military food chain. There were benefits such as having the best equipment and training in the world. Some of the really exotic electronics they used would not be known to the outside world for twenty years. Despite all the gizmos and training, it was still him and his men that had to get there, wherever there was, assess the situation, and get the job done. All was usually accomplished with no one knowing they had been there. At least in cases involving surveillance and intelligence gathering missions. The enemy almost always knew someone was there during direct action or assassination missions.

Things were changing, and Sean didn't quite know if it was a good thing or not. Two women had joined his company-sized unit as operators. One was a First Lieutenant and the second a communications Sergeant. His company was made up of officers, administrative staff, and operators that were the soldiers in the field. Several of the admin people were female. He had found them to be competent at their jobs, but he would never consider them as potential operators.

The two female operators were different. Both could think quickly on their feet and could carry their weight like all the other operators. Feedback from their first mission in Afghanistan had proven the added value they gave to their teams. No other operators had been successful in gaining intelligence from Muslim women.

Lieutenant Linda Sharpe had definitely shown leadership and ingenuity as team leader. She was five feet ten inches tall and a slender 140 pounds with short blonde hair. Sean decided she could be very attractive if she chose to be. She didn't look like she could carry a heavy pack and weapons for miles through the brush.

Her team found out quickly not only could she do so, but after ten miles hiking through the hills, she hardly broke a sweat. Her most distinctive feature was her piercing gray eyes. Secrets didn't last long in the Special Forces environment. Soon after Sean read the contents of her military personnel folder, the word had already leaked about this new Lieutenant who had graduated from MIT with a degree in Astrophysics, making her a real, honest-to-God rocket scientist.

Sean looked up as Lieutenant Sharpe knocked at his open doorway and walked in. Army protocol normally required anyone entering the office of a superior officer to knock and wait for permission to enter. After entry, the junior ranking soldier should march up to the officer's desk to salute and formally report their presence by uttering their name and rank followed by, "Reporting as ordered, Sir!" Special Forces dispensed with such formalities. Lt. Sharpe remained standing, however, until Sean motioned toward the chair across from his desk.

"What have you got for me, Major?" Sharpe was at ease but alert. After two missions, she had developed respect for Sean's leadership and his attention to detail.

Sean handed her a six inch thick deployment packet with SECRET stamped on the top and bottom. "Here's the background. You and your team will be heading into Afghanistan to locate and identify a new terrorist cell known as Jihadists of the Prophet, or JOTP. Our NSA friends have developed whispers of this new group, and the CIA could not develop any additional information. Your deployment orders are in the packet. You can get additional Intel with higher classification on the TOP SECRET computer in the Secure Work Environment. Be back here with your team at 0700 hours tomorrow morning with questions."

"Yes, sir," Linda said rising from her chair and began to walk out of the room.

"Sharpe?" Linda turned as Sean said her name. "I will be coming along as far as Kabul to evaluate your team's performance. Let the team know I'm only there because the IG ordered me to be there. Clear?"

After she read the truth in his eyes, Linda said, "Yes, sir." She then left to gather her team.

Sean hated it when the Army Inspector General made demands directly affecting his teams. Since Fontaine had become President, it seemed all of her appointees had placed everything military under a microscope. His sources at the Pentagon had told him the President's appointees had begun to gauge the military leadership's loyalty. The question was not their loyalty to the country, but rather their loyalty to the civilian chain of command. Would the military follow orders no matter what the orders were? The trickle-down effect was a dramatic increase in IG mandated inspections. Sean was very curious to note Special Operations Command seemed to be selected for most of the inspections.

This was one of the times he felt fortunate he was not married with kids. Within forty-eight hours, he would be on a military transport bound for Afghanistan.

CHAPTER 36
INAUGURATION - PLUS SIX MONTHS SEVEN DAYS

Shanghai, China
1430 Hours Local Time

General Hu's meeting with General Lao was arranged in secret. The covert protections used were normally reserved for only the top echelon sources of the MSS. Two different car changes followed before he walked into the back door of a mid-sized motel in Shanghai. These activities made Hu feel like a real spy. Spying in China had begun over 4000 years earlier, so the level of expertise from China's top spy was to be expected.

Hu's husky five feet six inch frame carried a round head with thick, salt and pepper hair. The hair nearly covered his thick, black-plastic tri-focal glasses. Upon entering the room, Hu found Lao standing at the third-story window. The scene outside showed a thick, bluish haze over the industrial area where the hotel was located. Lao turned and began the usual pleasantries by inquiring about Hu's family and his upcoming travel plans to Hong Kong. Hu did not miss the subtlety. He was not surprised Lao knew about the planned trip the following week. Lao probably even knew Hu was not taking his wife, and he would be both gambling and enjoying the talents of two attractive young women for a long weekend. It was Hu's first real break in over two years. Whatever Lao knew, he did not indicate surprise or a cause for concern.

"The General Secretary," Lao began after turning in Hu's direction, "is most pleased about the reports concerning the vaccine. He would want everything done immediately, but your progress is impressive." Hu bowed his head at this apparent compliment. Lao continued, "He has also informed me he has your assurance all reports would be entirely factual. We both know what he means by this order, don't we?"

Again Hu responded by a positive bow of his head. Lao continued. "Both the General Secretary and I know issues will come up that must be overcome. Sometimes these issues cause delays. Let us just say such issues can be tolerated much more than the surprises that would result if the General Secretary were not kept up to date. Let me be perfectly clear, Hu. The General Secretary will make decisions based upon the data you provide concerning your project. Inaccurate data will not be tolerated. Do you understand?" Again, Hu performed another positive bow.

Lao said, "General, I want you to look into my eyes and, in your own words, assure me you understand exactly what I mean."

Somewhat startled, Hu looked carefully into Lao's eyes and said, "The General Secretary's orders are perfectly clear to me, General Lao. I have also instituted similar protocols with my own subordinates to insure I, too, receive only accurate information. My scientists were disturbed to learn anything less would result in both removal of their balls and having their nearest female relative sent to the women's prison." None of the general Chinese population knew exactly what happened in the secretive women's prisons, but they knew women feared this punishment more than death.

"Good," Lao said with a small nod in Hu's direction. "Now report."

"General Lao," Hu said with more deference than he had used upon his arrival. "As I informed the General Secretary...," Hu let the statement hang momentarily. He had quickly decided not to say when and where the meeting had taken place. "We have validated the vaccine by infecting an additional twenty prisoners. Ten of the prisoners had received the vaccine twenty-one days before exposure to the virus. Ten prisoners had received no vaccine. Five of the prisoners received the vaccine only after exposure. None of those receiving the vaccine before exposure caught the virus. All ten of the prisoners who did not receive the vaccine caught the virus. Two of those receiving the vaccine after exposure survived after suffering severe symptoms. None of the five with no vaccine survived."

"How quickly did the symptoms begin after exposure?" Hu was not surprised that as Lao heard the report and asked questions, he showed no reaction to the description of the prisoners' agonies. Lao considered them to be only laboratory animals. Of course, Hu thought, that is all they were.

"Manifestation of the symptoms began from three to five days after exposure."

Lao said, "The General Secretary wants an additional 100 test subjects used to ensure the vaccine is both effective and safe for distribution. And General," Lao said softly, "the General Secretary, yourself, and I will receive the vaccine following this additional verification. We will get this vaccine at the same time, from the same vial of vaccine. Understood?"

Hu responded with deference, "Of course, General Lao. I will insure your representative will accompany mine to retrieve the vaccine from the laboratory."

"What is the timetable for vaccine production?"

Without hesitation, Hu responded, "Over 200 thousand are ready now and another 700 million will be ready by November. For purposes of priority, they are color-coded. The red doses are for critical government and military personnel. The green doses are for the next tier of less critical personnel and necessary civilians. The yellow doses are for the masses. Only the red and green doses will be effective against, shall we say, certain viruses? And, General Lao, barring something out of the ordinary, this timetable is accurate." Hu had revised downward the estimates he had been given by his staff, hoping his experience at gleaning accurate information would be on point in this case.

"General Lao, you will prepare the program for distribution of the vaccine?"

"Yes, Hu. In two months, my propaganda section will begin informing the people of the government's new program to immunize against the flu, which made people so sick last year. It will be announced there will be immunizations available for all; however, essential people must take it."

Outside of Beijing, China
1945 Hours Local Time

Meeting General Secretary Song again in his private garden in the country, Lao relayed the information he received from Hu.

"You believe General Hu properly understands the importance of delivering what he has promised?"

"Yes, General Secretary," Lao replied softly. "By November all who need to get the vaccine will receive it."

Considering the topic closed, Song redirected the briefing. "Status of the invasion exercises?"

Lao smoothly changed gears and said, "The People's Liberation Army reports all shore landing exercises were completed successfully, and all involved troops have returned to their barracks. My own people have reported, however, the exercises were a disaster. Equipment didn't work, and we lost significant resources in the ocean during the exercises. Landing craft leaked severely and swamped even in relatively calm seas. Surprisingly, no soldiers died."

Lao continued, "My analysts have concluded that except for one thing, the PLA would fare badly against the 290,000 man so-called Republic of China's military on Formosa. Your pre-invasion plan to use a tactical electro-magnetic pulse will shut down the extensive communications structure of the ROC military and the technologically advanced planes and missiles they have acquired from the Americans. One strike with the EMP generators will effectively send them back to the World War II era in weapons technology. So long as we can keep the Americans out of the battle, our army and navy will be successful."

Song's question was simple and to the point. "Is this assessment realistic? Or are your people telling me what I want to hear?"

Lao had not risen to this level of power without taking risks. "General Secretary, their assessment is as realistically accurate as I can get. Two of thirty analysts have assessed this plan to fail. I made sure they were not disciplined or demoted to encourage honest assessments going forward. All analysts were told to assume the Americans would not intervene. They were not given any reason for a lack of American intervention."

"Good, Lao. Keep me advised." With this response, Lao bowed and departed.

Song was always a realist. To avoid a spontaneous release of his building rage, he spent the next ten minutes in meditation. When hearing the report of disastrous exercises from Lao, he had nearly lost composure and exploded at Lao. Such displays were not acceptable for a great leader. He should call the General of the PLA to task for his inaccurate report on the exercises. Unfortunately, this action would cause either the General himself resigning in disgrace, or weakening his own staff by his firing those responsible. Instead, he called his Secretary.

"Wong, come to my office."

Upon Wong's arrival, Song relayed what Lao had told him concerning the exercise.

"Wong, I want you to place the PLA General's testicles in a vice and slowly squeeze them until he has reached the level of pain just short of intolerable. Then he should be informed I will remove him along with the next two generations of his family if inaccurate reports happen again." Wong was aware Song's use of the word remove meant quietly killed and buried in an unmarked grave.

Watching Wong leave his office, Song thought again how difficult it was to convince people to tell the truth. It reminded him of the old Soviet truism: you pretend to pay me, and I will pretend to work.

CHAPTER 37
INAUGURATION - PLUS SIX MONTHS SEVEN DAYS

Outside of Cronin, Kentucky
1745 Hours EST

Mike sat in Peter Worthington's study, savoring a generous glass of Blanton's fine bourbon whiskey. Before serving it, Peter had taken a single, large ice cube out of the freezer from his office bar. He placed it in Mike's glass to chill the bourbon without the fast melting of crushed or normal cubed ice, preventing the bourbon from becoming watered down.

"How goes the neighborhood preparations, Mike?" Peter was working on pouring bourbon from an oddly shaped glass bottle. The bottle looked like something from which a genie might emerge.

"They're going ok, I suppose." Mike said, with no small amount of frustration in his voice. "What are you drinking?"

"Willet bourbon," Peter responded. "A friend recommended it so I decided to try some. Kind of scarce. Had to go to the distillery in Bardstown to find this lovely bottle." Mike always marveled at how Peter found the best of whatever caught his interest at the moment.

"Come on, Mike. Everyone at the meeting two months ago seemed to be enthusiastic, and there are gardens everywhere in the neighborhood!"

"Yeah, Lauren's got everyone fired up about laying in gardens. I think food-wise the neighborhood could probably get by for two or three months. I'm not so sure we could make it through the winter." After a pause he went on, "I walked around the neighborhood last Saturday morning and talked to a couple of dozen folks. Only about half thought they had enough food and medicine for their family for two weeks. Less than a quarter thought they could make it through the winter. Near as I can tell, they just don't think it can happen here."

Peter let Mike sit and sulk for a moment before asking, "Have you noticed the construction I have going on in front?"

"Yeah, Peter. I meant to ask you." It had been two months since Mike had been to visit. No construction had started then. Mike had seen evidence of construction while he walked to Peter's house through the woods, approaching it from the back.

"Let's take a walk." Peter got up, and both men headed out the front door. Mike could see where a bulldozer had scooped out a cut where Peter's front yard had gently sloped downward, straight out from his front door. The house usually had a beautiful view of the shallow valley which was now marred by construction. The cut was about 200 feet out from the front porch of the house and was the width of Peter's house. There was a concrete floor in the cut with French drains and concrete walls coming up at least 20 feet from the floor. They had poured another concrete wall across the end to form what appeared to be a roofless basement. Steel beams and steel reinforcing rods crossed the width of the underground chamber to form a gently sloping roof, just below the level of lawn that had been in front of the house.

"Any idea what you are looking at?" Peter asked Mike with a large smile. Mike could only shake his head in amazement. "Tomorrow, a crew will come to pour the concrete ceiling to my new home addition. You're looking at what will be my storage and security bunker. Don't know if you noticed, but my house is made of poured concrete, too. You may have seen the window sills are pretty deep. That's because the concrete walls are two feet thick, just like the walls of the bunker." Peter let this announcement sink in for a few moments. He could see the wheels turning in Mike's head.

"Why haven't I told you about any of these plans before, you might ask yourself?"

Mike looked at Peter and just nodded his head once.

"In a word, I wanted to make sure I could really trust you, Mike. Let's just say the way you've been handling yourself lately, I think I've decided I would trust you with my life and the lives of my family. I want you to know if the worst happens, and the neighborhood gets overrun, you and yours have a place here. It can be defended and has all the necessities for my family and any number I think could be beneficial to insure all of our safety."

"I would, however, like for you to put just a little skin into this game. Would you invest some money into some long-term storage food?"

"How much are you talking, Peter?"

"Oh, not that much. Only five or ten thousand dollars."

"Sure, okay. I can add $10,000 from my savings if it'll help."

"It's not the money, Mike. I just want you to invested in the whole project. I've set up a company that has been buying and selling freeze dried emergency food. You know, the kind that will store for over twenty-five years? Considering all the government is buying up, it was only by promising I wouldn't sell to the government that two of the manufacturers would even sell to me. Right now my company inventory is in a warehouse just outside of Cronin. When this place is finished, I'll need your help to move it to the bunker. I'll have a small forklift to help, but we'll need to set up shelves for long-term storage. It will be beast work and will probably take a long weekend to get it all moved."

Mike realized what a reach it was for Peter to trust anyone to this extent. He was honored beyond words. A handshake was all that was needed.

CHAPTER 38
INAUGURATION - PLUS SIX MONTHS TEN DAYS

Washington, D.C.
1900 Hours EST

Su Ling was more nervous walking to the library to meet with Lisa than she had been for her final test at Charm School, which turned out to be easy for her. They had placed her and her classmates in competition at a party with forty or fifty diplomats and businessmen from at least three different countries. Their task was to identify and seduce the man or woman who had the most valuable information. Su had to have sex with the target and get some significant bit of information useful to her government. These tasks were to be accomplished with no one suspecting she was a spy working for the MSS.

On the evening of the final test, she had taken only thirty minutes to identify the gray-haired, diminutive Chinese-American man as someone of great interest. He was there to be part of trade talks from the United States concerning Internet hacking. He was the leading computer security man on the American team. He also could not take his eyes off her breasts. They were tastefully displayed in a blue silk dress with a plunging neckline. Her nipples stood up at every errant breeze from the air conditioning. She had on no underwear. Playing the role of the daughter of a Chinese diplomat, she could dress provocatively without coming across as a prostitute. Speaking with a cultured and slightly accented English accent, she was alluring, but not suspicious. She quickly learned her target, Steven, had recently suffered a bitter divorce and was angry at the legal system that gave "the slut" over three quarters of everything he had. The rest was easy.

Thinking back, Su remembered she had achieved her entire objective without having actually slept with the target. When she stroked him through his trousers, he climaxed in a few seconds. Although tempted to suggest he clean up in the bathroom and be done with him, she decided to give him a true night to remember. By doing so, she learned he had only one testicle and was a cancer survivor. He had also identified several Chinese hackers for the FBI. Afterward, he promised to do anything for her if she would only visit him in Seattle, Washington. He even promised to provide first class plane fare. That had been four years earlier. It was not until she was finally told her next target was Walter she understood why there was no follow-up on Steven.

It was with a great rush of emotions she saw Lisa and gave her a fierce hug. Even after thinking about it for these past few months, Su still didn't understand their attachment. Possibly her feelings could be explained if Lisa were her identical twin from a previous life. How else could she explain she was about to place her life and the life of her family into Lisa's hands?

"Hey, girl," Lisa said with a choked-up voice. "I've been worried about you."

Su's reading of Lisa's eyes told her the words of concern were true and uncomplicated.

"I know. That why I want talk to you." Su's normally correct English had even slipped back into one with a slight accent. Looking around cautiously, Su led Lisa to the last study room at the far end of the hallway and closed the door. She then pulled a tape recorder out of her purse and pushed the play button, placing it on a chair near the door. From the recorder came the sound of idle conversation from two women Lisa didn't know. Su then ignored her quizzical look and led her to the corner of the room.

Su said, "Can I trust you to keep a secret?" Lisa nodded with a questioning look on her face. "No, I mean trust you to keep a secret even from your father?"

"You haven't killed anyone, have you?" Lisa blurted out the question without thinking.

"No, no nothing like that. But I want to trust you with something that could get me killed or worse, get my family killed. Can I trust you?" She asked in the small voice of a pleading child.

Lisa's mind whirled and instantly considered several different possibilities. All of them could make her an accessory to some felony. She was the daughter of an FBI agent and had spent far too much of her youth watching crime dramas on TV. She was also the daughter of her mother, who had a huge amount of empathy. In less than a second, she knew her answer.

"You can trust me with anything." By that simple statement, she knew her kinship with Su was permanently sealed. The relief on Su's face caused her own empathetic heart to burst with love. Su grabbed both of her hands and tears poured down her face. They sat on two chairs while Su let the relief pour out.

After several minutes, Su pulled herself together and pointed to the recorder. It was still playing the conversation Su had recorded at the library two days earlier. "The recorder will cover our talk if anyone is outside the door listening. You will understand soon." Lisa blinked and nodded her understanding.

"My uncle Sung is not my uncle. He is an officer of the MSS. You know what MSS is?" Lisa shook her head no. She had previously told Su she knew about the MSS and KGB. This time she knew she really didn't know the answer in enough detail.

"MSS is like China's CIA and FBI combined. Sung is a very bad man who would do terrible things to me and my family if he suspect I talk to anyone here." Su paused to gather her thoughts and to give Lisa a chance to process what she said.

"If I don't do just what he tells me to, they will return me to China to be killed or imprisoned, and they would cast my mother and father out to starve or worse. I have no choice."

Lisa didn't disappoint Su and seemed to grasp the situation. "What does he want you to do?"

"If I tell you, you do nothing and tell no one without me saying, ok?"

"Ok," Lisa replied, but followed with, "but remember, I am an American. My father taught me almost anything can be overcome if you're smart enough and willing to do what it takes. Don't expect me to sit by the side and watch you suffer without at least looking for a solution. Can we agree I will take the Hippocratic Oath? I will do no harm?"

Su again gave Lisa a hug and said, "My heart has told me to trust you."

For the next twenty minutes, Su gave Lisa a condensed version of the story of her life. She spent more time on her childhood than the rest. When she came to the college entrance interview, she described in detail the MSS Officer who had manipulated her. Charm School only took five minutes, but Su could not keep the tears from streaming down her face again. Reliving the first few days caused the most pain. Lisa held both of her hands as she tried to describe just a little of her time there, without emotion.

"When I get here, Sung decides who I meet and what information I have to get from him." Su wasn't ready to reveal anything about Walter, at least not now.

"That goddamned sonofabitch!" Lisa said, in a hushed tone but with outrage. "I'd kill him right now, if you'd let me. That's slavery!" she hissed. Another pause was followed by, "You know you're in America now. Not only can they not do that here, but they can be arrested."

"No, you not understand. He is a diplomat. He has immunity from arrest. Worst anyone can do is to throw him out of country. They would then kill my parents and demand I be sent back to China." Looking at her watch, Su noticed their reservation time for the room was almost up.

"Time almost up. So sorry I cannot go to eat. If Sung or anyone from Embassy were to see, there would be very big trouble. Maybe we meet again in two weeks? At your apartment?" Lisa responded to Su's plea with a smile of agreement.

"Let's meet at my place, same time, and by then I will have thought of some options. Sister, this situation is *not acceptable!*" Again, warmth, and some confidence flooded into Su. She had made the right decision.

"Please keep promise and say nothing to anyone. And be careful about anything online. I know China monitors much of what Americans do online. Google of Sung's name may be dangerous. They even hack U.S. government employee information."

Reluctantly, Lisa said, "I'm good for my word, especially to you! But we will find a way for you to escape. End of story!"

Both women ended their meeting with a last hug. At Su's request, she left the room first. Lisa left five minutes later.

CHAPTER 39
INAUGURATION - PLUS SIX MONTHS TWELVE DAYS

The Mountains of Southeast Afghanistan
2015 Hours Local Time

When he came to Jasmine, Ahmed was furious. Even though she had just given him a daughter two months earlier, he backhanded her in the face before taking a strap from the wall and beginning to beat her back and bottom with it. She cried out with each strike. Her cries were just enough to let him feel he was causing her pain. Although there was pain, it wasn't much. She had stitched wool padding into the back of her shirt and skirt specifically to shield her from his blows. A man must vent his frustrations. The greater the man, the greater will be his frustrations, her mother had said. After ten such blows, and amid her tears and pleas, he stopped and lifted her skirt. His passion was hot and fast. It lasted only three minutes before he expended himself. She then took his head like a baby's against her chest.

"My husband, I am so sorry for what I did to cause you such misery. Please tell me what I did, and it will not happen again."

Ahmed lay with his head against her chest, breathing heavily. "You said we should get another aid girl to add to what the first one gives to our martyrs. This one has been crazy and out of her head since we took her. She was useless, so I gave her to my fighters. They needed a reward for the six fighters killed during her taking. I just had to kill her when she bit Mohammed in such a way he is no longer a man. Mohammed will martyr himself tomorrow and go to his reward, but really it is because he cannot bear to think of life without his manhood."

Jasmine lay quietly holding Ahmed as he calmed down. Ahmed said, "You will take very good care of the aid girl we have until the fighters are ready and able to travel. How soon will that be?"

"If they could get to their beginning point, they are ready now," Jasmine said softly as she stroked his hair. "What they are learning now is how to travel in Europe and the rest of the world. We are also getting passports and diabetic kits for each of them."

At Ahmed's confused look, Jasmine said, "You know they will need to disguise the virus in the diabetic kits to travel with it. The kits have syringes in them with insulin. I am told they will have to inject themselves regularly with plain water and know how to use test kits."

At Ahmed's continued confused look, Jasmine gently continued, "My husband, diabetes is a common Western disease mostly affecting fat people. You and your men are far too strong to have to deal with this disease. People with this disease have too much sugar in their blood, and their bodies do not make enough insulin..."

Ahmed abruptly slapped her in the face. "You are too smart for your own good, Jasmine. Make me forget I am angry with you." Jasmine hummed softly and rose to her feet to begin dancing. Her clothing came off as she danced to the beat of her own music. When she was naked except for the gold chain around her waist and another dangling between her breasts, he could not take his eyes off her. She danced rhythmically until she was dancing directly over his naked form on the blankets. She continued to sway as she lowered herself onto him. The dance did not end until after he had exploded into her again and fell asleep under her deeply breathing body. Her husband would never want seventy-two virgins after having experienced her, she thought with pride.

Outside of Washington, D.C.
1900 Hours EST

The Sunday after having met with Su, Lisa found herself seated at the dinner table of her parents' house picking at her food. Her mother was annoyed at her daughter's distracted demeanor. Then her empathy kicked in, and she said, "Lisa, what is bothering you so much? You haven't fallen for one of your professors, have you?" The mischievous smile on her face brought Lisa out of her daydreaming.

"Oh no, mom. I just have a friend who's in a bind. I'm trying to figure out what she should do next."

"Who is it?"

"Just a girl at school. I promised to keep everything confidential."

Lisa's mom showed she understood and said, "Sweetheart, you're a very bright woman whose judgment I trust implicitly. She's lucky to have you there to help." The smile on Lisa's face showed the love she felt for her mom and how much she appreciated her support.

Her mom laughed as she said, "I know you have recognized me stroking your ego since you were in the fifth grade. This time, I mean it!"

Her dad, Hugh McIntyre, looked up from his phone to ask, "Mean what, sweetie?" Both mom and daughter broke into laughter as once again they had shared a secret, right in front of her father, without his catching on. Some trained investigator, she thought. She then reminded herself how amazing her dad was when he focused on any specific problem.

"Oh nothing, dear." Lisa's mom said, with the usual mother-daughter conspiratorial tone. "Just some girl talk."

Hugh was used to both women in his home, leaving him perplexed and curious. Fortunately, he was a master at refocusing his attention to another subject. "Can you believe what the Redskins are doing now?"

Her dad described the latest trade moves by the Washington Redskins while Lisa again thought about whether she could say anything to her dad without betraying her trust to Su. Winding down on his complaints about the Redskins, she decided to change the subject.

"Dad, did you ever do the spy stuff at work?" The question was meant to be offhand, even nonchalant. Instead, it caught both of her parents' full attention. She should have realized the fruit did not fall far from the tree.

"Why the sudden interest in my career, sweetheart?" His question was asked by a loving father of his daughter, but it was also with the full focus of over twenty-five years of FBI training.

The little white lie came quickly to her lips. "I was talking with my advisor, Dr. Reynolds, last week, and he tried to convince me I had a future in the State Department. He then asked if I would do a little paper for him on the spies that hurt America most during the Twentieth Century. I wonder if you could point me in the right direction."

Hugh's focus softened, and he said, "Well, honey, there are a lot of books written on about it. With the Internet research possibilities, I'm sure you could zoom right in on what you'll need for the paper. How long does the paper need to be?"

"Oh, only about fifteen pages. It's supposed to be a summary of how foreign governments work against us here in the U.S."

"Whoa! That will take a lot more than fifteen pages. What's this guy trying to get you to put together? Maybe he wants you to create a bibliography for him? Then he'll write his own paper?" Her father's mind became creative when looking at a challenge.

"I don't know, but could be. Regardless, it shouldn't be too much trouble, so I'll hammer it out some evening over a cold iced tea."

"Honey, I haven't been in the spy business, but I do hang out with a number of those guys. If you need some specific, non-classified insight in how they do things, let me know."

"Thanks, Dad," Lisa said cheerfully. She thought it looked like she had some research she needed to do. Unfortunately, it had to be done the old fashion way and not through the Internet.

CHAPTER 40
INAUGURATION - PLUS SIX MONTHS THIRTEEN DAYS

The White House
1030 Hours EST

Katherine had called Homeland Security Director Dmitriy Roskov into the Oval Office for a follow-up report on the Chicago school shootings. Right after the shooting, she had called the FBI Director into her office for details. From him, she only learned what she could see on CNN.

"Roskov," Katherine said with her usual lack of civility, "what the hell have you done in the last five days to stop the next school shooting? You're from Chicago, right? Has any effort been made to seize guns there to get them off the streets?"

"Madam President," Dmitriy began in a reasonable tone of voice, "I will have to address your questions one at a time. So long as there are over a hundred million guns in the country, and kids continue to play violent video games, I believe the school shootings will continue to happen every so often."

"Video games? What are you talking about?" Katherine's temper flared once again.

"Madam President, despite what the game manufacturers claim, it is my belief children learn to solve their problems using a gun from the very games that take up most of their spare time. They don't learn to deal with other children and life in general. Instead, they play games to shoot and destroy anyone they perceive is evil. And with the Second Amendment to the constitution, there's very little we can do to take the guns off the streets."

"Goddammit, you worthless moron! That's the same shit the FBI Director was trying to feed me five days ago." Katherine had been totally incensed when the FBI Director had tried to speak to her about constitutional rights of gun owners. If they didn't have guns, she wouldn't have to listen to this shit. "The FBI Direcvtor even had the gall to look shocked when I ordered him from my office. My call to the Attorney General didn't bring much help. The bastard at the FBI has a ten-year appointment. Hell, the AG is supposed to be his boss."

Katherine took a deep breath, which seemed to calm her. "How much of what the FBI does could Homeland Security do?" She was already thinking how she could circumvent the FBI and their high and mighty morals.

"Madam President, the FBI's responsibilities are set out by federal statute. It will take an act of Congress to transfer any duties and responsibilities to Homeland Security. ATF is also under the Department of Justice and the AG. Heck, their name even says they have responsibilities for Alcohol, Tobacco and Firearms. If you want the guns off the streets, they might be a good place to start. Even with that, the Second Amendment is pretty clear."

Katherine didn't appear to have even heard Roskov after he had steered her to the ATF. She picked up the phone and called her Chief of Staff. "Burt, get the ATF Director scheduled to meet me in my office sometime tomorrow. Yes, it's about the same thing I had you direct young Baxter to do. Just get him on my calendar." She hung up and appeared almost surprised Roskov was still there.

"Anything else, Mr. Roskov?"

"No, Madam President." Walking down the hallway, Roskov had a funny feeling in the pit of his stomach. He hated guns in the hands of bad guys. On the other hand, he had been a cop for many years. He had seen his share of citizens whose only real protection from the criminals of Chicago were their guns. He then wondered if the President would fire him from his job if she knew he was a life member of the NRA.

Katherine called Susan Cassel's cell phone number. "Susan, I want your help later this evening. Please stop by the residence at ten."

Susan was getting better at helping her migraines and her levels of frustration. "Why can't people do what they are told," she thought as she tried to focus on the next item on her calendar.

Walking to her White House bedroom at 11:30 p.m. Katherine even had a slight spring to her step. She knew Susan would be waiting patiently in her sitting room. Upon arrival, she was not disappointed.

CHAPTER 41
INAUGURATION - PLUS SIX MONTHS FOURTEEN DAYS

Kabul, Afghanistan
1115 Hours Local Time

Once again, Major Sean Callahan was impressed with the incredible talent shown by his people. Despite jet lag and coming from a strange culture, his team had learned a great deal about the JOTP in only three days. Virtually all the intelligence had come from the work of Lieutenant Sharpe and Sergeant Amy Bonner. Wearing their in-country women's robes and veils, both women had gone to the market and then the river where three women were washing clothes and watching children. When Linda and Amy complained to each other in Arabic that all the good men seemed to be killed, it opened a conversation among the women. Two of the three had relatives in the mountains, and all hated the Afghan government and the JOTP. About Americans, they were only curious.

One of the three at the river had heard the JOTP had captured a Western girl a few months earlier, and she was teaching fighters to speak foreign languages. Even though the JOTP had lost over half of the men fighting for it, they continued to come recruit the boys in the area. They promised an ultimate martyr's death, but also the possibility of infidel girls before that happened. The foolish boys went off to learn to kill. The woman didn't know where in the mountains the JOTP base was, but thought they moved often.

Sean had observed Linda sending this intelligence by priority message to Special Operations Command, or SOCOM. Linda and Amy then went to a house on the outskirts of the village to talk to some women whose husbands had died. They did not take any other team members for guard detail. Linda explained they didn't want to scare away potential sources of information.

By 11 p.m., Linda and Amy were two hours late. The assistant team leader sent out a four-man patrol to the house identified on a satellite high resolution photo. Forty-five minutes later, the word came back the woman who spoke to Linda and Amy at the river had been overheard laughing about the trap she set for the two Americans. Under quick interrogation, they learned twenty JOTP fighters had Linda and Amy and had taken them to the mountains. When he heard the report, Major Sean Callahan took charge of the team.

"Radio, send a flash Intel report to SOCOM and get me real time satellite and infrared drone images of everywhere between here and the mountains. Gear up the team. We're heading east into the mountains as soon as the radio messages go out. Is everyone kitted up and ready to go?"

The Assistant Team Leader responded, "Affirmative, sir."

. . .

Four days after jumping off into the desert in pursuit of the captured Green Berets, Sean woke up in a hospital bed with a blinding headache. He ached all over and was quite disoriented. Sleeping in the chair next to the bed was First Lieutenant Linda Sharpe. She had several bandages on her face and head. Her arm was in a sling with her desert camouflage jacket draped over her shoulders. Her tan t-shirt was showing an attractive figure, with dog tags hanging between her breasts. With a shock, it all came crashing back.

Sean's team had been directed to the JOTP patrol by a Predator drone. It was after 3:00 a.m. as they were nearing the mountains. When his team was less than one hundred meters from the patrol, the Predator fired missiles at both the front and rear of the patrol line. It was presumed the prisoners would be somewhere in the middle. His operators then made fairly short work of the JOTP fighters using their night vision goggles and M-4 carbines. Sergeant Amy Bonner had been shot and killed by one of the terrorists just before he was killed by rifle fire. Linda Sharpe had been shot in the arm and had been beaten pretty severely when she was captured. Fortunately, the team medic rendered first aid and painkillers on the spot. Despite her injuries, Linda insisted on hiking to the extraction point without assistance.

The last thing Sean remembered was the blinding flash when the operator right in front of him seemed to disappear. It resulted from an improvised explosive device known as an IED.

Looking at her sleeping form, Sean tried to say Linda's name, but only croaked something unintelligible. She woke and gave him a big smile between swollen lips and two missing teeth. "Knew you would make it, sir."

"Water," he mouthed.

"Ok, sir. The nurse said you could have a sip or two when you woke up." She then poured a glass of water from a pitcher on the nearby table and placed it up to his lips for a drink. "They restrain your arms to keep you from pulling out the tubes and wires. Just a minute, and I'll get the nurse."

Linda walked from the room only to return with an American Army nurse. She checked him over carefully before asking, "Now if I remove these restraints, will you leave these wires and IV's alone?"

"Yes ma'am. I can do that. Thank you."

The nurse removed the restraints and told Sean, "The doctor will be in to see you in about an hour. Lieutenant, I believe they have cleared you to bring the Major up to speed?" Linda shook her head yes. "Ok then, press the call button if you need me."

Having had the sip of water, Sean seemed to be able to talk normally through his very sore throat. "Ok, where am I, and what the hell happened?"

"We're at the main army medical center in Wiesbaden, Germany. It is day four following my rescue, and you have already been through two surgeries. You probably know about Sergeant Bonner," to which Sean nodded in the affirmative. "Taylor bought it when he stepped on an IED as he approached the extraction chopper landing zone. The blast also sent several pieces of shrapnel through your body. A large piece took your left leg below the knee." Linda intentionally reported this news in the standard briefing tone of voice and with near mechanical precision. "We brought the lower piece back, but they could not save it. Looks like you will be bionic going forward."

Sean's eyes had redirected to the foot of the bed, where he saw the sheet flat against the bed where his lower leg and foot should have been. He registered its absence, but felt nothing, nor did he feel any psychological shock. That would probably come later.

"Sir, you will have up to a year of convalescent leave stateside for rehabilitation. And sir?"

Sean looked up into her eyes. "You came for me, sir. I won't ever forget it."

Before he could even get beyond the tears in her eyes and his own, she was hugging him as he lay in the bed.

CHAPTER 42
INAUGURATION - PLUS EIGHT MONTHS

Washington, D.C.
1010 Hours EDT

Eli Fredericks did not like to be kept waiting. Doing so usually resulted in immediate dismissal, and in egregious cases, in someone's financial ruin. This abhorrence to waiting did not translate to his own punctuality, however. He used his own tardiness to project his power and ensure whoever was waiting understood their place; he had always found it useful to make people wait for him. It usually caused nervousness and anxiety, and it reinforced his power over them and their dependence upon his good graces.

When he received the hand-delivered message from Chen Wen, it had said only:

"10:35 usual." Through past contacts with Chen, he knew to expect a trusted associate of Chen's to visit him at a coffee shop six blocks from his Washington, D.C. office building.

Eli had initially met Chen by invitation when he had traveled to Beijing several years earlier. They were introduced through mutual acquaintances. Eli felt it only appropriate he should attract the attention of one of China's top industrialists. Eli had moved hundreds of millions of dollars through one of Chen's banks during the course of several investments. Chen had met him while sitting behind a table. He never stood up, nor did he offer to shake hands. Eli was okay with this lack of social grace. He could tell by Chen's cold stare and fake smile he had found a man similar to himself.

Over the next decade, Chen had provided Eli with information resulting in his personal fortune expanding from tens of millions to over fourteen billion dollars. In return, Eli had insured Chen's known interests were not damaged within the U.S., either by act of Congress or crafty competition. Both men knew what they owed each other. Both were comfortable with this arrangement. Eli detested feeling like some low-paid spy. He did, however, understand both its necessity and Chen's overwhelming need to be in apparent control.

Arriving at the coffee shop, he received the most imperceptible nod from his man who had cleared the meeting area for bugs or surveillance. Potential interested parties included U.S. intelligence and any foreign intelligence service. It also included any criminal elements. Wu Chin was seated at the lone table in the back corner. It was secluded enough to speak privately, but not so segregated as to be conspicuous. He ordered simple black coffee at the counter. He hated the lattes, or other fancy coffee drinks. He then walked to Wu's table and sat across from him. Neither man looked at the other, as if Eli were merely taking an available seat. In busy East Coast coffee houses, this table sharing was a common practice.

In a cultured British accent and without looking directly at Eli, Wu commented,

"Something smelled burnt up by the register, don't you think?"

Eli responded, "No, I only smelled the hazelnut." It had taken Eli two sessions in a clandestine hotel room to learn to deliver code phrases smoothly. This exchange meant there were no listeners to their conversation, and nothing threatened either Wu or Eli. Eli did not like the feeling of meeting with retired MSS Officers who taught him to act like a spy. Patient explanations over time had finally gotten through. Be professional or be arrested or shot. After that, he warmed up to the whole spooky thing.

"It is good to see you, my friend," Wu said while looking at his Washington Post. "So sorry there was such short notice. My friend thought it important to pass on a word you will probably find of interest. China will stop buying almost all foreign oil twenty-four hours from now. This policy will last for exactly six months. As you Americans say, China has cut a deal with the Russians. They will supplement the oil China has stockpiled for the past year with additional Russian oil shipments."

Eli's mind whirled with both the overall financial implications and the potential for making money. His mind racing, Eli realized such a move would crush the world oil markets. China was the largest importer of foreign oil. Suddenly stopping purchases would instantly cause a worldwide oversupply of crude oil. The oversupply would drop the prices of crude dramatically, resulting in a ripple effect. First, the oil industry would collapse followed by all the other related industries.

Eli's first thought was he would have to begin immediately to move all of his investments out of dollar impacted areas and into precious metals. It was clear a global financial depression was about to follow. Like the Chinese, he had already moved a significant percentage of his personal portfolio into stocks of companies who held gold for shareholders. Those shares would be sold, again through straw companies and intermediaries. They would then be converted into physical possession of precious metals. Fortunately, he had been planning such a move for months, so within only a few days, they would deliver stockpiles of the metals to secure locations.

"How soon do you expect the public announcement?"

Wu responded in his usual dispassionate voice, "In twenty-four hours."

For the briefest instant, Eli looked at Wu directly to find Wu looking into his eyes, measuring. In less time than the blink of an eye, Eli became aware Wu had seen a glimpse of the rage he felt, having been essentially blindsided by what was world changing action. Twenty-four hour notice left him no time to get started on necessary acquisitions and left no time to use the information for power and political advantage. Trying to do everything over the next twenty-four hours would show he had advance knowledge of this event and would flag to the world he was in bed with the Chinese. What was even more infuriating was Wu could read all of this reaction from his glance.

Looking from his newspaper where he had redirected his gaze following Wu's announcement, Eli moved back to direct eye-to-eye contact with Wu. "Why the delay in advising me of this action?" His voice was cool and measured, however it included the subtle but unmistakable edge and the unveiled threat of a Japanese samurai sword in the hands of a master.

For just a moment, Wu's iron control slipped as he looked into the unblinking pale, green, round eyes of this American. Working directly for Chen had given Wu status, power, and relative protection from most threats in the world. In looking into Eli's eyes, Wu could see the malice and ability to order resources that could reach out anywhere in the world. Eli's eyes said Wu's messenger status would serve as an example for others. A long painful death for Wu and his family would send a message to all who would want to cross Eli. It would be a somewhat less than subtle message. At these levels, subtlety is most frequently used. Sheer power and vicious efficiency were also sometimes used to motivate certain responses. He had ordered some vicious actions himself, on behalf of and with the knowledge of Chen himself. Just like the Americans were known to say, "Just pushing the right buttons."

"This timing was not my decision," Wu said with some discomfiture coming out in his soft voice.

The very slight smile on Eli's dark face was even more chilling to Wu, who was not used to feeling fear. His stomach tightened when Eli continued, "Tell him for me of my level of disappointment in this breach of trust." The words and implication were Eli would take direct action to accentuate his disappointment.

"Tell me Wu," Eli continued, breaking protocol and verbally naming him in a public place, "how set in stone is this twenty-four-hour timetable?" After a pause, he continued, "An additional forty-eight hours would make all the difference."

Eli purposefully stood and turned toward the door. He then turned back and said, "I'll expect a response within the hour." He then turned and walked out. Wu understood Eli meant he should prevail on Chen to push back the timetable for a public announcement for an additional forty-eight hours.

Wu sat quietly in the coffee shop for a full two minutes, the minimum allowed by protocol and training. Sitting there, his heart and mind searched for inspiration for his next action, which he realized would likely determine whether he, and possibly his family, would survive. The wire on which he walked between Chen and Eli had suddenly become extremely high and thin. He was under no illusions after looking into Eli's eyes. He could see Eli was quite capable of ordering his seizure, torture, and death in the most unpleasant manner. Displeasing Chen by suggesting he change plans because of Eli was equally fraught with danger.

Wu thought about the power, prestige, courtesans, fine living, and the exhilaration of his position as someone able to get things done for Chen. All of it was worthless if he and his family failed to survive.

Two blocks from the coffee shop, Wu entered the limousine and picked up the secure satellite telephone from its case on the floor. Speaking in impeccable Mandarin, Wu said, "I must speak to him. Now." There had been no preamble or small talk.

The response from the other end of the line was, "Wait."

Ten seconds later, Chen said from the satellite phone receiver, "Speak." It was entirely lost on Wu that in a Western culture such a command would have been indicative of Wu being Chen's dog.

"He did not take it well, the late notice. His displeasure will result in possible negative reactions to include vindictiveness and sloppy or gross attempts to send a message to you, highlighting his displeasure. He wants an additional forty-eight hours, and his displeasure will be salved." After a pause, Wu continued, "He could be problematic with his contacts and influence. What are your instructions?"

From years of experience in dealing with Chen, Wu knew Chen had completely grasped both what had happened and its potential meaning. Chen's pause for consideration was only a few seconds. "Tell him in consideration of our friendship, there will be an additional forty-eight hour delay before they make the announcement."

"It will be done. Any other instructions?"

Chen responded, "No," and broke the connection. Wu sat for a moment without moving. To all appearances, he had successfully saved his life and the life of his family. At least he did not worry Eli would make an example of him having gotten what he wanted. Chen, on the other hand, could easily decide Eli should have been better managed by Wu, and both an example and replacement was in order. After a moment of thought, Wu let the matter drop. It was beyond his control now, anyway.

Wu then picked up the burner phone from a soundproof box on the floor and placed a call. In a thick Chinese accent, Chen said, "So sorrwee, but laurndry will be derayed for two mo' days."

"That is acceptable," was the response, and the connection was broken.

CHAPTER 43
INAUGURATION - PLUS EIGHT MONTHS ONE DAY

Beijing, China
0800 Hours Local Time

The morning after the conversation between Wu and Eli, General Secretary Song's Chief of Staff Wong Jie came just inside of Song's office door and waited to be noticed. Three minutes later Song looked up with raised eyebrows.

"General Secretary, Ching Kai requests five minutes of your time. He indicates there is some urgency." Song and Wong both knew Ching was the trusted mouthpiece for Chen Wen. Standing two meters, or six feet six inches tall, with dark hair and close-set eyes, he towered over almost everyone in China.

"Send him in."

Entering the room, Ching immediately went to the chair next to Song's desk and sat down. The move was to show deference to Song by avoiding the appearance of towering over him. It was also to show his status by not asking permission to do so.

"Your employer is doing well, Ching?" Song opened the conversation with the usual polite pleasantries. Upon their conclusion of politeness, Song waited for Ching to say his purpose in coming.

"General Secretary Song, my employer has a delicate request to make, which he hopes will be given your consideration." The pause following this statement was neither unexpected nor taken by Song to be out of place. "For several reasons, it is requested the announcement China will not be importing oil be delayed an additional forty-eight hours. General Secretary, we understand all implications involving this request."

So, Chen was not making the request lightly, thought Song. There must be a significant financial reason for the request. Such a request will also come with more than the usual compensation placed in various accounts around the world. He and his family had exclusive access to those accounts. It didn't occur to Song to question how Chen had learned of the plan. Since he was one of the two most powerful businessmen in China, Song presumed he had sources everywhere.

"That should not be a problem," Song said off-handedly. "Is there anything else?"

"No, General Secretary. My employer will be most appreciative of your consideration." Ching rose. A very shallow bow preceded his departure without another word.

Wong entered Song's office moments after Ching's departure. "Wong, do what is necessary to delay our announcement about our stopping oil purchases. The purchases can be stopped, but have the Ministry make up some reason for the momentary stoppage. A formal announcement can be made in three days."

"As you wish, General Secretary." Wong departed the office and immediately called to invite three key people to meet with him in one hour. They were given instructions to offer excuses for a temporary delay in oil purchases. Foreign suppliers were to be told the halt would only last a day or two. Three days later, the announcement would shake the world.

Song sat in his office following another ten-minute meditation session. He was well aware that by stopping oil imports he would throw the world, including the United States, into depression. It would also throw his own country into a financial tailspin. The trade ties across the globe were enormous, and such unexplained actions could draw severe trade restrictions. It would also weaken the U.S. economy. This result would weaken the American ability to respond to his planned invasion of Formosa.

· · ·

Katherine gave a scathing denunciation to her congressional liaison officer. These cold and withering chastisements had become regular occurrences. Only the recipient of her rage changed. Sometimes they came several times per day. "I don't give a shit what the Second Amendment says. If they want any spending reform signed into law this *decade,* they will give me just one little gun control law. Just one!" Both she and the liaison officer knew one would be just the beginning. She had already outlined a strategy provided by Eli's people that would, if it could get through Congress, permanently insure her power to do what needed to be done.

Between Eli's subtle suggestions, her liberal supporters, and the environmental people, there was barely enough time in her day to even think about what was important to her. It just seemed like she jumped from one fire to another. She had to continue to make time to further her own vision of where the country should go. Like everything, it had to be done in small steps, but her steps seemed to go backward lately. Since becoming President, Katherine had gotten virtually nothing through Congress, while her veto pen had nearly run out of ink. The opposition party people kept sending her bills that were dead on arrival. She didn't know why they wasted her time with such drivel. The smug Speaker of the House had the audacity to accuse her of blocking the country's move forward. Then he complained about her cuts to the military. She noticed he didn't complain about her using some of the money saved to augment the Special Forces and National Guard. If there were only a big enough emergency, she could declare martial law and do what was best for the country, she thought with frustration.

Outside of Cronin, Kentucky
1430 Hours EDT

Mike had just finished helping Peter move the supplies from the warehouse into his newly finished bunker. Every muscle in his body ached after three days of heavy manual labor. At least it was good exercise. He had shaved off eight pounds over the past three weeks between the exercise and cutting back on the beer. A grass lawn was growing on top of the bunker, and they had camouflaged the front entry to look like a small underground garden shed. Evergreen trees and vines had been planted to hide the visible parts of poured concrete walls. There was even a small room just inside the flimsy, wooden outside doors leading into what looked like a poorly lit underground garden shed. Hidden steel double doors were behind an old metal shelf covered with gardening tools. There was another hidden entry from Peter's house.

"How many people do you intend to feed, Peter?" Mike asked with amazement in his voice and written all over his face. The inside of the bunker had several rows of heavy-duty shelving bearing huge amounts of freeze-dried food and other materials. There was even a living space for over a dozen people off in the far corner and in a loft-like partial second floor.

"What I initially planned was twenty people for two years," Peter said. "Then I got to thinking about your whole neighborhood project thing and decided I could get more basic. I'm not even sure, but I added enough very basic calorie foods to feed at least another couple of hundred for three years or more. Might have gone a bit overboard by laying in a stock of heirloom vegetable seeds. What do you think?"

"What I think is consulting must be more lucrative than I thought!"

"I'd only tell you, Mike, but I did made a killing on the market since the 2008 crash. Wanted to get at least some of my money out of the market, so that's why I bought up the long-term storage food company. I think I mentioned it to you before. What you see is the stock I have on my inventory books, minus what I pay two employees to package up and ship whenever someone orders from my website. Enough inventory keeps coming and going to insure this stuff is not missed."

"All I can say is wow!"

"You know, Mike, with idiots like Kerry around it's probably a good idea if we keep this little project at the top secret level. Don't you think?"

"Absolutely! I won't even mention it to Lauren. By the way, did you hear Sean Callahan is coming home?"

"Really? Great!" Peter said with enthusiasm. "Last I heard he was at some Army hospital trying to heal enough to be fitted for his artificial leg."

"Yeah, Lauren talked to Penny who's thrilled to have her baby coming home to Mom's doting care. Guess the VA just didn't have the facilities to give him the best rehab. Hell, Lexington has one of the top artificial limb companies in the country. They work through the university and the rehab place in town. I think they're on government contracts. You know it took the personal attention of two U.S. Senators and a Congressman to get it done."

"Well, that's still great. How's he doing?"

"According to Penny, he's doing pretty well," Mike said. "Initially she planned to stay at the hospital with Sean indefinitely. But, that turned into only two days. Seems there was a pretty Lieutenant who has taken responsibility for his care. She's supposed to be quite a looker. Special Forces, too. I think she may get out of the military and plans to come back here to look after Sean. Must be quite a back story."

"Guess we'll find out when he gets here," Peter said.

"On another topic, Peter," Mike continued, "have you heard anything from Scott Shelby or Hugh McIntyre lately?"

"Kinda ominous that you mention it, Mike. I just talked to Scott yesterday. He's moved everything he's got into precious metals and construction materials. Think he even tried to buy out the entire stock at 84 Lumber. He said he talked to several people he trusts and thinks something big is coming down the pike very soon."

Mike responded, "The way Congress keeps fighting with the Fontaine administration, I did pretty much the same thing. Just between you and me, I pissed Lauren off by having her buy three rifles, and I bought a couple myself. Then I bought ten handguns from different private sellers at the gun show two weeks ago and bought a bunch of ammo for each of the guns. Guess you might say my new investment strategy is to buy guns and ammo."

Mike could see the understanding smile spread across Peter's face.

"Sounds kind of familiar," Peter said.

"Now that you mention it, Peter, would you mind if I stored some of this stuff in your bunker?"

"Sure, Mike. Happy to help. Oh, and when I talked to Hugh, he had to call me back late in the evening. He couldn't say much, but did say he expected something to happen. Kind of like waiting for the other shoe to drop, whatever that means. He asked if his wife and daughter, Lisa, could come out to visit if it looked like something might happen. Of course I told him Elizabeth and I would love to see his whole family anytime."

Washington, D.C.
2115 Hours EDT

Hugh McIntyre sat in his overstuffed chair in his man-cave. He was in a near total state of shock. Sitting in the other chair was his daughter, Lisa. For the past twenty minutes, she had been telling the most fantastic story he had ever heard. It far exceeded anything he had encountered over his twenty-five years in the FBI. The expectant look on his daughter's face showed she believed every word she had told him. He had not interrupted while she described how she had met Su Ling. He wasn't even surprised when she described how they had instantly bonded like sisters, no, even more than sisters. After all, she was her mother's daughter, too.

Her ability to empathize and see through people had always impressed him. It was the rest that was so stunning.

He had been tracking some extremely strange activities in the terrorist world. In recent years, analysts had given him briefings about many of the things the Chinese were doing. Even with what he knew about China, his first inclination was to believe Lisa was on drugs. Looking into her eyes, however, he knew that wasn't the case. The Chinese girl could be pulling one over on Lisa for some evil purpose. But even if it were true, it would be something he could determine through some very careful investigation. Hugh decided he would operate on the assumption Su was pulling something on Lisa, although he considered his daughter an expert in reading people. Anyone could, however, be fooled by a true professional.

"Honey, this story is unbelievable," he said gently. Seeing the look on her face, he quickly continued, "It isn't that I don't believe it. It's just going to take some time for me to think about some way to handle the whole thing. And you know I will have to meet this girl, right?"

"Yes, dad. I told her. But she's terrified of what will happen to her family and then to herself. Daddy, they made her into a sex slave!" Lisa's tears flowed.

Hugh took her into his arms and said, "You know sweetheart, your old man can be pretty good at this kind of thing. Let me see what I can do. Ok?" Lisa mumbled ok and snuggled closer in his arms. Hugh thought of different possibilities, but held off on everything until he met this girl, Su Ling.

CHAPTER 44
INAUGURATION - PLUS NINE MONTHS SIX DAYS

The White House
1045 Hours EDT

Katherine sat in the chair glaring at her advisors. Seated around the table were the Secretary of State, Defense, Treasury, Homeland Security, the Attorney General, and her Chief of Staff. Also present was the Chairman of the Joint Chiefs of Staff and the DNI. In chairs against the wall were Marc Baxter and Towanda Jefferson.

"First of all, I want somebody to tell me why the economy is going in the shitter. Anyone?"

"Madam President," said Treasury Secretary Seth Goldberg after clearing his throat, "when the Chinese suddenly stopped buying oil on the world market over a month ago, there was instantly a glut on the market. Oil prices were already way down because of Saudi Arabia and several other Arab countries pumping oil as fast as they could. The Saudi goal was to bankrupt the Canadians and those in North Dakota who were pumping all the oil obtained through fracking. Well, over the past couple of years, the Saudis were largely successful. World oil prices are way down. The Chinese were the world's largest importer. So when the Chinese stopped buying, the world oil market crashed from the glut of oil. Oil producers can't simply flip a switch and turn it off. Things have to be geared down."

"Okay, so oil companies lose their asses. They're swimming in money, anyway. Why did that cause the New York Stock Exchange to lose two-thirds of its value? And it's still falling!"

"Madam President," Seth continued, "the expression our nation runs on oil is true. Oil and Natural Gas touch almost every industry in the world. When the oil industry tanks, dozens of related industries supporting the oil industry go the same way. Most of North Dakota is now essentially out of work and looking for unemployment compensation."

"Well, goddammit, how long will it take before it turns around?"

"Madam President," Seth continued, "we don't know. This situation has never happened before. My best guess, and sadly that is all it is, it will take at least six months to even begin to see what direction a recovery will take. In the meantime, you will need to either work with Congress and dramatically cut the federal budget or plan to increase our policy of printing more money. I must add that as a nation, we're already over twenty-five trillion dollars in debt. The potential for catastrophic inflation, in the realm of hundreds of percentage points, is very high."

"Cummin, I ordered trade sanctions to be put in place on the Chinese. Why aren't they in place?"

The Secretary of State looked even more uncomfortable than the other men at the table.

"Madam President," Cummin said with resignation, "as you know, we have suffered some issues in our computer systems at State. The final draft of the trade sanctions will be on your desk for signature by the end of today."

State had been feverishly working with both the NSA and CIA to identify the cause of the shutdown and fix the computer systems. When he had reported to Katherine, it appeared Chinese hackers were responsible; she exploded in another tirade and accused him of wanting to go to war with China.

Cumin continued, "Our European allies have already put sanctions in place. On the Pacific Rim, only the Aussies and New Zealand have cut off trade. Japan, South Korea, and our other allies in the area have privately expressed fear of Chinese economic reprisals, so they have not done so. Unofficially, I have been told there is fear the United States cannot protect them from China going forward, and they are hedging their bets."

Katherine's response was instantaneous. "This meeting is over. I want a proposed plan of action from each of you to get us out of this mess. Yes, that means you, too, General." She was looking at the Chairman of the Joint Chiefs of Staff. "And General, your plan better not include war." She then stomped out of the room. Each person present looked around the room at one another. Resignation was present on a few faces, but most showed barely contained anger.

Later, Katherine sat in her sitting room with Susan rubbing her shoulders. With the stress leaking out of her body, she mumbled to herself. "Maybe this is the chance to do what needs to be done." Susan could tell she was merely talking to herself and knew not to respond.

"How bad does it have to get before I declare martial law… take control? Fucking Congress… tying my hands, saying it's my fault. Those fucking bastards will find out soon enough." She mumbled the last comment while dozing off in the chair. Susan suspected what she had heard was only the tip of the iceberg. Katherine's plan was already in place. She only hesitated over the timing.

When Susan finally got to Marc's place, she woke him up. "Marc, I can't believe it. She was mumbling about declaring martial law! Taking control from Congress! That's crazy!"

Half asleep and very confused, Marc pulled her into bed and said, "Get some sleep. Nobody's that crazy."

While Marc held her, Susan laid awake feeling the fear permeate the pit of her stomach.

CHAPTER 45
INAUGURATION - PLUS NINE MONTHS SEVEN DAYS

FBIHQ, Washington, DC
1345 Hours EDT

Unit Chief Hugh McIntyre sat at a small conference table in the FBI Director's office. The office was on the top floor of the Hoover Building at 10ᵗʰ and Pennsylvania in Washington, D.C. Hugh had waited for over two weeks for the private appointment he had requested with the Director by E-mail. The Director seemed happy to see one of his people who wanted to speak to him privately and just hoped this meeting wasn't about some personnel issue that was about to give the bureau a black eye.

"Hugh, I've seen you several times before. Why haven't you introduced yourself?" This Director was completely different from previous Directors. He claimed to have an open door policy, and he actually did.

"My apologies, Sir. You always seemed to be tied up whenever there might have been a chance."

"Well, never mind. Tell me about yourself." Hugh was ready for the question. He had heard from many others at FBI Headquarters about this Director and his genuine interest in the people working for him.

"I've been in the bureau for over twenty-five years, Sir."

"Now I remember," the Director interrupted, "I gave you your twenty-five-year key down in the auditorium." They give bureau employees a gold key in the shape of the FBI seal when they reach twenty-five years of service. This Director enjoyed doing so in a ceremony at the FBI Headquarters auditorium.

"Yes, Sir. That was me. I started in the Green Bay resident agency out of the Milwaukee Division. I worked Indian reservation matters until transferring to the

New York Office. Six years there led me to seek escape to the Counterterrorism Division here at headquarters." It was a common joke whenever agents were transferred out of the New York Office, they had escaped New York, referencing the movie by the same name.

"A few years later, I took a supervisory desk in Chicago before coming back here as a Unit Chief. Truth be told, Sir, I came back to be near my daughter. She's in grad school at American University."

The Director followed with several questions about Hugh's career and travels before saying, "Something tells me it isn't your career story that brings you to my office today."

"Well, Sir, that's true. What I'm about to tell you will sound unbelievable. I didn't believe it myself when I heard it from my daughter. That's why I have this folder. It contains evidence to show it is likely true."

"Well, let's hear it," said the Director.

For the next five minutes, the Director didn't say a word. He then picked up the phone and said, "Mrs. Leach, I will be tied up here until further notice. Unless it's very urgent, please see I'm not disturbed. Thanks." He then turned to Hugh and said, "Go on."

At the conclusion of his summary, Hugh said, "What I have in this folder are copies of my own personal investigation to date. It includes everything my daughter has told me, everything Su Ling told me, and logical background investigation done from a covert computer. I also have photos of Walter Fontaine in the company of a man I have confirmed is PRC First Secretary Sung Hong from the Chinese Embassy. Su Ling has trusted me with her life and the lives of her family." Hugh was looking intently into the Director's eyes.

The Director said, "Wait one," and then sat quietly for two full minutes. He was a brilliant man who had made a personal fortune on Wall Street before agreeing to become the next FBI Director.

After the minutes of contemplation, the Director said, "Who have you informed of this situation?"

"The only people who know anything about it are you, my daughter, Su Ling, and myself."

"How long have you known about it?"

"A little over a month, Sir. It was only two weeks ago I was able to get the photos of Mr. Fontaine and Sung outside the hotel where Su Ling was waiting. I was aware these allegations were so bizarre I needed solid proof and had to move with the highest level of care. I also knew if they were true, the need for discretion would be off the charts. That, Sir, is why I am here."

"And Sir?" Hugh interjected before the Director could respond. "I kind of looked at this one like what would I do if I were driving down a country road late at night and the car suddenly quit. I see a flying saucer landed in the field right off the road and little green men walk to my car. They look at me through the window, and then returned to their ship and fly off. The big question is, who would I tell?" After a pause, Hugh continued, "In this case, Sir, I chose to tell you."

"I appreciate the way you have handled this so far. You have obviously had a lot longer than I to think about this whole situation. How do you recommend we proceed?"

Hugh looked at the Director with no small amount of surprise. After a moment to gather his thoughts, he said, "My first inclination is to say I don't have a clue. Then my past military training kicks in. Never come to a commander with a problem without having at least some recommendation for a solution. Sir, I would quietly form a small task force made up of less than ten people. It should include the sharpest Deputy Assistant Director, Counterintelligence, that you can find and top people from every intelligence and surveillance discipline you think you need. I would also include the two best analysts we have. The task force will need to be operated from an off-site location. Background investigations should then be quickly and quietly conducted on all concerned. Once we have all we're likely to get from investigation, I would covertly interview Mr. Fontaine's Secret Service Protection Detail team leader. Sir, you may need to be part of the interview for our credibility. If he is not cooperative, you will need to be ready to immediately brief the President. From there, the next step is to interview Mr. Fontaine."

Throughout this description, the Director slowly nodded his head. He then grabbed his phone again. "John, this is the Director. Who is your best and brightest Deputy Assistant Director? Is he in the office? Please ask him to come to my office. And John, I will tie him up for a while and no one is to ask questions about it. Can you do that for me? No, no one. Not even you. Ok. Thanks, John." He hung up the phone.

For the rest of the afternoon Hugh, the Director, and the Deputy Assistant Director identified and recruited the task force. China was already the bureau's hot-button topic because of the world oil situation.

Frankfort, Kentucky
1645 Hours EDT

Kerry met up with his cronies again at the Pen and Ink Saloon. Mickey Blondiac and Freddy Dobson had been first to arrive. They were followed by Tank Monahan and John Chapman. Each ordered a drink, three of which were doubles.

"A toast to good friends," Tank said as he raised his glass. Unlike the others, he didn't sip his bourbon but tossed the entire double-shot down his throat. He motioned to the barmaid, a cute little brunette. She was already ordering another for him from the bartender.

"To good friends," everyone said except for Freddy. He sat off to the side playing a video game on his phone and didn't seem to care.

Kerry looked at John Chapman. "John, what do you hear from your friends here in Frankfort?"

"Well, boys," John began with a drawl, "everyone around here is just plain scared. Just about everyone I know has lost a small fortune with the stock market crash, and jobs are just plum drying up. On top of that, this damned right wing Governor seems to be hell-bent on saying no every time the unions or anyone else comes around for a state handout. Fucker even claims what the President is trying to do with the gun control is unconstitutional and won't fly in his state. Who does he think he is?"

General grunts of agreement were made around the table. Everyone had a deep and personal hatred for the new governor.

"Well, what about the National Guard?" Kerry asked quietly. He wanted to make sure no one close was listening.

"I have it on good authority the Commanding General has been told that if something terrible happens, he won't be answering to the Governor. He'll be activated and get his orders from the President." Everyone knew John's good authority was his brother-in-law, the National Guard Commanding General himself.

"Here, here," said Kerry. All then toasted to the statement. What John didn't know was right after the General had told a small gathering of politicians about these instructions coming from Washington, D.C., he had gone to see the Governor. Privately, he told the Governor he didn't care what the President said, his allegiance was to the people of Kentucky, the Governor, and the U.S. Constitution.

John continued, "I also talked to my contact at FEMA. He said that among trusted people at FEMA and in Washington, D.C., there were quiet moves to prepare for a federal takeover, if it becomes necessary. When I say take over, I mean they plan to take over everything."

Kerry said quietly, "Well, I guess you best get those contracts ready to lease out warehouses, Tank. Things are going to shit in a hurry, and I bet it won't be too long before the President takes things in her own hands. Then the rich bastards will do what they're told!" Again, the glasses were raised high in a toast. "And I've got some ideas where there might be stuff ripe for redistribution!"

CHAPTER 46
INAUGURATION - PLUS NINE MONTHS SEVEN DAYS

The Mountains of Southeast Afghanistan
1030 Hours Local Time

The JOTP had moved every three days since the drone attack on the disastrous patrol three months earlier. Ahmed was surprised there had been no follow-up attacks. He praised Allah at each of the five required daily prayer times for saving his fighters from additional attacks. That attack had cost him twenty men. One had survived long enough to tell about the captured American women and how the drone had fired missiles. The six American bullets taken from the man's body showed it also involved a ground force. He wondered why there had been no more patrols.

Ahmed also praised Allah for having protected his hidden base of operations twenty kilometers away. It was there he had stored all the equipment his brother-in-law, Ali, needed for his special work. Everything on the list had been obtained and carefully stored in sealed containers. They hid away even the propane generator and fuel tanks in the cavern.

Ahmed's chief lieutenant, Hadi, walked toward Ahmed's hidden position on the rocky hillside. "Allah be praised, great leader," Hadi said as he approached.

"Allah be praised," Ahmed said in response.

The report to Ahmed was made quickly and efficiently. "I sent Rasheed to pick up the Chinese infidels. They should arrive within the hour."

Ahmed responded, "I will meet them outside escape tunnel number four. You and twelve fighters will provide cover and security."

Then Hadi smiled slightly and turned to walk away. It exhilarated him to be a part of the plan involving the Chinese and felt Allah had chosen the JOTP to be his right hand.

Cho and his assistant found Ahmed sitting on a rock overlooking the flat rock on which they stood. Hadi stood just behind Ahmed and was prepared to translate.

"Allah be praised, and you are looking well." The tall Chinese infidel Cho had spoken in cultured Arabic. The bow of his head showed just enough humility. Ahmed overlooked his having spoken first.

"Allah be praised. Why have you come?"

Rather than be offended by the abrupt question, Cho said, "I come to ask when you and your men will be ready to change the world." Ahmed immediately understood Cho was cleverly asking how soon he would be ready to launch the infidel-striking virus.

Ahmed motioned for Cho and his assistant to approach for a more confidential conversation. Quietly, he said, "I have all the martyrs needed to fulfill Allah's will. Their training continues, and they will be able to travel in the West after only another month or two of training."

"You have a plan of how they can travel with the virus?" Cho was ready with a plan he hoped the simple-minded martyrs could learn within only a few months.

"Yes. They will travel with diabetic test kits and insulin shots." Ahmed was immensely proud of his ability to shock the Chinaman with his ingenuity.

Cho's face registered great surprise. "Good, that should work," Cho said with hesitation.

"When will the virus be ready?" Ahmed asked quietly, but with a hint of fervent emotion.

"I am told it will be ready by the end of the year, not next year." The fact struck Ahmed this dream might actually happen.

"How will you transport the virus here?" Again Ahmed asked his question with the mounting emotion he felt rising within himself.

Cho hesitated before saying, "I can have special medical people meet your martyrs in Europe and Mexico just before they will board their planes."

"No!" Ahmed's shout caused his security men to ready their rifles and look around carefully. "You will bring the virus here. I will see it is spread throughout the West!" Ahmed rose from his rock and walked away.

On the way back to Kabul, Cho said to his assistant in Cantonese, "That could be a big problem." His assistant agreed, knowing Cho was talking about delivering the virus to Ahmed in the desert. Cho ended the thought with, "That will have to be decided by the General."

This ends book one of *The First Coronation*.

Appendix A: Characters

I. Kentucky

1. Mike Broehm (Pronounced Brame and rhymes with frame)
Mike is an outwardly simple man who lives in a nice subdivision in Kentucky. He is married to Lauren, has two grown children and suffers from a weight problem, along with high blood pressure and pre-diabetes. He works as a research biochemist at a local university.

2. Lauren Broehm
Mike's wife. Lauren's parents died in a tractor trailer/car accident when she was in college. Lauren was 18 and her brother Marc was only 6. Lauren had helped her aunt raise Marc and was later appointed as Marc's guardian.

3. Kerry DuBois
Kerry lives in Mike's neighborhood and works for state government in the transportation cabinet. His background includes a Bachelor's in Social Engineering from UC Berkeley.

4. Jim Carson
Jim is one of Mike's hunting buddies, a CPA, and economist.

5. Fred Callahan
Fred is one of the few black men living in Mike Broehm's neighborhood and is Chief of Police in the nearby town of Cronin. Fred's is married to Korean-born Penny. His son is Sean Callahan.

6. Sean Callahan
Sean is a Major in the U.S. Army Special Forces Command (SOCOM) and commander of a Green Beret company and is the son of Fred Callahan.

7. Linda Sharpe

First Lieutenant Linda Sharpe is a Team Leader in Sean Callahan's Special Forces (Green Berets) Company. She leads an "A" Team of operators in the field. She's the orphan of two Army parents and just missed becoming a swimmer on the US Olympic swim team.

8. Rollie McDermott

Rollie is another of Mike's hunting buddies and a builder who can build or fix anything.

9. Peter Worthington

Peter is a university professor of mechanical and environmental engineering. In his mid-50's, he is a recognized leader in meeting environmental standards for exotic metals mining, through which he has become moderately wealthy. His land is connected to Mike Broehm's land. He is married to Elizabeth, who is a good friend of Lauren's.

10. Jim Webb

Jim is a semi-retired electrician who lives in Mike Broehm's neighborhood. He is a lifelong member of the IBEW (International Brotherhood of Electrical Workers).

11. Freddy Dobson

Freddy is Kerry DuBois' crony and the son of a wealthy East Coast family.

12. John Chapman

John is Kerry DuBois' crony and a former community organizer from Louisville, Kentucky who had been brought on by the previous governor to be his Lieutenant Governor. John is well wired with the unions throughout the state and was instrumental in organizing the get-out-the-vote effort to get elected. He convinced the Governor to pardon his friend and money man, Jerry "The Tank" Monahan, for the minor drug transgressions for which he was convicted fifteen years earlier.

13. Jerry "The Tank" Monohan

Tank is from the mountains of Eastern Kentucky. He accumulated a great deal of wealth from extortion activities targeting the coal companies back in the 1970s. He branched out into marijuana sales just before his arrest by federal and state agents. Tank owns the Pen and Ink Saloon in Frankfort through a shell company, where he has a private office and meeting room, including a very private entrance to an underground garage.

14. Mickey Blondiac

Mickey is a DuBois crony and the political commentator for the largest paper in Central Kentucky. He publishes a weekly column called *Blondi's Corner*.

15. Scott Shelby

Scott is a financial advisor who left Wall Street after his heart attack at 32 and opened up a small financial firm in the town of Cronin. He handles Peter Worthington's portfolio.

II. Washington

16. President Katherine Fontaine.

Katherine Fontaine is the ambitious wife of former Senator and former Vice President Walter Fontaine. Before her election as President, she was an attorney and a liberal to moderate Senator from California.

17. Walter Fontaine

A former Vice President, Walter left the office of Vice President with a strong belief he never wanted to be President, a stance which was not popular with his wife Katherine.

18. Su Ling

Su is both very attractive and beautifully accomplished in her ability to meet the needs of a man. They trained her at the MSS Charm School located outside of Shanghai.

19. Sung Hong

Sung is Su Ling's MSS handler in Washington, D.C. He acts as a de facto slave master and keeps a close eye on Su to insure she continues to service Walter and extract intelligence from him.

20. Don Stetson

Stetson is Katherine Fontaine's campaign manager.

21. Susan Cassel

Susan is an attorney and personal assistant to Katherine Fontaine.

22. Marc Baxter

Marc is a Columbia-trained journalism graduate and New York Times Junior Political Editor who joins Katherine Fontaine's campaign and then becomes a primary assistant to Presidential Press Secretary Marjorie Klein. Marc is also the younger brother of Lauren Broehm.

23. John Butler

Marc Baxter's administrative assistant in the White House Press Office.

24. General Roger Tignor

Air Force General Tignor is Katherine Fontaine's Director of National Intelligence. Tignor is one of the brightest minds in the military. He is in charge of all U.S. government intelligence collection.

25. Marjorie Klein

Marjorie is a woman in her mid-40's chosen to be Katherine's Press Secretary. She is a bright, professional woman who was formerly an editor for the New York Times.

26. Towanda Jefferson

Towanda is a black Georgetown University School of Journalism graduate who is forced upon Marjorie as her deputy by Katherine's need to placate wealthy donor Eli Fredericks.

27. Burton "Burt" Combs

Katherine Fontaine's Chief of Staff. He was a Senator who was recruited by Katherine right after she was elected President.

28. Bradley Pittson

Director of the CIA.

29. Donald Clayborn

Director of the National Security Agency (NSA).

30. David Cummin

Secretary of State under Katherine Fontaine. A holdover from the previous administration, he ends up staying due to his personal patriotism.

31. Seth Goldberg

Secretary of the Treasury under Katherine Fontaine.

32. Dmitriy Roskov

Roskov is Director of Homeland Security, a former Chicago Police Commissioner, and political hack who plays the political game well. He has both backbone and character.

33. Carlton Hathaway

Secretary of Defense in the new Fontaine administration. He was previously the Director of the Environmental Protection Agency (EPA).

34. Lisa McIntyre

Lisa is a graduate student at American University in Washington, D.C. studying a dual track of Chemistry and Biology. Lisa is the daughter of Hugh McIntyre.

35. Hugh McIntyre

Hugh is a Unit Chief in the Counterterrorism Section of FBI Headquarters.

36. Eli Fredericks

Fredericks, a graduate of Princeton University, is an extremely wealthy black man who has made billions through hedge funds and government contracts directed to minority contractors. He is a frequent visitor to the White House and the primary donor for Katherine's campaign.

III. Peoples Republic of China

37. Song Ren

Song is the Chinese Premier and General Secretary of the Communist Party in China. It places him at the head of the Chinese government. He is obsessed with retaking control of the Chinese renegade province known in the West as Taiwan or Republic of China and formerly as Formosa.

38. General Lao Tung

Lao is the head of the PRC Ministry of State Security (PRC version of the KGB). Lao has the ear of Song and is the perfect balance of a spymaster, an economist, and a politician.

39. General Hu Sengai

Hu is the General responsible for the PRC's "Special Warfare" arsenal to include nuclear, biological, and chemical weapons.

40. Wong Jie

Song's Secretary and de Facto, Chief of Staff.

41. Major Cho Chong

Cho is the bright up-and-coming MSS Officer sent by Lao to meet with Ahmed. Cho is fluent in eight languages, including Arabic.

42. Gong Xi

Foreign Minister, People's Republic of China. Gong does what Song and Lao tell him to do.

43. Chen Wen
Chen is a major industrialist in the People's Republic of China. He made his billions by knowing the right people within the Politburo and supplying military material to the PLA.

44. Wu Chin
Wu is Chen Wen's clandestine contact with Eli Fredericks, usually in Washington, D.C.

IV. Afghanistan Muslims

45. Ahmed al-Rasheed
Ahmed is the undisputed leader of Jihadists of the Prophet (JOTP), a radical Muslim group loosely affiliated with al-Qaida and ISIS (Islamic State). His second wife is named Jasmine. Ahmed has been recruited by Cho for future actions.

46. Abdullah Muhammad
Abdullah is the Imam (religious leader) and a close confidant of Ahmed al-Rasheed.

47. Ali al-Hadiz
Ali is the brother of Ahmed's second wife, Jasmine, and the rising star within the family. Ali just graduated from the University Of Kentucky School Of Pharmacy with a PhD.

Appendix B: Forty-Five Goals of Communism

Congressional Record--Appendix, pp. A34-A35 January 10, 1963

Current Communist Goals

EXTENSION OF REMARKS OF HON. A. S. HERLONG, JR. OF FLORIDA
IN THE HOUSE OF REPRESENTATIVES

Thursday, January 10, 1963

Mr. HERLONG. Mr. Speaker, Mrs. Patricia Nordman of De Land, Fla., is an
ardent and articulate opponent of communism, and until recently published the
De Land Courier, which she dedicated to the purpose of alerting the public to the
dangers of communism in America.

At Mrs. Nordman's request, I include in the RECORD, under unanimous consent,
the following "Current Communist Goals," which she identifies as an excerpt
from "The Naked Communist," by Cleon Skousen:
[From "The Naked Communist," by Cleon Skousen]

CURRENT COMMUNIST GOALS

1. U.S. acceptance of coexistence as the only alternative to atomic war.
2. U.S. willingness to capitulate in preference to engaging in atomic war.
3. Develop the illusion that total disarmament [by] the United States would be a
   demonstration of moral strength.
4. Permit free trade between all nations regardless of Communist affiliation and
   regardless of whether or not items could be used for war.
5. Extension of long-term loans to Russia and Soviet satellites.
6. Provide American aid to all nations regardless of Communist domination.
7. Grant recognition of Red China. Admission of Red China to the U.N.
8. Set up East and West Germany as separate states in spite of Khrushchev's
   promise in 1955 to settle the German question by free elections under
   supervision of the U.N.

9. Prolong the conferences to ban atomic tests because the United States has agreed to suspend tests as long as negotiations are in progress.

10. Allow all Soviet satellites individual representation in the U.N.

11. Promote the U.N. as the only hope for mankind. If its charter is rewritten, demand that it be set up as a one-world government with its own independent armed forces. (Some Communist leaders believe the world can be taken over as easily by the U.N. as by Moscow. Sometimes these two centers compete with each other as they are now doing in the Congo.)

12. Resist any attempt to outlaw the Communist Party.

13. Do away with all loyalty oaths.

14. Continue giving Russia access to the U.S. Patent Office.

15. Capture one or both of the political parties in the United States.

16. Use technical decisions of the courts to weaken basic American institutions by claiming their activities violate civil rights.

17. Get control of the schools. Use them as transmission belts for socialism and current Communist propaganda. Soften the curriculum. Get control of teachers' associations. Put the party line in textbooks.

18. Gain control of all student newspapers.

19. Use student riots to foment public protests against programs or organizations which are under Communist attack.

20. Infiltrate the press. Get control of book-review assignments, editorial writing, policymaking positions.

21. Gain control of key positions in radio, TV, and motion pictures.

22. Continue discrediting American culture by degrading all forms of artistic expression. An American Communist cell was told to "eliminate all good sculpture from parks and buildings, substitute shapeless, awkward and meaningless forms."

23. Control art critics and directors of art museums. "Our plan is to promote ugliness, repulsive, meaningless art."

24. Eliminate all laws governing obscenity by calling them "censorship" and a violation of free speech and free press.

25. Break down cultural standards of morality by promoting pornography and obscenity in books, magazines, motion pictures, radio, and TV.

26. Present homosexuality, degeneracy and promiscuity as "normal, natural, healthy."

27. Infiltrate the churches and replace revealed religion with "social" religion. Discredit the Bible and emphasize the need for intellectual maturity which does not need a "religious crutch."

28. Eliminate prayer or any phase of religious expression in the schools on the ground that it violates the principle of "separation of church and state."

29. Discredit the American Constitution by calling it inadequate, old-fashioned, out of step with modern needs, a hindrance to cooperation between nations on a worldwide basis.

30. Discredit the American Founding Fathers. Present them as selfish aristocrats who had no concern for the "common man."

31. Belittle all forms of American culture and discourage the teaching of American history on the ground that it was only a minor part of the "big picture." Give more emphasis to Russian history since the Communists took over.

32. Support any socialist movement to give centralized control over any part of the culture, education, social agencies, welfare programs, mental health clinics, etc.

33. Eliminate all laws or procedures which interfere with the operation of the Communist apparatus.

34. Eliminate the House Committee on Un-American Activities.

35. Discredit and eventually dismantle the FBI.

36. Infiltrate and gain control of more unions.

37. Infiltrate and gain control of big business.

38. Transfer some of the powers of arrest from the police to social agencies. Treat all behavioral problems as psychiatric disorders which no one but psychiatrists can understand [or treat].

39. Dominate the psychiatric profession and use mental health laws as a means of gaining coercive control over those who oppose Communist goals.

40. Discredit the family as an institution. Encourage promiscuity and easy divorce.

41. Emphasize the need to raise children away from the negative influence of parents. Attribute prejudices, mental blocks and retarding of children to suppressive influence of parents.

42. Create the impression that violence and insurrection are legitimate aspects of the American tradition; that students and special-interest groups should rise up and use ["]united force["] to solve economic, political or social problems.

43. Overthrow all colonial governments before native populations are ready for self-government.

44. Internationalize the Panama Canal.

45. Repeal the Connally reservation so the United States cannot prevent the World Court from seizing jurisdiction [over domestic problems. Give the World Court jurisdiction] over nations and individuals alike.

Appendix C: Excerpt from Presidential Executive Order 13603

Excerpt from Presidential Executive Order 13603, issued March 16, 2012.

(1) Sec. 201. Priorities and Allocations Authorities. (a) The authority of the President conferred by section 101 of the Act, 50 U.S.C. App. 2071, to require acceptance and priority performance of contracts or orders (other than contracts of employment) to promote the national defense over performance of any other contracts or orders, and to allocate materials, services, and facilities as deemed necessary or appropriate to promote the national defense, is delegated to the following agency heads: the Secretary of Agriculture with respect to food resources, food resource facilities, livestock resources, veterinary resources, plant health resources, and the domestic distribution of farm equipment and commercial fertilizer; the Secretary of Energy with respect to all forms of energy; the Secretary of Health and Human Services with respect to health resources; the Secretary of Transportation with respect to all forms of civil transportation; the Secretary of Defense with respect to water resources; and the Secretary of Commerce with respect to all other materials, services, and facilities, including construction materials.

Appendix D: Terms and Definitions

Charm School
Special school located outside of Shanghai, China where young women and a few young men are trained to exert sexual and psychological influence over others, usually men. This school is operated by the MSS.

DNI - Director of National Intelligence
The Director of National Intelligence (DNI) is the U.S. government official - subject to the authority, direction, and control of the President–that advises the President and other agencies about intelligence matters related to national security. He or she also serves as head of the sixteen-member U.S. Intelligence Community.

EMP - Electo-magnetic pulse
An EMP is a surge of energy that can be caused by a solar flare or high level nuclear detonation. It will burn up and render inoperable most electronic devices or circuits.

FEMA - Federal Emergency Management Authority
FEMA is a United States government agency contained within the Department of Homeland Security. FEMA coordinates the federal response to emergencies of all kinds, including hurricanes, tornados, floods and other catastrophic events affecting large numbers of people.

Formosa - also known as Taiwan
This island off the coast of Fujian Province, People's Republic of China (PRC) is also known as the Republic of China. Following World War II, the Communist insurgency defeated the Nationalist Chinese government, the remnants of which fled to the island of Taiwan and nearby islands. Under a democratic, capitalistic government Taiwan has flourished economically while the PRC remained closed until the early 1970s. The PRC Communist Party views Taiwan as a break-away province that will be eventually returned to the Chinese empire.

HRT - Hostage Rescue Team

The FBI Hostage Rescue Team (HRT) is the counter-terrorism and hostage rescue unit of the FBI. Its mission is to rescue American citizens and allies who are held hostage by hostile forces, usually terrorists and/or criminals.

Intel-Intelligence

Intel is the description for a group or agency that collects secret information or "Intelligence" about an enemy or area. Intel is the collected information used by decision-makers to form actions and policies.

JOTP-Jihadists of the Prophet

The JOTP is the Afghan terrorist group led by Ahmed al-Rasheed.

MSS - Ministry of State Security

The Ministry of State Security (MSS) is the intelligence and security agency for the People's Republic of China (non-military area of interests), responsible for counterintelligence, foreign intelligence and political security. It is headquartered near the Ministry of Public Security of the People's Republic of China in Beijing. It has responsibilities that are roughly equivalent to the old Soviet KGB and a combination of the FBI and CIA and is an organ of the Chinese Communist Party.

Nanotechnology

Nanotechnology ("nanotech") is the manipulation of matter on an atomic, molecular, and supramolecular scale.

PLA - People's Liberation Army

The Chinese People's Liberation Army (PLA) is the official name of the armed forces of the People's Republic of China. It is under the complete control of the Communist Party of China (CPC).

Proletariat Revolution

A proletarian revolution is a social revolution in which the working class attempts to overthrow the bourgeoisie. Proletarian revolutions are generally advocated by socialists, communists, and most anarchists.[13]

RPG - Rocket-Propelled Grenade

A Soviet designed shoulder-fired anti-tank weapon somewhat similar to a bazooka. It fires a grenade, powered by a small rocket. The grenade is made of a shape charge capable of penetrating light armor or building walls and spraying hot metal fragments after penetration occurs.

SOCOM - Special Operations Command

USSOCOM synchronizes the planning of special operations and provides SOF (Special Operations Forces) to support persistent, networked and distributed GCC operations in order to protect and advance our Nation's interests.[14]

SVR

The Foreign Intelligence Service of the Russian Federation (Russian: Слу́жба вне́шней разве́дки, tr. Salzhauer vneshney razvedki is Russia's external intelligence agency, mainly for civilian affairs.[15] It is roughly equivalent to the CIA.

SWE - Secure Working Environment

A space or office which is specifically designed to protect classified or sensitive information from access by hostile entities.

VA - Veteran's Administration

The U.S. Federal Government's agency responsible for administration of benefits earned by military veterans.

Waldorf Astoria

Luxury Hotel in New York City.

[13] Wikipedia United States Special Operations Command Website
[14] Wikipedia

ABOUT THE AUTHOR

The author is an attorney and retired FBI Special Agent. After growing up in the Midwest, he has worked and traveled extensively in the Northeast Corridor. Following college studies, U.S. Army Officer training, and a thirty-one-year career in intelligence, counterintelligence, counterterrorism, and public corruption, he was inspired to write a novel addressing the realistic potential future of America. The author is married with one son, lives in the Midwest and enjoys motorcycling, multiple sports, flying airplanes and service in the American Legion.

NOTE FROM THE AUTHOR

Word-of-mouth is crucial for any author to succeed. If you enjoyed *The First Coronation*, please leave a review online—anywhere you are able. Even if it's just a sentence or two. It would make all the difference and would be very much appreciated.

Thanks!
Carlton

Thank you so much for reading one of our **Military Fiction** novels.
If you enjoyed the experience, please check out our recommendation
title for your next great read!

Blown Cover by Mark Hewitt

2018 Pencraft Award Winner

"... a high-octane thriller that explodes off of the starter blocks and
races top speed to the final scene."

–AUTHORS READING

View other Black Rose Writing titles at
www.blackrosewriting.com/books and use promo code
PRINT to receive a **20% discount** when purchasing.

www.ingramcontent.com/pod-product-compliance
Lightning Source LLC
Chambersburg PA
CBHW011133100726
47898CB00009B/2966